BLUE FATE 5

PURSUIT

CASS TELL

BLUE FATE 5
PURSUIT

A novel from the Blue Fate series

destinēe *media*

PROLOGUE

"When do you think you'll get back to California?" asked the man in the dark suit. He turned toward a younger blond woman seated next to him in his rental car. They had just parked in the garage of the Brussels Hotel Royal. Before she answered, they climbed out onto the hard concrete and slammed the doors. The sound reverberated throughout the dark.

The man pressed his remote lock and set the car alarm. The woman finally answered, "I've just about finished my basic research. Once that's done, I can write up my thesis from anywhere."

They walked across toward the elevator, neither noticing the two men crouched behind a gray Mercedes parked near it. One of the waiting men had received a telephone call that the target car was coming. Their instructions had been to eliminate the two passengers, but at the last minute they were told to change plans. Someone thought the girl had possibilities.

"And you," she asked, the man, "When do you think you will get back to California?"

"Not soon," he answered, punching the up-arrow on the elevator. "Our task force is making progress, but we have a lot of work to do."

As the pair waited for the elevator, the two men raised up from behind the Mercedes, guns in hand. A second later, two silenced shots pierced the man's navy suit. He staggered backwards, reaching beneath his jacket for his holster. By the time he grasped his .38 special, he was on his back on the concrete, body quivering.

The young woman screamed and fell to her knees beside him, holding her hands to the wound.

One of the two gunmen crossed to her, and just as she raised a furious glare to confront him, he raised the butt of his pistol and slammed it against the side of her head.

She tumbled forward onto her uncle.

★ ★ ★

Turk sneezed, interrupting the morning silence. It was chilly in the northern Spanish forest, the sun not yet up. The only other sound was the occasional chirping of birds. Turk needed a cigarette and hated that he could not have one.

For two weeks Turk and his team had been on a manhunt. And then last night, they had spent bone chilling hours crouched low in a cluster of pines observing the set of old stone buildings circled by a stone fence and closed off by a wooden gate.

The small monastery consisted of three buildings that formed a 'U'. The bottom was the main building, and its sides were a huge stone barn and an attached chapel, distinguishable by its peaked roof topped with a metal cross.

A terrace filled the center of the 'U.' It was arranged with chairs and tables and blocked from the wind by a glass partition.

The men waited—and were they ever good at waiting by now. A tall man walked out on the terrace with a book under his arm and took a place at a table. Shortly after, a waiter came and poured him coffee. The man stared through the windows at the field and trees beyond, and Turk had the uncomfortable feeling that he and his men were visible, despite distance and camouflage.

Turk's men turned to him. He nodded and whispered, "Justin Collins."

They looked back to observe Collins whose only observable action was adding sugar to his coffee. A moment later Turk said, "I did my part. Now I go." He was antsy and brusque.

The team understood it was dangerous for him to be in Spain, or anywhere else in Western Europe. Turk had made it very clear that he would help them find Collins, but once that was done, Mustafi was obliged to help him escape. Turk needed to hide for a while. They weren't sure why and no one was telling them.

Turk turned and crept down the path through the shrubs and pines, towards the cars. He couldn't wait to drive to get to Figueras, get on the plane, and join Ziginiglou. The forbidden European air made him sweat.

The other men turned and began looking in the direction of the monastery. They had their man.

Now they needed the right moment.

CHAPTER 1

Abright November sun broke above the eastern horizon and its rays made rhinestones of the morning dew on the pine trees.

Justin split his gaze between the patchworked farm fields to the west and the thick pine forests to the east.

He and his family, oddly extended though it was, had settled into the estate. Justin had wondered how long Gloria and Chantal would be able to sustain their tenuous friendship. The last two days had included some silent meals and slamming of doors.

Justin sighed. They had the place for three months. It was renovated, but some monastery traditions were maintained. No telephone. No radio. No TV. It was a place for healing and recuperation. And for contemplation.

He picked up the book he had found in the monastery library. No contemporary best sellers to be found in there. The spines of most books on the shelves were ribbed and thick with bindings made long before modern glues. Justin rubbed dust from the rough, lined leather of the book in his hands. It was a collection of writings by a sixteenth-century Spanish mystic, St. John of the Cross.

He had been reading a poem over and over, all morning. Several lines kept running through him like water:

And when you come to the possession of all,
you must possess it without wanting anything.

How did that work? He wondered again at the dream he had on arrival here, the one that kept returning to his waking life. In it, he had been standing in a room packed to the ceiling with chests of Indian silks and precious gems, with Greek statues and African masks, with Moroccan rugs and Renaissance art.

He had spotted a painting partially covered by an inlaid table. It was of a mother and child. The mother and child Chantal had painted, the one still in his Paris storage unit. But when he looked closer, he saw that there were two mothers. And two children.

In the dream he had climbed over the stacked treasures, trying to move the table away and see the entire painting.

But when he reached out to touch it, the canvas went blank.

⋆ ⋆ ⋆

In her room overlooking the terrace where Justin was finishing his coffee, Chantal finished gathering her sketching supplies into a canvas satchel and did a mental inventory: paper, charcoals, pastels, clay eraser, fixative… gunshot wound. She had taken a deep breath and exhaled too sharply. She was recovering, but her body let her know it had a ways to go.

She took a gentler breath and buckled the bag closed, slowly transferring it to her right shoulder and heading for the stairs.

While she was still bedridden, Justin had brought her these sketching materials—all things he had remembered her bringing along on their car travels around the French countryside. Though she was primarily a painter, she required deliberation and much time to select her colors and canvases. Justin had not forgotten this.

On her way downstairs, she stopped in at Dora Vine's suite to see Sophie. Chantal needing to see her daughter's bright, innocent face before a day of tense, adult company. When she knocked on the door, Dora appeared, smiling. "Good morning Chantal, I thought you might want to kiss someone goodbye before you left." Sophie came thundering from across the room, dressed and washed and all three of her years engaged in the happy process of barreling toward her mother.

"You going to make art, *oui*?" she asked of Chantal's leg, having firmly embraced it before her mother had time to set down her bag and bend over for a hug. Extracting her lower limb from Sophie's arms, Chantal laughed and knelt down to hug her daughter. "*Oui, ma cherie.*"

She glanced up at Dora who wore a look of concern and sympathy. "It will be fine," Chantal said, releasing Sophie to let her rummage around in the bag of art supplies and standing up again. "I asked to go to the sea, and we all decided to go together. We have to start somewhere."

Dora nodded. "I am proud of you."

Sophie started jumping up and down at Dora's feet, "I want art today too, Dora."

"Well then, we shall have art," Dora said, picking Sophie up and holding her toward Chantal. "Kiss *maman* goodbye and we will go find your paints."

Obediently, Sophie gave Chantal a big, wet kiss and giggled. Chantal squeezed her fingers and kissed them, saying "The fingers of a *petite artiste.*"

Sophie started chanting '*petite artiste*' as Chantal thanked Dora and closed the door behind her.

Chantal reached the main hall just as Gloria came from the direction of the terrace with Justin. Gloria smiled at Chantal, "Are you ready?"

"Yes," Chantal managed, noting that Justin had dropped his hand from Gloria's arm as they had passed through the doors into the hall. She gripped the satchel strap even tighter. "Shall we go?" She fixed a tight smile on her face and walked straight ahead, through Justin and Gloria to the driveway.

But Chantal went straight for the back seat. On the passenger side. There she could make eye contact with Justin and not have to see Gloria at all. That, and she did not like to have an enemy behind her.

CHAPTER 2

Gloria reached for the radio dials and found some classical music that she turned low. This drive to the sea was going to be thin on the conversation side, she thought. Though she agreed with Justin that it would be good to give Chantal a change of scene and a chance to draw near the sea, she wondered just how good an idea it was for the three of them to pretend they were a functioning family out on a day trip.

She kept her eyes out the side window, noticing that she could observe Chantal in the side rear-view mirror, her ash-blonde hair glowing in the early morning sun that filled the car sideways.

Gloria moved her eyes to the landscape flying past them. She could smell the umbrella pines even before they saw them. Then came the hills lined with ancient vineyard lines. And finally—the sea.

Llanca. Where she had fallen in love with Justin and he with her. Where they had tried to start a life together. A life that Curly Grady and his news of the intact plane engine had thrown into discord.

And now they were going to her and Justin's one remaining place of harmony—their home. But they were bringing the source of discord with them. Chantal.

From now on, whenever Gloria closed her eyes and tried to return to those brief months alone with Justin, just married, she would also see Justin's resurrected wife alongside them. Sharing that space as she maybe always had.

As they neared the port town, Justin pulled into a vacant space at the Supermercat. "I'll just go and get some picnic things. Any requests?"

"Turrón" said Gloria.

"Madelines" said Chantal, at the same instant.

Justin laughed, "My two sweet teeth." As he closed the door and went inside, Gloria turned around with a puzzled expression that matched Chantal's. In spite of themselves, they both laughed.

* * *

From Justin's balcony, the November sea stretched calm and blue below the rough rocky coast that formed the peninsula that was the port town. A large man and his small dog walked by below on the path that wound from the fish market to a beach several inlets south.

Gloria stood at the railing, letting the faint breeze lift strands of her red hair into her peripheral vision. She wondered if this is how she herself was to Justin—faintly there and out of focus. Or whether she lay across his heart as heavily as he did hers.

A noise came from the kitchen. She could hear Justin pointing out to Chantal that the tea was in the cupboard near the sink. Gloria took a deep breath. This was her home, and she would be a generous hostess.

She released the railing, noticing that her palms were lined where the squared wood had left its imprint.

Justin was filling the kettle with water. As Gloria came in, he asked, "Would you like some white tea?" Her favorite.

"Yes, thank you," she smiled at him, almost able to forget that she could not go up to him and lace her fingers behind his neck.

Chantal was rummaging in her canvas sack. She looked up, "Can I set up my things on the balcony?" She did not seem sure whether to address this question to Gloria or Justin, so she just looked back in her bag.

"Of course," Gloria answered, gesturing toward the glass door with what she hoped was a genuine looking smile. Chantal nodded and went outside, closing the door behind her.

Gloria looked at Justin who had set the water to boil and was now leaning against the kitchen counter with his arms folded and an extra line in his forehead. Had that been there a few months ago? She did not want to miss an inch of change in him.

"How are you managing?" he asked.

"Not so well." She smiled to lighten the answer and continued, "But then you were the manager, I'm the banker. I just do what I'm told."

She came over toward him but stopped a couple of feet away.

She glanced out at the balcony where Chantal had begun setting up her sketching things in a corner, safe from any winds that might rise in the course of the morning. Justin joined her gaze, and it was several minutes later that he spoke.

"I have no idea what to do."

She placed her hand on his shoulder, giving it a faint squeeze. The sounds of the sea against the rocks came up through the open kitchen window. A distant, drowning rumble.

⋆ ⋆ ⋆

Chantal ripped another page from her pad and crumpled it. She felt like she was being watched from behind the sliding doors. She could never work with anyone watching. The blue pastel chalk she was holding snapped between her fingers, but she was surprised to find herself not angry so much as resigned. To what… this sad triangle?

She gently set the broken blue into it's place and reached for the red. Not exactly an oceanic color, but it was what she wanted in her hand. She held it to the paper vertically on its long side and pulled it quickly across, twisting it toward the end to a thinner line. A red horizon stretched in front of her. Or a red path.

She sprayed a swath of fixative across it and pulled it from the pad. After waving it a bit in the air to dry, she slipped it in toward the end of the sketch pad and pulled the lid down over her pastels.

When Justin had asked her yesterday if she needed anything, she had said the sea. Or, more exactly, she had told him she wanted to draw the sea. He hadn't realized how literally she had meant this.

To draw was to bring forth. And she needed to bring forth whatever part of her *had* died over this water. She squinted her eyes to a slit and the horizon blurred till she could not distinguish sky from sea. Then she closed her eyes completely.

When she opened them, she had no desire to continue drawing. The tea Justin had brought her had gone cold and so had her hands. She stood, then pulled open the door and went inside.

Gloria and Justin were in the living room, seated opposite each other on plush stuffed chairs. A fire was crackling. Chantal walked over to the hearth, sat sideways near the flames without blocking them and stretched her hands out toward the warmth.

The three of them sat there without speaking as the fire ate its way through wood and air in a crimson hunger.

CHAPTER 3

"Mr. Chairman, that concludes our preliminary investigations. We submit this to you for your consideration." The committee member from India looked up from the text he had been reading from for the past hour. "We are at your service for any questions."

The chairman of the committee, Dr. Nikomo from Zimbabwe, nodded his head, "Thank you Mr. Sanjee for your thorough summation." He then looked around the conference table making eye contact with those seated around it. "And thanks to you and your colleagues for your excellent work over the past five months. From your meticulous efforts, it appears that the allegations of misconduct cannot be substantiated ."

A few of the six other occupied chairs leaned back a notch and several members shuffled their papers together in satisfaction. The international committee was meeting in a small room in the Palais des Nations, the massive United Nations building in Geneva. Every person there was a seasoned politician appointed to the U.N by senior political leaders from his country. The paneled room had been hushed and attentive for the last hour of Mr. Sanjee's report.

Twelve months before, the directorship of the United Nations had appointed the committee members to 'carry out impartial, objective and thorough investigations into alleged wrongdoing within sub-organizations of the United Nations'. It had taken six months for the appointed individuals to be released from their previous posts to begin this work.

Mr. Sanjee tilted his head slightly from side to side in the affirming gesture of his countrymen and said, "That is correct, Dr. Nikomo. We made extensive investigations. We visited most of the refugee camps and other operations in question, and there has been no evidence of wrongdoing. After lengthy interviews with United Nations officials based at those camps, we find no authentication of offenses."

Dr. Nikomo placed his large hands on the neat stack of paperwork in front of him. His hands almost spanned the size of the sheets, dwarfing them. "And, may I respectfully ask, do you feel you adequately interviewed the alleged victims of suspected offenses?"

Sanjee returned Dr. Nikomo's serious expression with one of his own, answering, "We spent considerable time questioning the alleged victims. It was a long and tedious task. In our opinion, their stories were often inventions backed by no evidence. In fact, their facts were often confusing. In addition, listed victims refused to bring any charges, and the names of some of the alleged victims appear to be fabricated. With such circumstances, claims of wrongdoing cannot be corroborated."

Dr. Nikomo pursed his lips, "So, you are confident that your findings would stand up in a court of law?"

"Absolutely." Mr. Sanjee said immediately. "Outside of circumstantial evidence, at this point here is nothing that would prove any wrongdoing."

"What about non-governmental organizations? Did you find any inappropriate behavior there?" the chairman asked.

"The NGO's were outside the charter of our committee. We were asked to make an extensive and objective examination of field based operations of the United Nations."

"I understand," John Nikomo responded, finally leaning back himself, but looking around at the six members of the committee, all appointees from within various bodies of the UN.

The committee had been formed to check into claims that various employees within UN agencies had been demanding sexual favors in exchange for food and other supplies. Such rumors had been dismissed as fabrications of zealous news reporters who had unofficially and sensationally labeled the affair in Europe as the 'UN Sex for Food Program.' Officials were relieved that this story had managed to miss the United States media. In response to these allegations, the directorship of the UN had appointed an independent committee to determine if indeed any truth lay at the base of these charges.

With all eyes on him, Nikomo pulled himself straight again in his chair, "And I am assuming we have records of the interviews and evidence?"

"Yes." Sanjee pointed to twenty-five binders on a table along one wall. "There is the draft report including records of all our interviews."

"Gentlemen, do you feel there is anything else we need to look into?" Nikomo asked the room.

Sanjee, as spokesman for the committee said, "Over the past six months we have visited most of the refugee camps and distribution operations mentioned in the original charter list, although this has taken longer than originally expected. Certain events delayed our entry into some countries, and it took longer than planned to meet with the appropriate people when we arrived. We still need to visit several more countries from the original list, officials in some of the UN organizations."

"How long will that take," Dr. Nikomo asked.

"Three months may be adequate, but to complete a thorough investigation, we feel we need another six months."

"Six months?" the chairman questioned. He glanced at the binders in their symmetrical row. The UN had now funded the six committee members for five months. He resisted sighing and said, "This issue is of extreme importance, and we must ensure that the investigation is impartial and satisfies the exigencies of outside questions. Therefore I believe the UN Directorate will agree to an extension of the mandate."

"Thank you Mr. Chairman," Sanjee answered. "We will plan to remain faithfully at your service."

★ ★ ★

As the embers spat and sank to a chalky ash, Justin rose from his chair. "Anyone for lunch?" he asked. Gloria nodded and moved toward the kitchen. Chantal remained fixed on the hard stone hearth, mesmerized by the dead fire.

"Do you have more firewood?" she asked, slowly stretching her stiff limbs and not wanting the fire to expire.

"Sure, I'll get some," Justin said, diverting his route toward the kitchen by heading for the side door and down to the lower terrace.

Chantal joined Gloria in the kitchen and began absently pulling things from the grocery bag onto the counter. Without looking up from the carrots she was rinsing, Gloria said, "When we get back to the monastery, we should have a talk. Do you not think so?"

Chantal flattened the now empty bag and began to fold it in half and half again. "Yes. We should. Without Justin, you mean."

"Yes."

Gloria began slicing the carrots as Chantal made the smallest, foldable square out of the bag. When she let it go, it popped open through several sizes. "Can I help you?" she finally asked Gloria, who handed her two zucchinis and continued chopping.

Justin returned with an armful of wood and proceeded to relight the fire. By the time it was roaring, the fish was on the grill and the Collins household had appetites large as the fire.

★ ★ ★

After lunch, Gloria took a siesta, Chantal tried sketching again, and Justin went for a walk.

He soon found himself in the village, in front of Señora Pascual's. He opened her gate and went to the door, remembering the first, wind-blown time he had entered beneath its lintel in the company of the Señora's son and Jordi Pujols. Was that just less than a year ago? He shook his head—more like a dog ridding his fur of water than from disbelief. He knocked.

After half a minute, he knocked again. No answer. He was more depressed than he would have thought at her absence. He realized he had been craving a glass of her family liqueur and her matronly presence amidst the drying herbs of her cozy kitchen.

Even her cats were nowhere to be seen. He glanced at the winter garden and hoped she was doing well. Señora Pascual was strong as a horse but she had seen her share of years.

He left her yard, made for a plaza café and ordered a coffee. The waiter greeted him with pleasure, "Ah, Señor Collins, you have not visited us lately. What have you been doing these days?"

"Trying to solve my life," Justin replied, wondering if he ever would.

"Ah, *sí*. This solving of life—it takes all the life long, no?" the waiter said.

Justin just stared past him at the bright red table, worried that yes, it would.

He spent the rest of the afternoon walking through the hills where he used to run, but as the sun slipped behind them, he decided he had better go back home. If that's what he could call it.

Before he even opened his door, Justin could sense that he would be walking into a fight. They may as well have hung a sign on the lever "do not disturb—on pain of dismemberment."

He exhaled and entered. He was right. They weren't just arguing, they were yelling. Chantal occasionally in French, Gloria occasionally in Spanish. Justin's heart contracted in pain. Whoever said catfights were entertaining had no true regard for the women doing the fighting.

They broke off long enough to notice him. He met a pair of green eyes, then a pair of blue ones.

Before they had a chance to continue, Justin took a deep breath and raised his hands slightly into the air. In supplication or placation, it was difficult to tell. "When my family reached an impassable crisis," He began, "My mother would not cook dinner. She would take my father and I to a restaurant where we would be forced to behave. If only to save our pride." He looked at both Chantal and Gloria. "We may not have much else to save, so we may as well."

With this he headed for the door and opened it in exasperated invitation. No better option presenting itself, the two women filed out in stony silence and headed for the car.

CHAPTER 4

The drive back to the monastery was as silent as dinner had been. The three of them had eaten at a small place in the village that neither Gloria nor Justin had been to. In unspoken agreement, they avoided their favorite spots and the memories that would have hung in the air with the scent of familiar food.

It was late when Justin pulled up to the monastery entrance and let Chantal and Gloria out. "I'll go park the car," he said. "Sleep well, both of you."

"Goodnight," said Gloria, reaching over to squeeze his hand on the steering wheel before she got out of the car. She started toward the building.

Chantal leaned up toward the front seat and placed a surprise kiss on Justin's temple, saying nothing. She too left the car, pulling her bag with her and closing the door.

Justin watched the two women pass through the entrance and be swallowed in the dark.

He sighed and completed the circle of the drive, continuing back up a path toward the garages. He locked the car and headed for the monastery, noting the dramatic lighting made by large spotlights embedded at the base of its outer walls.

He pulled the carved door open and let it close with a resounding thud behind him. All this atmosphere of ages. Passing through the dining hall, he could almost see long rows of heavy wooden tables lined with men in rough, brown robes, their invisible and silent faces bent over bowls of soup.

He shivered at the thought of all the subdued passions these walls had absorbed. Part of him—a very small part, admittedly—wondered if he shouldn't just enter a brotherhood and give up this precarious relationship with the two women he loved. The two wives he loved.

The click of his footsteps on the wooden planks sent small echoes off into corners as he reached the massive staircase leading up to the second-floor bedrooms.

Chantal, Gloria and he occupied the six bedrooms in this wing. Each room boasted high ceilings spanned by aged wooden beams from the days of wealthy secularism that had proceeded the building's use as a monastery. As much as he enjoyed rustic charm in theory, Justin was glad to have recently renovated bathrooms, complete with bathtub and separate shower.

Dora had a large suite in the downstairs wing, with a bedroom each for her and for Sophie, his precious little Sophie. Dora wanted to take care of Sophie, and Chantal had agreed, since she was still recovering from a gunshot wound. During their months of captivity in Tunisia, Dora had become like a grandmother to Sophie.

He was certainly paying a high bill to enjoy these facilities, but finances were the last of Justin's worries. Though at first Dora Vine's exorbitant gift had shocked him, he had already begun to enjoy the benefits of his new and unexpected fortune. Because of the pain his family had endured in during the process of the merger and after, Dora had insisted that he would receive fifty million dollars in cash from the sale of Vine Industries and three percent of Unipac's shares.

This added up to about a billion dollars.

He intended to invest the majority, but right now, he needed to invest a little up front in the most important relationships in his life.

Relationships. That was what occupied his mind day and night. Had he made the right decision by bringing everyone down here together? At the time, it had seemed the best option. Recently, however, he felt like the entire place was strung with high-tension wires, and a single false step would zap him.

He hadn't told Gloria and Chantal about the money yet. He wanted to make sure they were physically and emotionally stable before announcing that they were multimillionaires. No telling what would happen if he added that complexity on top of everything else. Dora agreed to keep the secret until the time was right.

Justin stopped by Chantal's room. Before he had finished thinking about whether he should, he had opened the door and looked in. As timing would have it, Chantal was just emerging naked from the bathroom, drying herself with a towel.

She jumped when she saw him and quickly pulled the towel around her and smiled.

"I'm sorry if I scared you." he said, closing the door behind him. "Did today wear you out?" The glimpse of her uncovered body sent him back to the days when he had known her every contour as well as his own. He suddenly remembered a constellation of freckles across her lower back that he used to kiss.

She seemed thinner now, but what he'd seen before the terry cloth covered her looked as lovely as ever.

"*Au contraire*," she said, smiling even more. "I feel like doing something."

He had forgotten the quirk of her eyebrow and lips when she was being playful.

"How is the wound?" he asked.

"Healing quickly. Do you want to see?" She moved toward him.

"Yes," he breathed, trying to remember why this was not a good idea.

"Sit on the bed."

She sat down next to him, her thigh pressed against his. She dropped the towel and tucked it around her waist. In the soft lamp light, he looked below her left breast at a round pinkish red mark.

"It looks better," he said, running the pad of his forefinger around it. "I'm so thankful it wasn't a few more inches over." He moved his fingers toward her heart.

"You mean centimeters?" She smiled.

"Whichever you prefer," he said, returning her smile and meeting her eyes.

CHAPTER 5

Vejay Sanjee entered the upper floor restaurant of the Geneva Hilton Hotel where a waiter in a white dinner jacket directed him toward a table. The waiter pulled back a chair and Sanjee seated himself to a view of Lake Geneva out the window beside him. Beyond the lake stretched the city it was named for, and beyond its limits, the Alps.

The last flush of alpenglow was still coloring those mighty white mountains a rosy pink as the sun prepared to break above their ridges.

Sanjee ordered a coffee. A moment later the waiter returned with a silver pot and poured Arabica coffee into a fine porcelain cup. Sanjee inhaled deeply of the fragrant liquid, added cream and sugar, and enjoyed the sunrise.

He looked around, noting that no other diners sat in the restaurant—one of the most expensive restaurants in Geneva. Every table was laid with crisp white linen and a crystal vase of fresh-cut roses. As Sanjee was finishing his scan of the dining room, he saw a man enter.

The man wore a dark business suit, white shirt and red silk tie. Lionel Banneret, the director of the United Nations Agency for Trade Development. Sanjee had seen him before at official functions within the United Nations, but had never met him personally. Rumor hinted that Banneret had considerable influence within the United Nations. Some even said he was being selected as a candidate for the Secretary General position.

Banneret crossed the room in long, straight strides. A man in his mid-fifties, he wore his age well, his curly black hair barely grayed at the temples, his warm smile almost unlined.

As Banneret approached Sanjee, he extended his hand in the manner of a practiced politician, firmly shaking Sanjee's. "Good morning Mr. Sanjee. I am so pleased you could join me here. I apologize if I am late."

"Oh no, you are not late. I was a bit early," Sanjee smiled, gesturing at the seat across from him.

The waiter materialized and pulled a chair back for Banneret.

The waiter said, "The usual, Mr. Banneret?"

"Yes, thank you."

A few minutes later, Banneret was adding sugar to an espresso and replying to Sanjee's thanks for meeting there. "No, it is my honor. I am so pleased to meet with you. We could have met at my office, which is not far from here, but I need to leave this morning to fly out to the field, so I thought it would be more convenient to have coffee together. I just apologize that I don't have much time."

"I fully understand and am thankful we can meet in such a lovely place," Sanjee said, watching Banneret appreciate the view. Banneret's agency was on the list of organizations his committee was investigating. His eyes slipped down to his watch. Seven o'clock. He stifled a yawn. An hour and a half before he usually woke.

Banneret brought his gaze back to the man across from him, "Once I am back in Geneva, I propose that we have a less-rushed meeting. But because of my time constraints, I'm afraid I must go straight to your concern. I am assuming it has to do with your committee's recent investigations?"

"Yes, " Sanjee replied. "We gave a preliminary report yesterday, and as your agency was on the list, I thought it might be of value if we were to meet informally, just to ensure adequate communication lines in the future."

Banneret looked at the Indian man, nodding, "Tell me, has your committee discovered anything?" Banneret asked.

"Nothing," Sanjee answered. "All allegations of misconduct seem to be a prefabricated attack on the integrity of the United Nations." He paused. "But, I must say, there were several interviews against some agencies of the United Nations that were…" he paused.

Banneret spoke softly though no one was around to hear him, "May I ask if the UN Agency for Trade Development was implicated?"

Sanjee lowered his voice. "Nothing substantial. But I have personally handled these interviews and do not believe they are without basis in fact."

Banneret set his empty cup down, "If that is the case, I need to have details. If crimes have been enacted, then we must see that justice is served. That is a fundamental basis of the United Nations." He made a fist and continued, "But if these accusations are unfounded, they are quite heinous. We work so hard to improve the conditions of humanity across the world. I am grateful there are conscientious officials like you," he relaxed the fist and used it to gesture at Sanjee, "who can objectively verify that these accusations are unjustified."

* * *

"This coffee tastes like shit," Turk said, slamming his cup onto its saucer with enough force to spill some of the offending liquid. "They call it Turkish coffee, but it is like drinking mud. I miss the coffee in Istanbul." He slouched, thumping his elbow onto the table and leaning the side of his head onto his hand.

He sat opposite Ziginglou at an outdoor café table facing a dusty street in Pec, Kosovo. It was a quiet town near the border with Macedonia. Only an occasional car rolled past them on the street.

"Be thankful you are here," Zigniglou told him both with words and a knobby-knuckled finger pointed at Turk.

"Why should I?" Turk said, shifting against the hard metal back of his chair.

"We are out of Western Europe and you are not in jail."

Turk looked across the small round table at Zigniglou, his compatriot.

They had worked for the same organizations over several years, and Zigniglou was often right.

But Turk was in the mood to complain. "I don't like the Albanians. For hundreds of years they worked for the Ottoman Empire—for *us*— now we have to work for them." He made a grimace as if this were at least as distasteful as the coffee he had just spat out.

"At least it is work." Ziginglou tilted his head down in the manner of a reprimanding parent, "And they made good their part of the bargain. Work that got us out of Western Europe."

"But I had to help them find Justin Collins. That was two weeks of moving around, with no sleep. Or if there was any sleep, it was in the back seat of a car with a bunch of stinky Kosovo Albanians."

Zigniglou raised his hands in the air and looked toward the sky. "But, you are now here, and in a few days you will be rested. Plus, the work is easy."

"I suppose so," Turk said. "Just guarding packages. What are you doing for them?"

"The usual. Accounting. Keeping track of shipments and payments. Bookkeeping."

"Why do you think they want Collins?" Turk asked.

Ziginiglou straightened in the chair, raising his head upward toward Turk, his outsize nose casting a striking profile. "I will give you some strong advice. Don't meddle in their affairs. Just do everything they ask and don't ask questions. Anyone who asks questions is eliminated. I have seen it with my own eyes during the two weeks I have been here. Just be smart and be careful."

Turk returned to his self-pitying slouch, "We were stupid to sign those papers back in France. We confessed to killing Jacques Tapic, but we didn't do it. And they gave the papers to the police in France. Now police everywhere will be looking for us."

"I know," Zigniglou said, having replied the same way to Turk's repeated complaints, "but we had no choice. Those men with the guns pointed at us were hard characters. They give me the shivers, the large one with the steely blue eyes and the muscular Spaniard with the barber's razor."

"If I find them I will kill them," Turk declared, finally animated..

"You want to avoid men like that," Zigniglou stated. "If you value your life."

"For the way they treated me I will kill them and then go back to Istanbul," Turk vowed, slamming his hand on the table hard enough to rattle the cup in its saucer. Turk looked at his unfinished beverage, adding "And decent coffee."

CHAPTER 6

It was almost time for breakfast by the time Justin quietly pulled Chantal's door shut behind him. He did not immediately let go of the door knob, but stood there staring down the hall. When he finally shook off his daze, he blinked and realized he was looking at Gloria's room.

The lingering pleasure that surged through his body stilled. Just beyond that door, his wife, his other wife, cradled their three-month-old child in her womb.

He walked down and rested his head against the wall near her door. He had committed himself in all honesty to her too, thinking Chantal dead. He had entered into the journey of marriage with both of them. No surprise that he ached for them both. But here in a monastery, of all places, where such ways of the flesh were sacrificed.

For the last few nights, he had awakened in the dark to reach for—which woman? Either. But his hands had groped only cold sheets. He had wanted to wait until the three of them came to some kind of decision about their future. Now he had gone against his original intentions and interfered with the possible resolution of their situation.

Psychologically, things were getting worse. But physically, things were improving. Justin noticed that after only a week, Chantal was resting much less and seemed to be moving easier. She had gone out on several short walks, and color was returning to her cheeks.

And then there was the rosy red flush that had bloomed on her face this morning—she had expended significant energy to get it there.

Gloria too was advancing well through the early stages of motherhood, with only a bit of morning sickness to bother her.

Justin went to his own room and showered. After pulling on khakis and a t-shirt, he glanced at himself in the mirror, rubbing his palm across the stubble he didn't care to shave. His green eyes looked worried.

He walked downstairs to the dining hall. He was surprised to see Gloria eating breakfast with Dora and Sophie.

Justin smiled at her, then looked away, afraid that her matching jade

eyes would recognize the troubled soul that shown through his. And
that she would guess what had happened.

"Good morning," he said to the table in general.

"Good morning," Dora replied.

Gloria nodded slightly in his direction, keeping her eyes on her
croissant that she seemed more intent on rotating than eating.

"Papa," Sophie cried out, leaving her chair and running to Justin.
He took her in his arms and gave her a kiss on the cheek, glad to have
innocent and uncomplicated love at that moment.

"I'm going to go for a short walk," he said.

"Be careful," Gloria said, looking up at him as she said it.

"I will." He knew what she meant. She always said that before he
went jogging or out for a walk. Several months before, during one
of his runs, he had been forced over the side of a cliff by a car when
someone had tried to kill him. He had spent several days in the hospital
in Figueras with a slight concussion.

"Justin, would you have time to talk today?" Gloria asked as he
turned to go.

"Sure," he replied. "Do you want to come walking with me?"

"No, I'd like to finish my coffee. We can talk when you get back."

"You're sure?"

"Yes."

Chantal appeared in the dining room doorway, wearing wide-leg
linen pants and a pink cotton blouse that complemented her radiant
complexion.

"*Bonjour,*" she said.

"You look good. Color in you cheeks," Dora said, smiling at her.

"Feeling much better," Chantal replied, pulling up a chair.

Gloria attempted a smile.

Justin put Sophie down and she scurried over to Chantal. Chantal
drew her close and kissed her forehead.

"Mama. I go paint," Sophie said, as she ran across the dining room
and headed for her bedroom.

"I better keep an eye on her," Dora said. "She's becoming quite the
artist, just like her mother. But she likes to taste the paints."

Dora left Justin, Chantal and Gloria to themselves.

No one spoke for a moment.

Justin broke the silence, "I'm going to walk now. I won't be long."
He wanted to let the two women talk alone almost as much as he
wanted to escape.

When they were alone, Chantal lightly asked Gloria, "How are you today?"

As Gloria looked over, she noticed dancing light in Chantal's eyes, even though the cloud of weariness still circled them. "Fine, how about you? You look much better."

"Oh, I much feel stronger," Chantal beamed, quickly picking up two croissants, the marmalade dish, and a large lump of grapes.

At the tone of Chantal's voice, a strand of fear knotted with the pain in Gloria's empty stomach. She watched Chantal more carefully, in search of something she couldn't define. Chantal did indeed look vibrant this morning, and if pulling grapes from the vine and chewing them could be sensual, Chantal was making it look that way.

Gloria put down her coffee and looked straight at Chantal. "We agreed we were going to talk."

"That's right," Chantal said, stabbing her knife into the fig preserves with a loud thwack.

"When?" Gloria demanded more abruptly than she'd intended. She watched Chantal's knife come away clean from the croissant and then pause in front of Chantal's chest. It looked poised to strike. Instead, Chantal set it with elaborate precision across the top of her plate and then placed both elbows square on either side of her breakfast.

"As soon as you are prepared to be civil."

Gloria glared and pulled her chair back from the table. Standing up to leave, she said over her shoulder, "And I wait for the same conditions from you."

CHAPTER 7

Chantal watched Gloria walk away and took a furious bite of her croissant. But she had dolloped a mountain of the sweet fig jam on it without noticing, and this promptly landed with a splat on her slacks.

"*Zut!*" she said to her sticky lap, standing up. She punched her fists to her sides and stamped her foot on the terrace. Right into the rest of the fallen preserves. She stormed off toward the residential wing, leaving fainter and fainter splotches of jam on the terrace and ignoring the waiter who was scurrying toward her with a white towel.

In her room, she yanked off her pants and dumped them in the laundry bin, careless as she never was to rinse out the spot first.

She sat on the bed with a thump, and then let her torso fall backward, hands twisting in the sheets she had shared with Justin just hours ago. She closed her eyes and brought a swath of fabric to her face, trying to smell any trace of his cologne or sweat. When she opened her eyes, she saw the white of the bedding and shivered.

Nothing so sterile as white. Her bedding had always been colored or patterned or both. Two weeks ago, she had been lying in a Nice hospital bed. White everything. Gloria had stood between her and Justin, holding each of their hands, setting the groundwork for the agreement to work together as friends and find a way to… what? Accept that one of them would remain with Justin and the other would calmly pack her bags and head off with her child and start over?

Friendship. I think not. Chantal thought. She rose to her elbows, then off the bed. From her closet she pulled another pair of pants from a hanger without looking at them.

Gloria. She thought. Then aloud to the mirror she said, "She stole my husband," wanting to feel justified in saying it. But as she made eye contact with herself, she knew it was not that simple. The circumstances had been unusual, to say the least.

Everyone thought she had died in a plane crash over the Mediterranean. "Maybe it would have been better if I *had* died," she said to the mirror. But as with the other statement, her reflected double did not let her get away with it. She frowned at the woman frowning back at her.

As much as she knew that Justin was a man who needed a woman to love him, she felt betrayed that he had found one after only fourteen months since he had heard of her "death."

During her captivity in Tunisia, imagining their reunion had helped to keep her sane. How many times had she envisioned Justin locking her in his arms, tangling his fingers in her hair. She had tasted his lips in her dreams.

And then last night. Finally to have him body and soul. She smiled, hugging herself, and crossed to the window.

But in the midst of reliving a particularly pleasant memory from the previous evening, she found herself staring at a fly trapped between window panes and wondering: had Justin also slept with Gloria during the two weeks they had been here?

She dropped her hands to the window sill and stared down at the terrace and the countryside beyond it. Justin was talking with the waiter who had cleared the breakfast things. They were laughing. She loved the way he laughed, his head slightly thrown back, smile spread all the way across his face.

Then Justin turned and headed toward the gates of the monastery. She watched his tall body as he took long strides down the main road toward a small forest. He had done the same thing in Paris, going for long walks alone along the Seine or in the twisting passages of the Left Bank. As she with her studio time, he needed his solitude. Even more so now with herself and Gloria on his mind.

As Justin approached the forest, Chantal noticed a sudden movement in the bushes. She had just enough time to process a fleeting worry of whether predatory animals prowled the forests when one appeared in front of Justin.

A man with a gun.

* * *

Gloria finished brushing her hair and reached for a ribbon to tie it back. She looked at the red hairs entwined through the brush bristles, wondering when they would start to go gray. And when they did, would she be with Justin to compare laugh lines and age spots? She had planned on growing old with him, and now she did not know whether they would even be able to celebrate their first anniversary together.

She pushed back from the dressing table and went to her closet for a light cardigan. The days were cool.

Breakfast had not exactly been a success. Neither had any of this, actually. But she was determined to make some progress—in any direction—so that the three of them did not have to continue in this hateful purgatory forever.

She lifted the cross that hung at her neck and kissed it, sending up a silent prayer for help as she did so.

"We are going to speak like adults if it kills us," she said to the cross as she left her room and headed for Chantal's.

Just as she came to Chantal's door and raised her fist to knock, she heard Chantal shriek, "*Mon Dieu, non!*"

Gloria yanked open the door and ran inside to see Chantal pounding at the glass window pane which was stuck in its grooves.

"What is wrong?" Gloria asked, immediately at the window. She saw nothing but forest. Chantal gathered her breath, registered Gloria's presence and started running for the door.

Gloria grabbed her arm, and insisted, "What is wrong. Tell me."

"He had a gun. Justin fought. Then there were more men. One of them stuck a needle in Justin's arm. It happened in seconds. They took him away…"

Chantal had now frozen in terror.

Gloria still had her by the arm, which she was squeezing hard. "We will find him."

CHAPTER 8

"We may not find him," the well-padded village police chief shrugged in unflustered resignation. He and a skinny policeman looked at each other, gesturing sideways with uplifted palms that it was out of their hands. Late morning sun was burnishing the leaves of the bushes and trees around them where Chantal had seen Justin abducted. In ordinary circumstances, it would have been a gorgeous morning.

"But then again, you might," pressed Chantal, also in French. They were close to the French border here and most everyone spoke the language of their neighbors. That, and she did not speak Spanish. Chantal was far more animated than the two mustachioed men with badges who seemed more intent on making it home to find a bottle of *Pastis* in the cupboard than a silly American lost in the woods.

Gloria fixed both men with a Catalan glare, and the second policeman coughed then leaned down in the ditch and began fanning his arms through the weeds.

"Did he have any enemies?" The chief asked.

"Not really," Gloria said, trying not to sound like she was hesitating. How on earth could she begin to explain the events in Nice?

"Not r—" Before the chief finished making Gloria's answer into a question, the skinny policeman interrupted, pointing to something in the bushes.

"Chief. Look here."

Everyone was at his side in a second, bending over a leather wallet.

The chief picked it up with a handkerchief and said, "We will have this checked for finger prints."

"What's inside?" Chantal asked, holding her breath.

The chief opened the wallet by its corners and with the handkerchief, "Some Euros and Swiss Francs. Also some US Dollars. No credit cards. Look," he pointed, "identification papers. At least they look like identification papers. I don't recognize the language."

Chantal leaned closely over the papers. From a small photo, dark eyes stared out from under black, unruly hair. Even as small as it was, the image made her spine tingle. "I don't know the language either," she said.

"Nor I," said Gloria, who had also moved closer for a glimpse of the mystery man.

"We need to take this to Gerona to have it examined," the chief said, finally gathering his duties to him like armor and relishing the fact that solid evidence had been found. To his wiry deputy, he said, "And the central command needs to be notified so they can inform all police and border guards to watch for Mr. Collins." Gerona was the largest town in the area, about thirty kilometers away.

"Please go quickly," Gloria said.

"Is there anything we can do?" Chantal asked.

"We will work as fast as possible. Can you come down to the police station so we can ask more questions, perhaps go to Gerona where they have more infrastructure?" he asked.

"Yes, of course. Anything to help," Gloria replied. "Can we call a friend in Llanca? He may be able to help?"

"What friend?" The police chief asked with a look of grudging courtesy.

"Jordi Pugols."

At the name, the police chief's mustache twitched. "How do you know Jordi Pujols?"

"He is a friend of my husband's," Gloria replied.

"Does he have anything to do with this?"

"No. But he is a helpful resource locally," Gloria said, wondering if she regretted bringing Jordi's name into this.

"I think we need to ask you some questions," the police chief said, his eyes narrowing and the mask of incompetence thinning. He gestured toward the police car, "May we offer you a ride to Gerona?"

$\star\ \star\ \star$

Two hours of stale air and stale questions later, and Chantal and Gloria were tired, hungry and irritable. The windowless room at the Gerona station was threaded with stripes of smoke from the cigar hanging from the lips of the town's assistant chief of police. Chantal started to cross her legs under the metal table for a countless time before her knee hit its underside with a hollow thud, again for a countless time. She grimaced and tried to find a reasonably comfortable position on the stiff, straight chair and wondered who willingly chose dull beige as the color to paint their walls.

Chantal looked sidelong at Gloria whose posture had softened. She seemed equally melded to her chair and eager to bolt from it.

When questioned about the last months, the two women only gave information that was known to the public, mainly about Chantal's kidnapping and captivity in Tunisia, how the insurance investigator Curly Grady had rescued her, and how she had been shot during the rescue. Nothing of the incident with Jacques Tapic, the hostage-keeping mastermind, was disclosed. The reason they gave for the entire Tunisia incident was that the abductors wanted a ransom for Dora Vine.

"And, what was your husband's role in all of this?" the policeman asked, exhaling into the tobacco stratosphere.

"None," Gloria replied.

The policeman leaned back and pointed his cigar at them, "You have a strange situation. Two women married to the same man."

Chantal looked for signs of amusement or leering. Finding none, she said with an edge anyway, "That's our business, thank you."

"But does it have anything to do with your husband being taken?" he asked, wedging his elbows into the meager papers in front of him.

"Not that we can think of," Chantal answered.

"And Jordi Pujols. What does he have to do with this?"

"Why is that important?" Gloria asked.

"Mr. Pujols has a reputation."

"Go on." Gloria had straightened slightly from her slump.

Another puff of smoke. "A year or two ago the Russian Mafia was moving into the Costa Brava, buying up land. It was suspected that they planned to bring illegal operations into the area, drug trafficking and the like. Supposedly Jordi Pujols gave them a message."

"What kind of message?" Gloria asked.

"It was bloody."

Gloria and Chantal remained quiet. They knew Jordi's reputation as a protector of honor.

The chief continued, finally stubbing out his cigar into an ashtray impossible mounded with its predecessors. "We have no proof, and no one was ever directly associated with the incident. Nothing came of the rumor, and the police let it go. But, if your husband is acquainted with Jordi Pujols, then it might be possible that someone was trying to get back at Jordi by going after one of his friends."

"I don't think it has anything to do with that," Gloria answered.

"Then what other ideas can you give me?" the policeman asked. Both Gloria and Chantal sighed as they watched him reach for another cigar from the small tin at the desk's edge.

"Nothing," Gloria articulated clearly, leaning forward.

They sat in silence until young policeman walked into the small room. "We have information," he said to his seated colleague.

"What is it?" the chief asked.

"The identification papers are for an Albanian, from Kosovo. We did a search with Interpol, and his fingerprints were found on the wallet, along with someone else's."

"Perhaps Mr. Collins'," said the chief, nodding.

"Maybe Justin pulled the wallet out of the man's pants while they were fighting," Chantal offered. "Who is this man?"

"His name is Zog Merkat."

CHAPTER 9

"Zog?" Chantal shot up an eyebrow at the name.

"Yes, *madame*," The young man said. "Zog was a famous Albanian king, a tyrant, but nonetheless admired by many Albanians. Some name their children after him. At least that's what I learned during the past two hours of researching this." He wiped the back of his hand across his forehead to matte the damp that had formed there. He did look as if he had been focusing up close for too long.

"What can you tell us about him?" Chantal asked.

"He is a low-level member of the Kosovo Mafia, if you want to call it that."

"Low-level?" Gloria was relieved at the adjective but still worried.

"In Kosovo there are numerous gangs, many competing against each other. They are often family-run."

Just as the policeman was warming to his topic, his superior took over. In a voice that reminded Gloria of her boss when he was waxing professorial, the chief continued, "In Western Europe over fifty percent of the drug trade and prostitution are controlled by these gangs. In some countries, it's as high as seventy-five percent or more, and they are often responsible for violent crimes, such as bank robberies and murder. The drugs, mostly heroin, come through Kosovo on their way to Western Europe from Afghanistan and other countries in that area. The prostitution is run with girls from the Balkans and Eastern European countries who are promised legitimate jobs in Western Europe. The offers initially sound fantastic, but once these innocent girls accept, their identification papers are taken away, they are threatened or drugged and then sold into the brothels of Western Europe.

"That's horrible," Gloria said, bringing her hand to her mouth. "Why is this still going on?"

The chief lifted a weary shoulder. "Our politicians aren't willing to admit the problem and make the effort to resolve it. These gangs are becoming a huge problem." He noticed that the junior officer was still standing nearby and shooed him away with his ringed right hand. The man bowed out, opening the door for the briefest of air currents and then closing them back in the fog.

"What does that have to do with Justin?" Chantal asked. "Where does this Zog come in?"

"We don't know." The chief continued, thankfully distracted enough by his lesson to continue without smoking, "From our investigations, all we know about Zog Merkat is that he was arrested last year in Germany for trafficking young women. He was held for a day in jail in Berlin. Afterward, they took him to the Swiss border and told him never to come back. That is a common problem in Europe. One country just exports their problems into another country. Still, it is rather strange that he was held for such a short time. From the records we received, it looks like he didn't go through normal legal proceedings." He made a look of distaste at what would evidently never be his own error.

"So what are you going to do now?" Gloria looked over at her, sure that she too was irritated at the feeling of uselessness. It got under her skin and made her want to scratch. Chantal would probably want to scratch someone else.

"We will write a report and add him to a list of wanted suspects that will go to all the countries in the European Union. That is all we can do for now, unless you can think of any further information that might be helpful."

"That's all?" Gloria exclaimed. They had taken Justin over three hours ago and could be well into France by now. If the police couldn't help, what where she and Chantal going to do?

"We can't set up road blocks. There are just too many roads, and the abductors could be in France by now, but we will continue to investigate. Maybe they will call in asking for a ransom," the policeman was saying.

Chantal did not appear to be listening. "Can we have photocopies of his identification papers, as well as the translations?" she asked, standing up and finally ending the question session with one of her own.

* * *

Laszlo Vartek said *"Pardon,"* as he squeezed past two small, elderly women who were pulling on their fur coats. After passing them he looked back and caught the eye of Jordi Pujols who was reaching out to help one of the women with her coat. The woman looked up at Jordi with worry writ large across her face. Jordi's gave her a tiny smile, a short bow, and moved forward to join Laszlo.

Laszlo looked around the tearoom and wondered if they were in the right place. He did not see many empty chairs, and most were occupied by elegant, elderly women seated around small circular tables eating finger sandwiches from doily-covered, three-tierd serving platters.

Laszlo hated finger sandwiches. They were usually smaller than his fingers.

Finally, he spotted Stefan von Portzer who had raised a hand from his tailored cuff and jacket sleeve and was gently waving it in Laszlo's direction.

Stefan was unmistakably himself, dressed in a conservative Viennese jacket and a green overcoat that lay draped across the seat next to him. On the seat with the overcoat rested a green felt hat with a feather on the side.

Laszlo navigated his way through the tables and the curious glances of discreet dowagers. Jordi walked behind him, also trying to look at ease. Neither man was very successful. A small poodle dog stuck its nose from beneath one of the tables giving them a suspicious sniff as they walked by.

Somehow, Stefan fit in the tearoom without being feminine like the majority of its occupants. His black hair, peppered with gray at the temples was combed into a low wave Cary Grant would have admired. And the women who would have admired Cary Grant would—and did—more than admire Stefan von Portzer.

As Laszlo finally made it to the table, Stefan set down the French newspaper he was reading and stood, giving the men a smile. But Laszlo saw that Stefan's face was unusually serious. No light quips of weather or politics this afternoon.

Stefan shook hands saying, "Laszlo, Jordi, thank you for joining me. Please be seated." He motioned to the two empty chairs around the table.

Laszlo and Jordi sat down in chairs not designed for men of their size. Laszlo felt like he was in a little girl's playhouse. He hoped he did not break the chair. He sat straight, not leaning back into the brittle piece of furniture.

Stefan looked around, "This is a wonderful place. I always enjoy coming here when I visit Brussels. The coffee is marvelous and the pastries and chocolates are exquisite." Stefan nodded toward one side of the room where an extensive display of cakes, tarts, pastries and chocolates stretched from wall to wall.

A waitress came by in her a dainty white apron, took their order, and in a few minutes came back with three espressos and a choice of pastries. Next to the pastries she placed a plate of pralines and small round balls of dark chocolate.

Laszlo looked around the room and said, "This is certainly a contrast to where we were last night."

Stefan's eyes narrowed. "I know. Please tell me what happened."

Jordi reached across and took a ball of chocolate, popped it into his mouth and raised the small coffee cup to his lips, trying to fit his finger into the narrow, porcelain handle.

Laszlo lowered his voice. "It was a hotel near the train station. We got there too late. Our informant led us to one of the men involved in the murder of George Kent, and the abduction of Anne. It was a sleazy hotel, if you even want to call it a hotel. The man was dead on the floor of his room, a bullet hole in his head."

"Did you find any clues?"

"None."

"But, you are sure he was involved in the murder?" Stefan asked.

"Fairly sure. It seems he was contracted by the gang of international drug dealers being investigated by Kent and his task force," Laszlo eyed the confections in front of him and then ignored them. "It took quite some work to track down this information."

Laszlo and Jordi had been working together for nearly two weeks. They had questioned half of Brussels, working their way through the underground network, following up on leads, and gathering information.

"Do you know who contracted him?" Stefan asked, reaching for a praline.

Laszlo nodded, "There is conflicting information, but it seems it was a gang operating out of Berlin."

"You don't have any information as to why they would kill the uncle and not her?"

"Nothing. We haven't gotten close enough to any reliable sources, but we can speculate," Laszlo said.

"It is strange that they have not contacted the police to ask for a ransom," Stefan said. "There must be other motives." He puzzled over these and his praline, then continued, "Perhaps they haven't made the connection that she is related to Paul Kent the CEO of Unipac and Sam Oliver."

"Perhaps," Laszlo said, his thoughts on this fiercely striking Anne Kent and the photo Stefan had given him. He had the photo in his pocket, but quickly decided he had better not recall her image at this moment.

"How good is the lead in Berlin?" Stefan asked.

"A gang is implicated. We have a name but not much to go on."

Stefan eyed the cup of espresso that he hadn't touched. "Sam Oliver and Paul Kent are very grateful for your efforts. As you know, they will spare no expense to find Anne."

Stefan looked up at the men seated next to him. "How soon can you be in Berlin?"

CHAPTER 10

The front of the Gerona police station opened out onto a busy street. Gloria and Chantal headed down the sidewalk toward the train station. They ignored the traffic and sounds and each other, not speaking until they were in sight of the station.

"Why did you want copies of the identification papers?" Gloria finally asked in English. She did not like speaking Chantal's native tongue unless it was necessary—as with the police department. English put them on more equal footing.

"I thought I might check with Stefan Von Portzer to see if he has any ideas."

"Justin's friend in Geneva?" Gloria remembered the suave, well-groomed man at her and Justin's wedding that fall.

"*Our* friend," Chantal corrected, jolting Gloria from pleasant thoughts of her wedding day.

With a businesslike tone, Gloria asked, "How can he help?"

"Stefan is a very resourceful and had many contacts. It was he who helped us in Nice. We should find a telephone," she said, nodding at a cluster of pay phones inside the main hall of the station.

"Okay, but first let me call Jordi." Gloria reached into her purse for a phone card and address book with the number of Eusebi's barbershop in Llanca. All calls for Jordi went to Eusebi's. She dialed the number.

"*Diga*," a voice answered.

"Señor Eusebi?"

"Yes. Who is this?"

"Señora Collins."

"Ah, Señora Collins. How are you and Justin?"

"Not good." Gloria explained that Justin had been abducted. She took a shallow breath to steady herself as the fact that it had happened sunk further into her consciousness. Then she asked for Jordi. A few seconds later, Gloria hung up the phone in disappointment.

"What's wrong?" Chantal asked.

"Jordi isn't there."

"Where is he?"

"He left for Brussels a few days ago. It seems that Mr. Sam Oliver's niece was kidnapped. There was a shooting, her uncle was killed, and she disappeared. The police are working on it, but Mr. Oliver asked if Jordi and Laszlo Vartek could help. They went to Brussels."

Chantal stared at Gloria as if she had made this up. "Another kidnapping? I've got to call Stefan." She took the phone and dialed through to Geneva, first to Von Portzer's home number and then to his office. There wasn't an answer in either place. She hung up with force and started walking away from the phone to a bank of benches where they sat down facing the flow of travelers and their various baggage.

"Do you think he went to Brussels along with Laszlo Vartek?" Gloria asked.

"Quite possibly. Laszlo works for Stefan. But who knows. He may just be sleeping later than his usual noon." She made a face as if she was familiar with his sleeping habits. "Did Eusebi say where Jordi was staying in Brussels?"

"No. He said they were moving on to Berlin, but he doesn't know when. Jordi called him two days ago just before they left. Eusebi hasn't heard from him since then. She gestured at Chantal's purse where she had stuffed copies of papers from the police station. "What information do we have?" Gloria asked.

"Photocopies of someone's identity papers. That's all."

A man lumbered past with an enormous duffle bag slung over a meaty shoulder. Each step dragged to the left under its weight. Not until he had passed was his tiny wife visible, hidden in his right shadow as she had been by man and bag.

Gloria thought for a minute, "If this Zog can be found, then he would lead to Justin, wouldn't he?"

"Yes, of course." Chantal's attention had wandered to the bakery display. The croissants would surely be greasy and stiff, but breakfast had been a long time ago.

Gloria was continuing, "We know the town where Zog Merkat comes from. Probably someone there will know where he is." She stood up. "I'm going to Kosovo."

"You're what?" Chantal swung her head from croissant to a very determined looking Gloria.

"Zog's identity papers said he was from a town called Pec in Kosovo. I'm more likely to find information there—to buy it if necessary—than anywhere around here. If I find Zog, I can find Justin."

"Then I'm going with you," Chantal stood next to her, and Gloria noticed for the first time that she must be an inch taller than Chantal.

"You're not well enough," Gloria said.

"I am well enough," Chantal insisted. "We both want Justin to be safe, and two travel more safely than one."

"I can do it on my own."

"But I am going with you."

A young girl walked by in the hand of her mother, looking up at the two women facing each other with hands on their hips, saying nothing and saying everything at the same time.

CHAPTER 11

"Do you have to do that?" Gloria winced as Chantal shook her fingers out after cracking all their knuckles.

"Yes," Chantal said to the oval window which was filling with the Rome runway as their plane touched down in the dusky haze of an Italian evening. Now and then, her joints ached. She wondered if it had anything to do with the poor nutrition they had received when confined in Tunisia. But she said nothing to Gloria.

They had scheduled a flight to Podgorica in Montenegro the following day. From there they would have to find a way across the border with Kosovo to Pec. It was the quickest way that the travel agent had found, despite all of Chantal's flirting with the man.

Once through their arrival gate, the two woman walked straight for the entrance. They had agreed to travel as lightly as possible, and so had only one small bag each. They skipped the baggage claim and headed for the line of taxis and took one to a hotel the driver recommended nearby. Its neon sign announced it had earned two stars for its drab accommodations.

As the taxi pulled away, they exchanged looks of resignation. The lobby attendant booked them two rooms for the night and handed them keys attached to unlosable wooden carvings of local attractions.

Chantal turned her roughly-carved St. Peter's over and looked to see if the sloppy artist had bothered to claim his or her work. Wisely, no one had.

"Are you hungry?" Gloria asked her.

The train station croissant had certainly been stiff. And now so were her muscles. They had done so much sitting today.

"I could eat something," Chantal said, as her stomach made audible agreement.

Gloria laughed softly, "Mine sounds like that all the time."

Chantal had almost forgotten Gloria's pregnancy. She remembered being ravenous the day long when she had been pregnant with Sophie. She was surprised to realize she felt guilty that she had not thought of Gloria's need to feed two.

"Shall we meet in the bar in fifteen minutes?" Chantal suggested.

"That's fine."

They took the elevator up to their rooms, Gloria to the third floor, Chantal to the fourth. Chantal laid her small travel bag on the bed. It was just large enough for a sweater, her passport, a few personal articles, and of course a drawing pad. Traveling light was no understatement. They had each only brought one change of clothing. Fashion was not going to be an issue this trip. Rubbing her faintly aching knuckles, Chantal missed her rings. She had left them behind, not wanting to wear anything that would attract attention. And her jewelry pieces of choice—chunky square wooden rings, estate chokers and such—were not exactly your average accessories.

It was early November. The days were starting to become cool, and the nights were cold. Since leaving Nice, Chantal hadn't had an opportunity to shop, so Gloria had loaned her a warm wool coat for the trip.

She lifted the coat from her bag and tried it on, turning to inspect her image in the full-length mirror. Gloria was slightly larger than she, but the coat fit. The dark green color suited her, *though probably not as well as Gloria with her red hair,* she thought.

Laying the coat aside, she examined her form from the front, then turned to see her profile. Smooth shoulders, narrow waist, and legs that Justin had certainly not complained about last night.

Just last night. She steeled herself not to worry, to quell the anxiety with hope.

If she could paint herself at this moment, the canvas would be covered in a palette of blood-orange and Prussian blue colliding in Cubist perspectives, all sides of her visible at once.

She splashed cool water on her face and patted it dry with a fresh towel, reanchoring herself in a paintless but colorful reality. Well, maybe not this room. She frowned at the curling wallpaper, faded to a shadow of its former pattern.

Arriving in the lobby, she found Gloria seated at a small table sipping a glass of mineral water.

Chantal joined her, Thinking of nothing else, she asked, "How is your room?"

"Basic. And yours?" Gloria was poking at the lemon floating on her ice cubes.

"The same."

"Do you want something to drink?" Gloria handed her the small printed beverage list just as the waiter brought them bowl of dull-looking crackers. Chantal took a cracker but declined the drink offer from both the waiter and Gloria, "No thank you. I'll wait until we get some food."

When the waiter left, Chantal paused a beat before asking, "Have you been thinking about tomorrow?"

"A little," Gloria said, as she lost interest in her lemon wedge and looked up at Chantal "Pec can't be that big of a place. Surely someone would know where to find this Zog Merkat."

"Zog. Sounds like something out of a comic book," Chantal smiled, imagining masked eyes, and cryptic, initialed body suits in primary colors. But the reality of this man, especially in the context of Justin's abduction, was hardly comic. The faint smile faded from her lips and she said in a lower voice, "We'll have to be careful."

"I know that," Gloria said, a hint of exasperation shaping her words.

"Well, I didn't mean…" Chantal broke off, holding up her hands, "Never mind. I think I will order a drink." She hailed the waiter who was passing and asked for a glass of wine.

"I think we should start by talking to the local police," Gloria directed.

"Is that really the best tactic?" Chantal asked.

"What else do we do?"

"There might be other options."

"Such as?" Gloria asked.

"Find his family, a friend, someone who has inside information. They may not be willing to talk with the police."

"You make it sound theatrical," Gloria told her, green eyes accusing.

"Look, unless we are open to ideas, we will never find Justin."

"It was my idea to go to Pec," Gloria reminded her.

"And it was my idea to take copies of those identity papers," Chantal countered.

"We may never find Justin if we do it your way."

"And what happens when we find him?" Chantal asked, locking eyes with her rival and planting her elbow precariously near her glass of Chianti. It glowed fiery red in the candlelight and cast its shadow across the table toward Gloria. Chantal spoke each word as if it existed alone, "And if he chooses me?"

Gloria tilted her head, unperturbed. "Justin isn't like that,"

"Like what? You have known him so very long. What, less than a year?"

Gloria only responded to her first question. "He is honorable and gentle. He will do what is right."

"What makes you think you know him? I was with him for five years." And last night, she almost added, but restrained herself. She would not let this woman get under her skin any more than she already had.

"Maybe, but he has changed. I know him now."

"I doubt it," Chantal said, standing up from the table first this time. "I will have dinner sent to my room."

Without waiting for Gloria's reply, Chantal grabbed her glass and headed for the elevators. Once the lumbering machine had rattled down to the foyer, she stepped inside and hit the four. As it started its ascent, she slumped against its back wall, feeling like she should be headed down instead.

If she could tolerate it, she'd work with Gloria just until she found an opportunity to lose her. Then she would find Justin on her own.

If she got to him first, maybe he would choose her.

And only her.

CHAPTER 12

"We are crossing border," the driver said. "Pec is twenty five kilometers from here. It should take less than an hour." They bounced along a winding dirt road in a dented and rusted Mercedes with 'Taxi' lettered on the side. Every pothole jolted them into uncomfortable awareness that the springs poked up through the seat padding.

Gloria looked for any indications that they were crossing more than roads in sorry condition. She must have missed the signage. She sighed.

Broken only by necessary communication, a wall of silence had fallen heavily between Gloria and Chantal since they checked out of the hotel in Rome.

Flying over the Adriatic Sea on the way to Podgorica, Gloria had watched Chantal gaze out of the tiny airplane window at the magnificent blue below. During the flight, Chantal had taken her drawing pad from her bag and made several sketches of the sea.

Gloria wondered what Chantal thought of air travel. Belatedly, she realized that their flight from Barcelona to Rome had been the first time Chantal had chosen to board a plane since the high jacking. A current of unexpected sympathy added to the twisting in her stomach that was her morning sickness.

She crossed her hands over her womb, and imagined cradling the child growing there. Justin loved little Sophie at least as much as she already loved this small life.

She closed her eyes, remembering the days Justin had spent staring into the sea, grieving for his wife and daughter. But he had made his peace with their loss and asked Gloria to marry him. What if she were Chantal? If she returned from the supposed grave to a pregnant wife… Now her heart lurched in rhythm with her stomach. She pressed the button for a flight attendant and ordered a ginger ale.

★ ★ ★

Shortly after they landed in Montenegro, they had found this taxi driver. He agreed to take them to Pec, Kosovo for five hundred dollars, "not through the normal customs." The travel agent had told them that, although they could travel in Montenegro as tourists, they needed visas to enter Kosovo. Applying for a visa would take time that they did not have. When they briefly explained their situation to the driver, he merely gestured for them to get in the car.

From Pristina they drove north on the main road toward Serbia, reaching the town of Potje after seventy-five kilometers. Another fifty kilometers west took them through the larger town of Ivangrad. Generally the traffic flowed smoothly, but occasionally a car would try to cut a quick pass around a slower-moving large truck, veering back into its lane within centimeters of the oncoming traffic.

After Ivangrad the taxi driver turned off the main road onto the well-worn dirt one that they were currently bouncing along.

Dry brown hills jutted up around them, rocky and covered with sagebrush. The driver, who had been silent for most of the trip, said, "We are past border now. Must be careful."

"Why?" Gloria asked.

"NATO makes patrols for border. Smugglers. Not wanted people. Also, there are bandits. They steal from smugglers or ask money."

They drove on and met a small van. The stern faces of the driver and passenger stared directly forward as they passed.

"Smugglers," the driver said, nodding to himself.

"What are they smuggling?" Gloria asked.

"Many things."

"Like what?"

"Whatever people want. When they go that way they take drugs, cigarettes. Maybe people. When they return they bring food, clothings, car part or maybe weapons. Smuggle both ways."

"Are there many smugglers?" Gloria asked.

"Many. As I say, we must be careful. There are many gang, and they no like each other. If they stop us they may can ask for money." He paused and looked in his rearview mirror. "And two pretty women. It is dangerous."

Both women shifted in their seats at this and, for the first time since beginning this probably futile rescue mission, they exchanged glances with no malice in them. But fear was hardly a happy runner-up.

"Do you know Pec?" Gloria asked in the direction of the front seat.

"What do you want to know?" the driver asked.

"How big it is, people who live there…"

The driver looked at them in his rear view mirror and asked, "Why are you going there?"

"To find a friend," Gloria replied. "We want to know what happened to him. Do you have any ideas for finding someone there?"

"Pec is big town," the driver replied. "Maybe one hundred fifty thousand people, maybe more. Before NATO bombed there were fifteen percent Serbs, now less. Now mostly Albanians. KLA was very strong, mostly bandits. Now KLA factions control drugs smuggled to Europe. Why does NATO and the UN support these bandits? We no understand." He paused as if forgetting something. "In Pec not all people are bad, but have caution."

"How do you advise we find our friend?" Chantal asked.

"Do not go to police." Chantal glanced at Gloria who kept her eyes on the driver. "They will look for your visa in passport and then fine you, maybe put you in jail. You can never trust them. They work with the gangs. I take you to small hotel near center of Pec. Not many hotels. If you have one hundred dollars and give it to man who runs hotel, he find your friend. If you also give me one hundred dollars I will talk with him to make setup."

"OK. But we pay you after you speak to your friend," Chantal told him.

The driver smiled.

Chantal took a piece of paper from her sketch pad, wrote, 'Can we trust him?' and held it in Gloria's direction.

Gloria glanced at it and shrugged her shoulders.

"In five kilometers we reach Pec," the driver said. He came around a long curve and slowed down. A car parked crossways blocked the road ahead. The driver put on his brakes and came to a stop while a cloud of dust engulfed the taxi. A man in a long-sleeved red shirt was standing in the middle of the road with a gun in his hand.

Through the dust settling behind the taxi, Chantal saw that another man had come behind their car. He was bald and wearing a checkered blue shirt. He also held a gun.

"Not good," the driver said, gripping his steering wheel. "Bandits."

CHAPTER 13

Justin lay on his back, the spinning sensation in his head making him feel like he'd just stepped off a merry-go-round. He opened his eyes, attempting to focus on something to hold the world still for a moment.

Footsteps sounded nearby, and he slowly turned his head in their direction. The horizontal world gone vertical, he saw blurry image of several sideways doors opening and gravity-free men walking through them. He blinked hard, and a single man's form slowly came into focus leaning over him. Justin righted his head.

The man set a tray down beside him and lifted a glass of water with a straw to Justin's lips, commanding "Drink."

Justin struggled to lift his head and sip from the straw. His mouth was dry, and the little bit of water that he could suction up tickled his parched throat.

The man unwrapped a candy bar and put it to Justin's mouth. "Eat," he said.

Justin laid his throbbing head back down and let the man break off small pieces of chocolate covered nuts and nougat into his mouth.

Another man appeared and undid the straps pinning his hands to the floor beside him. Justin watched him release another strap around his ankles—he had not noticed that his feet were bound too. He could barely register that his head was still attached to his torso, let alone that his limbs were attached to that.

They lifted him up from the ground in slow motion. His legs felt like Jello underneath him. "Where 'm I," he slurred.

"We take you to toilette," one of the men stated.

"Wha'dya want w' me?" Justin managed to mumble when they brought him back to the room.

"When drugs wear off tomorrow, we ask you questions. Soon we bring you more food."

Justin's eyes fell closed under their own weight. He lost consciousness again.

* * *

The red-shirted man walked to the driver's window. Both women had their eyes on his gun. He said something to their driver who turned to them, "He wants us to get out of the car."

"What for?" Chantal said.

"Be careful, dangerous," the driver said. "Do what he asks." He heaved himself from his vinyl seat and stood against the door frame.

The bald man in blue had moved to the rear of the taxi. He held his gun casually like some ordinary work tool—a window squeegee or a garden trowel.

But the gun was his ordinary work tool.

Chantal stepped from the taxi followed by Gloria. The bald man stepped toward them, waving his gun back and forth, but keeping a steady and interested eye on the two women.

The front man spoke to the driver again who nodded and turned to Chantal and Gloria, "They want to know what we are doing here."

Chantal answered immediately, "Tell them we are going to see a friend in Pec."

"I'm not sure that's good enough," the driver faintly shook his head.

"It will have to be," Chantal said back.

The man knocked his gun against the side of the car and barked at the driver.

"He wants us to answer his questions, not have conversation between us."

Gloria repeated Chantal's answer, "Tell him we are here to see a friend."

The driver spoke to the man and exchanged more words.

"Who is your friend?" the driver asked.

"A man named Zog," Chantal answered, adjusting her posture.

The man laughed and said something to the driver.

"He said there must be a thousand Zog's in Pec."

The bald man laughed with them, speaking to his cohort who said something to the taxi driver.

"They want you to pay them money."

"What for?" Gloria asked.

"For passage to Pec."

"How much?" Chantal asked.

"A thousand dollars."

Gloria and Chantal looked at each other and then back at the bandit. They knew that if they paid that much money up front, these men would certainly believe they had more.

"We don't have a thousand," Chantal replied. "We can give them a hundred."

The taxi driver translated to the man in the red shirt who laughed.

The bald man was studying the women. He started talking while waving his gun toward his car.

The driver translated as ordered, "He wants you to get in their car."

"Why?" Gloria asked, a bead of sweat forming along her temple.

"They get more than thousand dollars for each of you if sell you to a gang. He said you both be worth much money."

Chantal spat in the direction of the driver and red bandit, "Tell him to go to hell."

Gloria put her hand on Chantal's arm, "Chantal, be careful. Let's give him his thousand dollars." Chantal shook off the touch.

"Please, you no talk to yourselves," the driver said.

"I'm not paying the money," Chantal said, folding her arms as if sealing the matter.

"Then what do you want to do?" Gloria asked.

The man in the red shirt raising his voice at the driver. The driver turned to them patting his hands in the air in an effort to placate and reason with them, "He says you talk, he shoot."

"Tell him to shoot," Chantal said, her face a challenging snarl.

Taken aback by this foreign woman's determination, the man in front spoke again to the driver, but kept his eyes on Chantal, and brought his gun up to aiming height.

The driver repeated, "You both to get into his car. Now."

Gloria began moving as directed.

"You can kill us first," Chantal yelled in French.

The man behind the taxi came forward, grabbing Chantal around the waist and lifting her off the ground. She began scratching at his face and kicking, trying to get her foot into his groin. Gloria moved toward them, but the man in red grabbed her arm and pinned it to his side, laughing. He poked his free elbow in the taxi driver's direction and said something in a way that suggested the driver would agree with him.

"He says he likes you," the driver said to Chantal. "That you will be worth much money."

Chantal began hitting and clawing at the man, shoving his shoulders backward in an untrained but instinctive effort to wrench herself free. Sharp pains shot from her healing bullet wound, and she gritted her teeth. The bald man pushed her toward their car.

Just as Gloria swung her head around for any diversion, a line of cars became visible heading toward them on the road. When the man holding her saw the approaching vehicles, he flung Gloria's arm from him and pulled at the man struggling with Chantal, gesturing at the road. They ran for their car, jumped in, and sped off in the opposite direction.

Chantal and Gloria were left standing in the middle of the road, shaking as the swirl of tire-stirred dust rose and fell on them.

The driver sank back down into his seat. "United Nations Peace Force. KFOR," he announced, though neither woman had had the breath to ask him. "They will ask why you are here." He sighed. "You should think of a better story this time."

CHAPTER 14

Illuminated by a fluorescent blaze of lights, Laszlo Vartek and Jordi Pujols walked down the office hall. They passed the nameplates of various small companies in advertising, technology, and consulting. When they came to a door emblazoned with 'Protective Services GMBH', they stopped. Laszlo signaled for Jordi to follow him inside.

A small reception area adjoined several offices. Laszlo walked across to one of them, glanced inside and saw a man seated in front of a computer screen.

"Horst, that will ruin your eyes," Laszlo said.

Startled, the man looked up. When he saw his visitor, a smile broke over his face, and he pushed back in the wheeled desk chair, hand to his heart, "Laszlo, you scared me."

"I have a way of doing that," he said, nodding at Horst.

Horst pushed his glasses back up his nose and pointed that appendage toward his monitor, "Just doing some web surfing to figure out where I want to go on my next holiday."

"Business is that good?" Laszlo asked. "The last time I was here you were in those run-down buildings. What happened?"

"They tore them down to put up some gigantic government building," he shrugged then brightened, "But better than that, business has been great. More and more "big" people are asking for protection." Horst rose and looked over at Jordi who had not fully entered the room, but had remained standing near the door, swarthy and silent. Horst went on, "Actually I need to hire a few more people. I know I can't entice you to work for me, but what about your friend there?" he pointed at Jordi. "Looks like he can handle himself."

"More than you know," Laszlo replied. "Horst Schneider, let me introduce you to Jordi Pujols."

The two men shook hands.

"Are you bringing me business?" Horst asked. "Last time you hired a security team for a big party here in Berlin."

Laszlo remembered. It was a social event Stefan von Portzer had organized. The guest list had included a large number of key politicians. "No. This time we are looking for information. Here in Berlin."

Horst's eyes narrowed. "Who are you looking for?"

"Someone was kidnapped in Brussels. A young woman, twenty-four years old. Her name is Anne Kent. The police are looking for her. We have been engaged by her family to do some parallel investigations." He remembered too well the photo of Anne Kent he had in his pocket. The girl was striking. He worried that her abductors would think the same thing.

"You mean you can go places and do things that the police can't," Horst smiled, but with a wry twist in his lips.

"Yes. Something like that."

"Why did you come to Berlin?"

"Mr. Pujols and I managed to find the trail relatively quickly. We think the kidnapping involves a gang of drug dealers. The police were already making involved. A task force of policemen from the U.S. and Europe are investigating an international drug ring. The girl's uncle, a detective from California, was on that task force until a few days ago, when he was murdered in the parking lot of a hotel in Brussels. Anne Kent was with him when the shooting took place, but no one has seen her since. We interviewed several leads in Brussels. A fairly reliable source in the underworld named several major drug dealers. It seems there are two connected organizations. One handles southern Europe, the other northern Europe. The northern one is based here."

"Did you say you 'interviewed' them?" Horst asked.

"Yes."

"I bet you did. But, if it was drug related, why did they take the girl?"

"We need to find out." Laszlo looked like he would.

Horst jerked his head in the direction of a cluster of chairs nearby. "Have a seat," he said, following his own advice and going on, "What information do you have about this 'organization' in Berlin?"

Laszlo sat, but looked as if he were still standing tall. "A knowledgeable source said that the head gang is run by a Klaus Schubach. He operates a large network and had the most to lose from the investigation in Brussels. One of the kidnappers talked too much and told our source he was working for Schubach."

"Did you find the kidnapper?"

Laszlo nodded. "Unfortunately he was dead. Killed. The price of disclosing confidential information. We were too late. But we believe Schubach was involved. Do you know him?"

"I don't know him personally, but I do know about him. He is, er, extreme."

"You mean 'extremely' bad?" Laszlo's face shifted into what might have been the shadow of a smile, as if this were a pleasing challenge.

"*Ja.* He controls a drug cartel worth hundreds of millions of Euro. No one trusts him, everyone is afraid of him. He's ruthless and manages to keep out of custody. No one ever has any evidence against him, and he has so many minions under him that no one ever gets near him. And," Horst narrowed his eyes a bit, "rumor has it that he has political backing."

Laszlo cocked his head to the side, "Someone is protecting him?"

"Seems that way. Politicians backing drugs. But that's not all." Horse expelled a breath "There's human trafficking too."

"You mean women?" Jordi asked. Horst blinked in surprise. Jordi had not said a word, even when being introduced

"Not exclusively," Horst said to him, "but yes. Let me ask something. Was the girl, this Anne Kent, pretty?"

"More than pretty," Laszlo said. He reached into his pocket and pulled out the photograph he had already carved in his memory. It was taken at a family picnic at Sam Oliver's house in Santa Cruz, California the past spring. A young woman with auburn hair looked out at him, her dark eyes filled with laughter. She wore a cropped, fitting t-shirt that revealed a flat brown stomach above long denimned legs. She held her hand out toward the photographer, in a failed attempt to keep her photo from being taken.

"*Schön.*" Horst whistled and said, "Looks like she has spirit too."

"And brains," Laszlo added. "She is finishing a doctorate at Cambridge."

Horst paused. "If she is in the hands of one of these gangs, they will ransom her for money or trade. Have they called in and asked for money?"

"No. That's what is troubling us."

Horst nodded. "Prostitution is a huge business in Germany, and not much is done to stop trafficking of women. German politicians are the first clients to line up at the door. A young, beautiful woman sold to the right person can bring a high price. Schubach is a big player in that business."

Jordi spoke a second time, "How can we meet him?" His accent on the word 'meet' made Horst swallow.

Horst turned to him, face serious. "That would be difficult. He lives just outside Berlin in a guarded compound. He comes and goes in a private jet."

"Does he have an office in Berlin?" Laszlo asked.

"Yes, on Guberstrasse. When he is in town, he is often there. But like his estate, his office is well-guarded."

"Every protection system has its vulnerabilities," said Jordi, standing up and closing the conversation.

CHAPTER 15

"*K*illed, not thrilled." Anne Kent tossed her hands in the air. To say she was having trouble communicating with the two girls in the room with her was an understatement. They spoke a little English, but better French. Anne's French was just plain bad.

She had tried to explain to them that her uncle had been shot and killed. Right before her eyes. And then that a man had smashed his gun into the side of her head.

One of the girls, the taller darker one asked her in English, "How long you with men?"

Anne answered slowly, hoping to be clear, "I do not know. They drugged me. Medicine. Sleep." She put her palms together, held them to the side, and laid her head on them to indicate sleep. She straightened, "I have traveled to several places. I don't feel the drugs any more."

The girls nodded their head.

"Is there any way to escape?" Anne asked.

"Escape?" the smaller one asked, her eyes brightening.

Anne motioned with her hand. "To go."

"Ah, *escale*."

"Yes, *escale*," Anne nodded eagerly.

"No good," the larger girl said. Her dark face dour at the reality of their situation.

There was noise at the door. A mid-sized man opened it and stepped into their room. Anne recognized him as Edouard, one of the men who had moved her from place to place. And the one who had stared at her the most.

He closed the door behind him and leaned against it, ignoring the two girls and looking directly at Anne, "*Demain tu va. Il y a quel qu'en qui a payée beaucoup pour toi.*"

Anne thought she understood, but she turned to the girls and asked, "What did he say?"

"He say tomorrow you go." The darker girl said. Someone pay for you. Many money he say."

"Pay for me! What does he think we are, slaves?" She turned to him but continued to speak to the girls, "What century does he live in?"

Edouard didn't understand what she said, but understood he had translators and said, "*Mais maintenant tu est pour moi. Je te veux pour mon plasir. Vien avec moi.*" He stared at Anne for a moment, turned to the taller girl and said, "*Traduire.*"

The smaller, pale-haired girl said, "He say now he want you. For pleasure. To go with him." The girl's young eyes betrayed the knowledge of what was being asked of Anne.

Anne did not move as a sense of enormous horror descended on her. The thought of being taken by this man, forced by him. Raging disgust replaced the horror. Her blood felt hot and thrumming and every kick box class she'd taken at college started to rise under her skin.

Eduard took Anne's stillness as an act of submission. He smiled, stepped toward her, and grabbed her arm, "*Vien.*"

With one adrenaline-packed movement, she shot out her leg, torso going horizontal as she smashed her foot into Edouard's groin, driving upward against his pelvis in one pounding thud.

"Ahhhh," Edouard breathed, sinking in slowest motion to the hard tile floor.

Anne followed that kick with another plus a punch. And another. And another.

Edouard doubled over, one hand to block blows to his face and one to his throbbing groin. He fell to the floor.

Anne drove her foot into his ribs and felt snap. She kicked again and again, aiming at his face and neck, an uncontrollable anger rising within her as she remembered the sight of her uncle sinking dead onto the ground.

The two girls sat on the bed watching, arms around each other and mouths gaping.

Two men rushed into the room. One grabbed Anne from behind but she wiggled in his grip, got her teeth onto his hand, and bit hard.

He released his grip, but still had a commanding position. He pushed her forward on the bed, a chokehold around her neck. He squeezed hard, immobilizing her, and cutting off her breath for a moment. When he released her, he said only, "Stay." He got off her and went over to help his friend lift Eduard off the floor.

They supported Eduard through the door. He remained doubled over, groaning with each slow footstep.

Anne rose from the bed, looked out the unlocked door, and watched them move to the end of the hall. They disappeared up a flight of stairs. She took advantage of the moment to move down the hall in the opposite direction toward the other flight of stairs.

The next floor down seemed to be the ground floor—the stairs opened into a large entrance area. Seeing no one, she crossed the entrance space and opened a wooden door. Just beyond it stretched the beautiful sight of an ugly, busy street.

She pulled the door wide as footsteps thundered down the stairs behind her. She had one leg out the door when the other was grabbed from behind and she was yanked back.

The door closed on the street and her freedom.

The second the bandit's dust had settled, two open jeeps rolled up the road, bringing a brown cloud with them. Four fully-armed soldiers in camouflage sat in each vehicle. When they pulled up even with the taxi, they braked.

One of the soldiers got out and saluted the driver and the two women. He wore the insignia of a sergeant on his sleeve. The other soldiers kept their eyes on the women.

The sergeant said something in the same language the bandits had spoken, and the driver replied.

The soldier said, "He said you speak English."

Chantal saw a small French flag sewn on his shoulder and she replied, *"Oui, et le Francais."*

The other soldiers laughed.

The sergeant switched to French. "Are you French? What are you doing here?"

"Bandits just tried to rob us. It is fortunate you came at the right time."

"In the car that just drove away?"

"Yes, there were two of them," Chantal replied.

Gloria stayed silent, and by the paleness around her mouth, Chantal guessed she was not feeling well. In confirmation, Gloria's hand went slowly to her stomach. Chantal could here her taking deep, slow breaths.

"There are many people like that around here. It is not safe." The sergeant said in his clipped, commanding voice. Despite the dust, his uniform looked smart and was worn with pride. "Who are you?"

"We are with the International Red Cross and have been sent to Pec to follow up on refugee issues." Chantal lied, the words leaving her mouth before she even realized she'd opened it.

The sergeant nodded, "There is much of this in Kosovo."

"We are part of a documentation team," Chantal continued, warming to her deception, but wary of giving herself away. She wanted to get away soon. Gloria looked like she needed to sit down.

"Pec is over that way," the soldier said, motioning with his hand in an Easterly direction. "Why are you in a taxi with Montenegro license plates?"

"We just went over there to get away from Pec a little bit."

"I understand," the soldier said, "but why not take the main road?"

"As part of the International Red Cross assigned to Kosovo, we are not supposed to visit surrounding counties. Please don't tell anyone." She caught the eyes of a soldier on her, and he wasn't making eye contact.

"Does she speak French?" the soldier asked, nodding toward Gloria.

"Yes, adequately," Gloria answered, a bit of color was coming back to her face.

"Ah, the accent of a Spanish woman," the soldier laughed.

Gloria smiled thinly back.

"That was quite frightening, to meet those men," Gloria said, "but you saved us. You are brave to be here." Chantal tried not to smile.

The sergeant lifted his chest to fill out his uniform, "Just doing our duty as part of the international peace force."

"Will we be safe now?" Gloria asked.

"We will escort you back to Pec. Where are you staying?"

It was back to Chantal's fib, "Where the internationals stay." She knew she took a chance, but if there were people from international organizations in Pec they would all be staying at the same hotel.

"The Hotel Balkan?"

"Yes, that's the one," she did a mental wipe of her forehead. "And thank you for escorting us. We feel so much safer with you." She gave him the full force of those blue eyes.

"Let's go," the sergeant commanded, waving at the drivers in the two jeeps.

Chantal and Gloria practically fell back into the taxi. Gloria was holding her stomach again. Under her breath, she said to Chantal, "I never thought I'd be grateful to sit again on this awful upholstery." Chantal said nothing until the taxi driver started the car and they were driving down the dirt road between the two jeeps full of soldiers.

Then she sank back against the seat. "I'm surprised it worked."

"You told a good story," Gloria admitted.

"I don't know where it came from," she said, wearily surprised. Then she sat up straight and turned to Gloria, "What if they had asked for our identification papers?"

"I already thought of that," Gloria said, closing her eyes and leaning her head back as another round of mistimed morning sickness surged through her. "The bandits stole them."

CHAPTER 16

Justin opened his eyes to light. It filtered in through an opaque window. He blinked and looked up—bars. He tried to sit up, but felt straps around his wrists and ankles anchoring him to a bed. He tried to focus on the mattress, but he had a splitting headache.

He resisted the urge to return to unconsciousness. *Think, man,* he told himself. Where was he? The last thing he could remember clearly was walking down a road near a forest and then fighting with men. His ribs were sore.

Then he remembered. He had been at the monastery with Chantal and Gloria. And with Dora and Sophie. How long had he been gone, and had anyone noticed his absence?

Someone had found him there. Someone who was willing to go to the trouble of taking him and holding him for questioning. Justin tried to ignore the steady pulse of pain crossing between his temples as he ran back over the past months. Gloria. Finding Chantal. Yass.

And the killing of Jacques Tapic.

Bingo. That had to be it. That and a significant chunk of money from Tapic's empire that had landed in Justin's hands.

Those hands were securely tied at the moment, but he wriggled them anyway, wincing at the chaffing. Head clearing, he surveyed the small room. It had just enough space for the single metal framed bed that he was horizontally familiar with at the moment, a small wooden table and a white plastic chair. Under the table sat a metal pot.

The walls had been painted a pale, glossy green, but probably not during the Cold War, Justin guessed. Large brown spots spread across the wall, puffing out the paint. There were also smaller dark spots everywhere. On closer inspection, they proved to be smashed spiders and blood-filled mosquitoes.

Just as he was wondering whether it was mosquito season, he heard a key turning in the lock. The door was constructed of solid metal door, but it swiveled open easily to reveal two men, one holding a tray. They entered and the empty-handed one released the straps on Justin's wrists and ankles.

Justin sat up slowly, his head throbbing.

"Lunch," one of the men said, pointing to the tray on the table.

On the tray waited a plastic cup with black coffee, a long piece of baguette and two cubes of sugar wrapped in paper.

"Metal pot for piss. Otherwise we come sometimes to take you to toilette."

Justin rubbed his forehead. "What do you want from me?"

"Mustafi wants to ask questions?"

"Who's Mustafi?"

"The man who asks questions," the man said, laughing.

"Where am I?"

"In a room." Both men laughed and backed out of their answer, relocking the door behind them.

Justin stood up stretched until things snapped and popped back into alignment. He went to the plastic chair and sat down. Making a grimace at his starchy provisions, he removed the wrapping from the two sugar cubes and dropped them in the coffee. There was nothing to stir with.

He picked up the baguette and bit into a crust so hard it scratched his gums. The surprising pain of it finally jolted him through the final haze of whatever drugs had coursed through his system.

Aloud to the barred window, he asked, "And just where is it I have the privilege of receiving such fine service? I'd like to send my compliments to the manager." He sighed and started to flick at the sugar cubes wrappers. He picked one up.

In small letters it read, 'Sucre S.A., Torino, Italia'.

★ ★ ★

The small convoy headed for Pec—a battered taxi sandwiched by two jeeps full of soldiers.

"Be careful of the French soldiers," the taxi driver said to his rearview mirror, making eye contact with Gloria and Chantal in turn. "They are with the bandits."

"Why do you say that?" Gloria asked. She was getting annoyed by the topic of bandits.

"On certain shipments, the French soldiers escort trucks to the border that cross into Albania or Montenegro."

Chantal looked puzzled, "What's wrong with that?"

"When trucks reach border, protection of trucks is turned over to gangs. If good and important things are in trucks, then local police take over protecting." The driver paused and returned his eyes to the road long enough to swerve around a gaping pothole. "And we know what's in the trucks," he added importantly.

"What's in them?"

"Cigarettes, drugs, women."

Gloria shivered at the last 'item'. "How do you know?"

"We know. But it is better not to tell anyone. Better for your health." He laughed. "French soldiers getting money. Someone giving orders to them. Don't trust French soldiers. And be careful of police in Pec. Gangs are paying police. They turn their heads the other way. Better I take you to hotel of my friend. Not Hotel Balkan. French soldiers will know you are there."

Gloria wrinkled her forehead at this and glanced over at Chantal. *She looks as unconvinced as I do,* Gloria thought.

The convoy picked up speed after they merged onto a paved road. They roared along, passing an occasional house with peeling paint and chickens pecking at dirt in the yard. After a kilometer the houses were packed closer together and interspersed with larger buildings that shadowed their shorter neighbors.

Gloria was ready to recant aloud her former appreciation of the back seat padding when they slowed into the center of Pec. She certainly would not be searching for postcards of this place. Soot-stained shops with faded signs lined the street which led to a large town square with parched brown grass and little else. Children played there while women chatted under the shade of a few large trees.

The jeeps stopped in front of a building whose faded sign barely read 'Hotel Balkan'.

"Not good to stay here," the driver said.

"We prefer here," Gloria said with authority.

His shrug was more like a flinch, "Your choice."

Chantal paid the driver the remaining three hundred dollars they owed him. He got out, opened the trunk and pulled out their two small travel bags.

The sergeant was approaching them. "Do you need any help?"

"No thank you," Chantal answered, "But thanks again for saving us back there." Gloria was happy to let Chantal take over from here. She was tired. All this stress could not be good for the life inside her. She breathed a silent prayer for the unborn child who lay in her womb.

"My pleasure," the sergeant answered. "How long will you be here?"

"Not long," Chantal said, businesslike, "We just need to do some research."

"In three days we will be back in Pec. May I invite you to dinner, along with my commanding officer?"

Chantal looked at Gloria. "We may be gone by then, but if we are here, please stop by."

"Here. I'll carry your bags to the hotel."

"No, thank you. They are not heavy," Chantal smiled, taking her bag as she declined. Gloria did likewise.

"Okay, see you in three days," the soldier made a gesture that appeared to be half-bow, half-salute. He marched back to the jeep and commanded his driver to leave. The soldiers in the two jeeps waved as they rolled by.

Chantal and Gloria entered the hotel lobby, passing a lady half-heartedly sloshing a mop over tiles that no amount of scrubbing would ever make white again. An unshaven old man sat, rumpled as his faded blue shirt, behind the reception disk. He glanced up when they entered but made no greeting.

"Do you have any rooms?" Chantal asked.

"Sixteen rooms in hotel. All taken." He waved a hand. Gloria could not tell whether it was to indicate the number of full rooms or to dismiss them.

"No free rooms?" Chantal asked again.

"Depends," the man answered, finally giving them half his attention with a rather nasty, wet cough.

Chantal rolled her eyes at Gloria and fished ten dollars out of her purse.

The man took the money and put it into his shirt pocket. "Only one room free," he said.

"Only one?" Gloria asked.

"Others taken. UN people. Aid people. Doctor people. Business people." He reached to a board behind his chair and took a key. "You pay with credit card or money, Euros or Dollars?"

"Credit card." Gloria handed him her Visa.

The man took an imprint of the card and gave them the key. "Next floor up, room twelve. Breakfast served in room down here in back. No dinner. Restaurant down street."

They climbed the stairs and followed the threadbare purple carpet down the hall to their room. High ceilings and an ornate multipaned window made the sagging double bed appear distinctly out of place. Clearly the hotel had seen better days.

Chantal and Gloria looked at each other, mirroring each other's exhaustion. In the last—how many hours?—they had traveled by airplane and taxi all the way from Rome to Pec, crossed the border into Kosovo, and barely escaped being captured and sold as prostitutes. Now here they were in a tattered old hotel, in a country where their only mild guarantee of safety seemed to be money.

And as for their trip's purpose, they still had no clear plan for finding Zog.

Chantal walked over to the bed and pulled back the cover with thumb and forefinger. After checking the fabric, she raised her head and dropped the bedding back. "At least there aren't any bugs in the bed." She made a gesture of wiping her hands anyway.

They both laughed.

Gloria gave Chantal a weary smile and suggested, "Let's see if we can find food we can say the same thing about."

CHAPTER 17

A miasma of cigarette smoke hit them square in the eyes as they entered the restaurant. Groups of men sat around greasy wooden tables drinking tea or coffee and clear alcohol in small shot glasses. Some were elbow-deep in discussion and others chatted casually in slouches.

The door banged shut behind Chantal and Gloria, and all heads swiveled in their direction.

The two women made straight for a small table in a corner of the room. They were conscious of their observers but pretended oblivion. A waiter approached them and said something in what must have been Albanian.

Chantal squared her shoulders and asked, "Do you speak English?" She waited and the man didn't reply. "*Le Francais?*"

The man shook his head.

"*Español?*" Gloria tried.

The man shook his head again. He held up a finger for their attention, then made a cup of his hands as though drinking. When Chantal nodded, he then used a hand to mimic forking food into his mouth. Satisfied with his performance, he walked away.

"What was that?" Gloria asked.

"I guess we just ordered something," Chantal shrugged. She gave the room a covert glance and saw that most of the men had returned to their conversations. A few heads still focused on their table, their eyes unblinking and transparently interested.

The waiter returned and set two glasses of tea on the table and two small glasses of the clear liquid they had seen in front of most every other customer there.

Gloria lifted her glass, smelled it and tasted a few drops. "Strong as Spanish brandy, but different. More like an Italian Grappa, I think."

Chantal raised her glass, glanced over at a nearby table of men watching her, and swallowed the liquid in one quick gulp. Noise of appreciation went up from the men. Gloria continued taking her time between small sips.

Once again, the waiter came to their table. This time with two plates piled with boiled potatoes and chunks of meat. He placed it before the women and left in silence as before.

Gloria looked at the food, "At least it's been cooked long enough to kill all bacteria."

"Not exactly a fine French restaurant." Chantal sniffed and tasted the meat. "I think it is boiled lamb."

Gloria stabbed a piece with her fork and bit at an edge. "Not too bad actually, whatever it is. It will fill our stomachs."

"What is it that Justin sometimes said?" Chantal asked. "Beggars can't be choosers."

As soon as the words left her mouth, she sensed Gloria's demeanor change from humor to worry. Chantal swallowed, finally grasping— over greasy food in a smoky, dingy restaurant—that Gloria's heart was just as filled with Justin as was hers.

★ ★ ★

At a large house on a hill in southern Pec, a staff member of the United Nations raised his crystal stem glass, swirling the honey-colored contents. When his wine had stilled, he looked through the glass's belly at the room he was sitting in. The medieval tapestry and Louis XIV sideboard across from him lost their rectangularity in the broad glass's curves.

He lowered the wine until he could see the large man seated across from him under the tapestry—his head also appeared wide and round.

Setting down his glass, the UN man pushed back his third course and said to the man's head that had returned to its normal proportions, "I need entertainment tonight. Make sure she's ready when the meal is finished."

"It's been taken care of, sir. She is already waiting in your room." Zog Merkat knew his boss's standards. And what he did to anyone who failed to meet them. Zog had been careful to choose a girl accordingly.

"Better than the last time?" his employer asked.

"Yes sir."

"She better be." The man looked Merkat in the eye and paused for several seconds, flicking at his empty glass. "Is the next shipment ready?"

"Yes, the itinerary is complete and the shipment will leave when you are finished upstairs."

The man frowned. "Which itinerary?"

Zog was quick to answer, "Through Montenegro, on the ferry, and then up through Italy. Don't worry. I will travel with it to supervise."

"What's in it?" He wiped his lips with a linen napkin.

"Twenty packages and five whores, including the one waiting in your room."

"Don't call them whores. Call them immigrants." The UN man looked annoyed. "If for some reason the truck ever gets stopped, it is important that everyone in the organization is using the proper terminology."

"Yes sir. Five immigrants."

"And in the twenty packages?"

"Afghanistan powder, the finest heroin. Worth a fortune on the streets of Europe."

A waiter entered the room carrying a bottle of brandy and two snifters, also crystal. He placed a glass before each man and filled them with aged brandy.

"Is everyone cooperative here?" The man asked Merkat.

"Yes, throughout Kosovo. The international representatives stay out of our way and the soldiers are helpful when we need them. The political appointees from the European Union concentrate on putting political institutions in place. Basically they make an effort to stay out of our business. We had a good business before NATO bombed the Serbs, but now it is thriving. Before the bombing, our main constraint was the Serbs. Now the biggest problem is rival gangs."

The man wrinkled his tan brow, "Can't you deal with the rival gangs?"

Zog grimaced, "We try, but for centuries we have been groups of rivals, families competing against each other, fighting against each other. There is much more rivalry here than in the Italian mafia."

"Well, see what you can do to bring this all together. It would be lucrative to gain control of all the business going through Kosovo." The UN man smiled at this possibility.

"I understand. We are trying, but it's not that simple. My compatriots shift their alliances quickly." He sipped his brandy then asked, "When do you leave?"

"Tomorrow morning. Tomorrow evening I need to be in Brussels for a meeting of some UN officials and members of the European Union, and then I want to get home to meet the shipment and to plan for a large private dinner at my home. The shipment will be useful for this purpose. I want some of the 'immigrants' to be brought to my place for entertainment."

Zog changed the subject, "Are investigations still taking place around the 'food exchange' program?"

"Some of my colleagues were not very discrete." The UN man frowned. "It is now under control. I know the independent group was going to investigate the refugee camp near Pec." He gave Zog a faint nod. "I thank you for your fast efforts to dismantle the camp and help people return to their homes in Kosovo. The independent group has now become a typical UN committee." He smiled, "They will spend years in meetings with no results."

"That's good news. I was afraid they would show up here. It would have been bad for business if they had discovered that we used the exchange program as a source of supply for the brothels of Europe."

"Speaking of 'immigrants,'" the UN man began, "has the one upstairs been readied?"

"Yes. The usual light sedative."

"How old?"

"Seventeen."

Zog's boss, Lionel Bannaret, rose from his chair. "Until tomorrow then."

He left the room thinking that next time he would demand a boy, only younger.

CHAPTER 18

After dinner and Chantal's second glass of the local alcohol, the two women left the restaurant and started down the dim street.

Both women kept casting her eyes into the dark corners and alleyways for any unusual movement. And both breathed deeply when they stepped through the doorway into the small lobby of their hotel. The old man was slumped over behind the reception desk, snoring into his shirt pocket.

They went up to their room and Gloria asked, "Do you want to shower first?"

"No. Go ahead."

Gloria went to the bathroom and after fifteen minutes emerged with a towel wrapped around her. "Lukewarm, but luckily not cold. It's all yours."

Chantal went in and sat on the side of the tub to undress. She was too tired to stand up. She looked down at her side, touching the pink spot where the bullet had entered. Maybe fighting with the bandit hadn't been such a good idea. In retrospect, she had been crazy to challenge him like that. But she had acted out of an adrenaline rush. And an instinctive response to the awful threat of being violated again.

She turned on the water and tested it. Gloria was right—it was tepid but adequate. She filled the tub and soaked her sore body. Lathering herself with the simple bar of soap, she relished the act of cleansing and closed her eyes. She did not want to imagine what filthy situation Justin might be in, but her mind sprinted from Hollywood dungeons to Chinese water torture and anything in between.

She dried off, wrapped herself in the towel, and poked her head into the room. Gloria had already taken a place on the left side of the bed. Chantal wondered what side Gloria slept on with Justin? She went to her bag and pulled an extra large, blue t-shirt out. Back in the bathroom, she pulled on the t-shirt. It was one she had taken from Justin and she liked having it against her skin.

As Chantal crawled into the right side of the bed, it bounced up and down, sending Gloria up and the sheet down. Before Gloria fully righted her covers, Chantal had seen that she was sleeping with nothing on.

"Sorry," Gloria said, not sounding like she really cared. "I sleep, as you would say, *au natural*."

"Never in pajamas?"

"Maybe as a little girl, but the Spanish nights are hot in the summer. I grew accustomed to sleeping only with a sheet."

Chantal said nothing and lay still on her back. Sleep seemed a faraway thing, and she tried to clear her head to welcome it. After staring at the ceiling for an hour, she turned over carefully.

The mattress rolled like a waterbed, and Gloria sleepily murmured, "Careful."

On edge from the frustration of not being able to fall asleep, Chantal meant to say she *had* been careful. But all the events of the last days boiled, mixed and merged together and she barked, "I could have done this on my own."

She regretted her words as soon as they hovered in the air above their heads.

Gloria opened her eyes, startled at Chantal's outbreak, and turned to her, "*I* was the one who decided to track down this Zog. The scene you made with the robbers could have gotten us both killed. We have to be more cautious."

"I refuse to let men like that have their way," Chantal replied. "You would have mildly gone along. You don't understand how they can treat you."

"I would rather be alive than dead," Gloria said lowly, green eyes glowing even in the dark. "Alive and able to plan my escape later instead of getting killed right on the spot because of stupidity. We were lucky the soldiers came along."

"I would rather be dead than be with men like that."

"You should use your head."

Chantal's head was, at that minute, on full throttle. Images of her Tunisian captivity blurred into the fight with the bandit. Chantal wanted to yell about pain and violation, but all she could think to say was, "Go to sleep."

Gloria yawned, "I *was* asleep."

★ ★ ★

Jordi and Laszlo walked slowly past a large building on Guberstrasse in East Berlin. They had come from the western part of the city, and the architectural differences—even with the wall long gone—announced themselves in grimy grays and weeded sidewalks. These block structures had been hastily built when the Soviet empire had spread it's tasteless uniformity as far as it could reach.

The men paused. Laszlo handed Jordi a cigarette and Jordi lit both, taking in details of the building's entrance.

Laszlo was used to cities like this, and as much as he hated to admit it, these neighborhoods felt like home. As a child in Prague, he had run through streets that could have been right around the corner from where they were standing.

After years of working for Stefan von Portzer in Eastern European cities, he understood why Schubach would have an office in this side of the city. First, it would be easy to find large office space for low cost. But second, and more importantly, it would be anonymous—a place where people would turn a blind eye to his business affairs. And it would be easy to find and hire people willing to bend the rules.

The building where Schubach had his offices looked just like the rest on the outside, but Laszlo suspected that inside it would be much different. Schubach had money.

Laszlo and Jordi dropped and crushed their cigarettes and walked into the building. On the ground floor several rows of mailboxes were imbedded into one wall. Laszlo wrote each name down on a piece of paper.

"Do you think all those companies belong to him?" Jordi asked.

"We will find out."

CHAPTER 19

Banneret couldn't remember any of the others being this pretty. Well, maybe the black girl at the refugee camp in Sierra Leone. Back then the UN Sex for Food program was working just fine. It was a pity that girl hadn't lasted through the night. She was only thirteen or fourteen years old and had little stamina.

He shut the door behind him and saw the girl look up from the wooden inlay chair next to the bed.

He smiled at her lonely, lost face. She had light ivory skin, unusual for an Albanian girl. Her eyes were slightly glazed.

Banneret locked the door. "Hello." He smiled. Do you speak English?"

"Yes, a little," she replied, her face tight with lines of worry around those glazed eyes.

Banneret took in the room with its polished wooden floor, pastel wall paper, and large double bed with silk sheets pulled sown. The silk glowed in soft lamplight. He knew this was quite a change from the room she had at the compound. The standard was two simple bunk beds on an unfinished wooden floor surrounded by bare concrete walls.

"That's good," he said. "Where did you learn English?"

"In school, in my village."

He looked at her clothing. Simple jeans—probably made in eastern Europe—and a striped red and white cotton top. She was nervously shifting her dirty white tennis shoes across the carpet.

"You learned it in school?" He repeated.

"And last summer. I work for my aunt Corina who has restaurant near sea. Tourists come. Good chance for speaking English."

"You speak very well." He had slowly come closer to her chair.

"May I ask why I come here?" Her voice was slow.

"I too look for opportunities to practice my English," he said, bending his head toward her. "And to get to know people,"

"You already speak very good English," she said, unable to concentrate enough to be skeptical. She looked at him with her light brown eyes, their lids slightly drooping under long lashes. Banneret loved unconscious sensuality, and here was a fine example.

"But, I asked for someone to talk with, to be with. Didn't they tell you?"

"No. Not really. The man who brought me here was not kind."

"I will make sure he is punished," Banneret answered, sitting next to her on the bed. "We need to treat our guests properly. Tell me how you got to Pec. I am very interested in you."

She looked at him, relaxing slightly, her body slumping in the chair. "A man came to my village and made offer to help find work in Germany. Factory there wants workers and workers make much money. More in one month than anyone makes in one year in my village. I speak with my mother and father and they say it is good idea, to make money for Huzo."

"Huzo?"

She looked down. "He is my boyfriend. We spend many hours talking about future." Her hand slipped off her lap.

"Tired?" he asked.

"Yes, long travel in back of truck."

"Here. That wooden chair is not comfortable. The bed is soft. Sit here." He motioned to the bed with his hand.

"No thank you," she replied. "It is enough comfortable here."

"I insist," he said, taking her hand. It was the firm and calloused hand of a working girl, but still young enough to be soft. He rubbed his thumb into the valley of her relaxed palm.

She resisted for a moment and then stood up. She was tall and came up to his chin. Her head bobbed forward and he smelled her thick brown hair. She stumbled into him and he guided her to the bed.

"Very tired," she said.

"There. That's better," he said. "The bed is soft and more comfortable. Now, tell me about Huzo."

"Huzo?"

"Yes. You said he was your boyfriend and that you were going to work in Germany to make money for Huzo."

"Huzo is mechanic in training, two years older than me. When finished with training next year, he wants to work for local mechanic store and then some day have his own mechanic store."

"Mechanic store? You mean his own garage, where they repair cars?"

"Yes, repair. Many cars to repair in Albania. It is good business."

"Two years older than you. How old is he?

"Nineteen."

"So, you are seventeen?"

"Yes. My birthday is in four months."

"I thought you had to be eighteen or older to work in the factory in Germany?" He asked, pretending disapproval.

She attempted a conspiratorial smile, "I tell them I am eighteen."

"So, you love Huzo."

"Oh, yes, very much."

"How much do you love him?"

She looked puzzled, "I no understand." She wobbled and put her hand on the mattress to keep from falling over.

"I'm just curious. Have you loved him?"

"Loved him?"

"Have you been with him alone? Have you made love to him."

Her eyes opened wide. "Why do you ask? Of course not. We wait for marriage. I wait for him. Only for him."

Banneret smiled. "That is excellent."

She put more weight on her arm and it gave way. She fell on her side. "I'm sorry," she said, slowly sitting up.

"Don't worry about it. You are very tired. And you look hot. It would help to loosen your clothing.

"Why?"

"Because you are hot." He reached down and pulled one tennis shoe off her foot and then the other. "Like I told you, that's better." She wasn't wearing socks. He reached up and undid the button on her jeans, sliding the zipper down.

"No," she said, blinking her eyes in attempt to focus.

"You will feel more comfortable. It will be okay." He pulled the jeans from her hips and then grabbed the hem, pulling them off her legs. She had fine, white shapely legs. He ran his hands over them. "Now, doesn't that feel better?"

"No. please," she said. She struggled to sit up.

"It's warm in here," Banneret said, feeling his own heat rising, "Please take off your top."

"No. I can't."

"Yes, you can. You must. Don't you want to make me happy?"

"Make you happy?" She had frozen in place, the wrongness of the situation seeping through her drugged fog.

"Yes. Take it off." He reached over and lifted the cotton top up, pulling it over one arm, then over her head and the other arm. She wasn't wearing a bra.

"I must go," she said, reaching for the shirt Banneret had already tossed to the floor.

"You will stay," he said. With one hand he pushed her onto her back.

"I should go. Please," she pleaded.

"No. You will stay. We need to speak English."

"My English no good."

"Good enough for me." He kicked his loafers off, undid his pants and dropped them. And then he pulled off his minislip underpants.

CHAPTER 20

Morning light filtered through a crack in the curtains, and Chantal opened her eyes. She did not recognize the room. And someone was lying next to her…

A Kosovo hotel.

With Gloria.

She looked over without moving her body and saw that Gloria was still deep in sleep, facing Chantal. Gloria's thick red hair ran off the pillow in long, sweeping curls.

Though the sheet hid Gloria's belly, Chantal looked in that direction, wondering when Justin's child would begin to make its presence known.

Chantal reached down to touch her own stomach, recalling taut skin stretched thin over her growing womb. The flutter of Sophie's kick inside of her had been an exquisite feeling. As exquisite as the love in Justin's hand as she had taken it and placed it on her belly so he too could feel the movement. She tried not to imagine Gloria taking Justin's hand and doing the same.

Her eyes rested on Gloria's sleeping face. She reminded Chantal of an angel. But a sensual and mysterious one, like the nudes of Courbet.

Gloria opened her eyes in the middle of Chantal's nineteenth-century art historical comparison.

"Did you sleep?" Gloria asked.

"*Ca va,*" Chantal replied. "Like sleeping on an uncomfortable cloud."

Gloria laughed. "You snuggled against me last night."

"I what?" Chantal sat up at this.

"You almost pushed me off the edge. But… it was comforting not to be alone." Her voice faded.

Chantal got out of bed and wondered why Gloria did not seem to be bothered by her snuggling—was almost thankful for the closeness. Chantal went to the bathroom, took a quick shower and dressed. When she re-entered the room, Gloria rose unabashedly from bed with no robe and took her turn in the bathroom.

Before she had thought about it, Chantal found herself taking out her drawing pad to sketch Gloria's nude form. Unlike drawing class nudes, this model bothered her.

Justin had touched and loved this puzzling contradiction of a woman. Gloria was a controlled, intelligent banker. And she was an uninhibited woman willing to walk casually through a room without clothing.

With her charcoal pencil still in hand, Chantal also tried to remember Gloria's face when she was sleeping. But after a few lines, she was already displeased with the results. She would return to it later.

Gloria emerged from the bathroom and began pulling on her pants and shirt. She had tied her hair back from her face in a pony tail that showed off her small silver hoop earrings and the thin silver cross resting in the hollow of her throat.

Chantal thought, *she looks lovely.* A slight tinge of jealousy intruded on her admiration. When Gloria had tied on her shoes, Chantal said, "You may want to put the cross away. Most of the people here are not Christian."

With a strange look in her green eyes, Gloria said, "It represents my beliefs. I don't care what they think here."

For the second time before breakfast, Chantal was taken aback. Had she just inadvertently asked Gloria to deny the faith that she herself also felt so strongly about? "I apologize," was all she could think to say.

Gloria nodded and said in a faraway voice, "The cross is from my mother. It reminds me of my faith."

"We need that now, don't we." Chantal stated rather than asked this, setting aside her sketch pad and closing her travel bag.

"More than ever. I shake inside and am afraid I will lose the baby."

Chantal looked at her hands, no words coming to her rescue.

★ ★ ★

Gloria saw Chantal at a loss and steeled herself to say no more of her fear. She arranged a nonchalant smile on her face and decided to give Chantal something other than her own worries to think about, "What do you suggest we do now?"

"We need to find Zog," Chantal said immediately. Gloria realized they were on a first name basis with a man as yet still a shadow.

"Yes, but how?"

"Let us get breakfast downstairs. Me, I need strong tea to start the day. Then maybe we might talk to someone at the reception desk."

Gloria hesitated, but decided to bring it up again anyway, "And you don't like the idea of going to the police?"

"Yesterday I had the impression that the police might be a problem." She then conceded, "If what the taxi driver said was true."

Gloria sighed, "I came to the same conclusion. I am sorry I was so insistent. I probably needed to pick a fight."

Chantal had been heading for the door. Hand on the knob, she paused. A few seconds later, she looked down, "Me too. I was also demanding and said hurtful things. I'm sorry."

It was Gloria's turn to be at loss for words.

When they approached the breakfast area, several men were already seated at the tables. They took obvious notice when the two women walked in. A small buffet was laid out on a table against one wall. It was sparsely laden with bread, jam, sliced cheese and hard-boiled eggs, and a single pot of coffee.

Chantal sighed at the lack of tea. Seeing this, Gloria reached in her purse, pulled out a small tea bag and handed it to Chantal.

"I always travel with a couple bags of my own tea," Gloria said with a smile. Chantal returned the smile and kept the tea bag, asking a sullen server for a mug of hot water.

The women served themselves and sat down at an empty table near a couple of men who were finishing their breakfast and a conversation. In English.

"So how long is your assignment?" one asked the other.

"Three months."

"What are they asking you to do?"

"Go from town to town to survey the status of the local police and then write a report."

"Sounds typical—reports, reports, reports. That's all the UN is good at."

"Look. It keeps us in business. Some UN official asks for a report to be written and we do our job, right?"

"As long as they pay."

* * *

Turk took careful aim at the ground and spit a wad of saliva next to his foot where. It landed near the hole of an anthill. He waited and then he watched two large black ants struggle to crawl out of the bubbly mass.

He was laughing at their effort as a swarm of ants began to crawl over his shoe. He felt some go up his pant leg and he wildly shook them off. He dragged his foot over the top of their anthill, bringing it down in a fast, crushing motion. He bent over to watch. The colony of ants collectively sensed something was wrong, and they quickly became a vibrating mass of movement.

He watched in delight, finally finding something of interest during the boring-as-shit job they had given him in Pec. He took out a cigarette. Lighting it with a match, he inhaled and then took the matchstick and stuck it upright in the wad of saliva on the ground, just for the hell of it.

His job was to keep guard, and be on call at all hours. Like last night. He had gotten very little sleep. His back now hurt from never sleeping on a proper bed. He had only been here for a couple of days and was wondering how long he could put up with the nothing.

They said to guard the packages, as though he didn't know what was in them. He wondered how stupid they thought he was. They were dealing drugs big time.

Ziginiglou had advised him to take it easy. To take the time to get rest. Ha. Last night he was told to keep guard over a UN truck. He did what he was told and had stood there for a long time outside the truck. But he got cold, and finally around midnight he crawled in the cab and fell asleep.

At some point he was awaken by noise, got out, and found two of the Albanians loading boxes into the truck.

"Help us," one of the Albanians had commanded.

"No. I was told to guard the truck." To show his authority he pulled a pistol from his belt and flashed it in front of the Albanians. "If I help you, then I can't guard. My job is too important."

They just shrugged their shoulders and finished their work, tearing some floor boards out of the bottom of the back of the truck, loading the boxes into the opening, and replacing the boards.

After the boxes were loaded, they brought out girls who climbed into the back of the truck. One of the girls had to be carried. Blood caked beneath her nose, and her left eye was swollen closed. She wore jeans and a wrinkled stripped cotton shirt. She was barefoot and they just threw her white tennis shoes into the back of the truck after they had lifted her in. One of the Albanians mentioned afterwards that she had been given to some official for the night.

Turk felt a twinge of pity for her and for the other girls, but there was nothing he could do for them. And anyway he thought, how could one feel any pity for girls who were so stupid. What did they think? How naïve to believe the men who offered them enormous amounts of money to work in factories in Europe. How did they think they would get jobs with no training, no experience?

Most of these girls were poor, and the thought of all that money messed with their reason. Well he didn't really blame them. He got his start that way when he was offered money to work for gangs in Europe. It was a natural migration from growing up in the back streets of Istanbul.

Standing over an ant hill outside a Kosovo warehouse, he wondered just where it had gotten him.

Working for Tapic had been different. At least there had been action. But back then he had to work with Yass, and that was something else. Yass was always treating him as an inferior, like some lost infidel. Life without Yass was a relief. He smiled, remembering a particularly nasty job he had helped Yass with.

Perhaps Ziginiglou was right. It might not be so bad here. *Just do your job and don't ask questions.* Still he dreamed of going back to Turkey, maybe running a fancy restaurant in a seaside resort, drinking Turkish coffee and smoking Turkish cigarettes. That would be better than working for the Albanians.

Last night he had gotten only a couple of hours of sleep in the truck's cab before it had to catch a ferry in Montenegro, one that would take the truck to Italy. He was pleased to see Zog Merkat go with the truck. Turk had spent two weeks traveling around Europe with Zog when they were looking for Justin Collins. Zog was almost as bad as Yass. But he was part of the Merkat gang—a different thing altogether.

Zog Merkat, Mustafi Merkat. Too many Merkats, like an enormous pack of rats from the same litter, and they thought they were so superior to everyone else.

Yes, Turk was pleased that Zog was gone, but there were still more Merkats here telling him what to do, barking orders.

Now, things were quiet, the early morning sun beating against the stone wall of the building behind him, very little traffic in the street. He had plenty of time to play with the ants.

He took another deep drag of his cigarette and then bent low over the anthill. A black ant had crawled to the top of the matchstick, like a sailor climbing to the top of a mast.

Turk exhaled the smoke in his lungs, aiming it toward the matchstick, thoroughly enjoying the ant's confusion.

Not able to be truly pissed at the stupid ant, he searched for someone to focus his hatred on. The two men who had questioned him in Nice came quickly to mind. The large blond one with the blue eyes and the rock hard Spaniard. The evil bastards who had forced him to sign that paper saying he had killed Jacques Tapic.

That signature had ruined all his chances of working in western Europe. After everything he had done to get established there.

He straightened up and stomped his shoe on the matchstick.

★ ★ ★

Ready to begin her day now that she had downed her tea, Chantal approached the reception desk and asked, "We are wondering if you might help us find some information."

"That depend."

"We are trying to find someone who lives in Pec."

"I know many people. Live here all life."

"Then maybe you might know of a man called Zog Merkat. We would like to find him."

"I know Merkat family."

"Could you tell us how to find him?"

"Information cost."

Chantal looked at Gloria who reached into her bag and pulled out a ten Euro bill. She handed it to the man."

By way of explanation, the man pocketed the money and said, "We have little in Pec."

"How can we find this Zog?"

"Bad family, Merkats. You must be careful with family of Zog."

"Is there someone who can help us?"

"Always someone to help, but it cost." He scratched his left armpit.

"How much?"

"Hundred Euro."

"We will pay, but you will tell us where we can find Zog Merkat."

"Give me hundred Euro and I will find out information." He shrugged as Chantal eyed him suspiciously, "I have to pay people."

Chantal looked at Gloria again. And again Gloria nodded and took out another bill. One hundred Euros this time.

"Wait here," the old man said. He turned and walked out the back door.

CHAPTER 21

Chantal and Gloria waited thirty minutes in the small reception area before the old man walked in, breathing heavily.

"Zog not in Pec," he said.

"We expected that," Chantal replied. "Where is he?"

"In Europe."

Gloria pursed her lips, "That is not very helpful."

"I say he in Europe."

"That means nothing to us," Chantal sniffed. "We are in Europe now. Kosovo is in Europe," she added for his benefit should he be unaware of his country's continent.

"I mean he in Western Europe. He there for two years."

"Where in Western Europe?" Gloria asked slowly as if speaking to a child.

"My friend not know, but he try to find out. Not easy to find information. Zog belong to most important gang in Kosovo. He work for them. They not like questions. My friend try and find information, but he must be careful. He try and find exactly where is Zog. In two hours you go to meet him."

"Where?" Chantal asked.

"Empty buildings not far from here. Buildings near main center of Zog's gang. My friend meet you to give most information."

The old man took out a piece of paper and drew a small map and then pointed to it with his bony finger. "Hotel here." He then made a circle in the air to indicate that was where they were standing—he too appeared to have doubts that the people he was speaking to were aware of their location. "Go three streets. Go right one street, across stone bridge over dry river. Broken empty houses on other side. Walk inside door of first house. My friend be there in two hours. Don't go to left after bridge." He shook his head. "Very dangerous. Many bad men work there."

* * *

Justin waited in the small room. When he heard a key turn in the door, he stood up. The metal door opened to three men. The two who had served him breakfast and another man, much more muscular. He looked just like a bouncer at a Barcelona club Justin had once visited.

"Come," one of the men said.

"Where to?" Justin asked.

"To another room."

"What for?"

"To ask questions."

"What kind of questions?"

"Just come."

The man grabbed Justin's wrist and started to pull on it. Justin yanked it back. Immediately the other men rushed him. He managed to hit one of them on the jaw with a stunning uppercut, but the muscular man grabbed his left arm and was twisting it behind his back.

The remaining man grabbed Justin's right arm while the one he had hit regained his composure and fury to tackle Justin around the waist, driving him back against the bed. Justin butted him on the nose with his head and the man released his grip, but the other two men now had control of Justin's arms, and the thug had Justin's arm twisted high behind him. Justin stopped his struggle, letting his body rest against the mattress. A deep pain shot through his shoulder.

The men sensed his surrender. They lifted him from the bed, and the man with the smashed nose said, "You come now." Blood ran from his nose and dripped off his chin.

They led Justin down a hall and into a much bigger room. "Sit in chair," the man with the bleeding nose commanded, pointing to one of several metal chairs. They tied his hands behind him, and the three men took up positions around the wall.

Within two minutes another man arrived. Unlike the thugs, he was well-dressed in an understated, practical manner. He pulled a chair opposite Justin and facing him. "Mustafi wants to ask you some questions." He fixed Justin with a look that suggested he knew what these were. "He is not here now. He will talk with you when he returns, but first I ask you some questions."

"Is that why you went to all the trouble to bring me here?" Justin asked. "We could have had coffee on the terrace. Would have saved everyone a lot of time and trouble."

His questioner was not amused. "You have information. Mustafi wants it."

Justin waited.

"First question. What do you know about Jacques Tapic?"

"About who?" Justin asked.

"Jacques Tapic. French businessman. What do you know?"

"He is a businessman, like you said. Most people in Europe know about Jacques Tapic." Justin shrugged.

"He *was* a businessman. He was killed. Why?"

"It was in the newspapers," Justin replied. "They said it was mafia related, or something like that."

"That is all you know?"

"Yes."

"Okay. Second question. Mustafi knows the story about your wife. Also in the newspapers." His eyes glittered at that. "She was kidnapped. And an insurance investigator, Mr. Curly Grady, went to Tunisia and freed her. Is that true?"

"Yes. He tracked her down and freed her."

"You say that is true?"

"Yes."

"Now, third and final question. What happened to the small office in Nice, the one managed by a Mr. Ziginiglou? Everything was cleared out and disappeared. Where did it all go?"

"What are you talking about?" Justin asked. "I don't know a Mr. Zig-glig—however you say it, nor an office in Nice."

"Thank you Mr. Collins," the man replied, rising. Justin tried to place him. He did not sound Albanian. "Mustafi will ask you more questions tomorrow when he returns from Monaco. He just wanted to see how you would reply to the first three. To see if you were telling the truth" The questioner fixed Justin with a hard glare, and continued, "We know you have not told the truth."

"Of course I told the truth," Justin said, beginning to feel uneasy.

Ignoring this the man made a casual hand signal to the three men by the door, turning his back on Justin as he did so. "We want to show you what happens to people who don't tell the truth. Without looking back, the man left the room, saying "We do hope you will tell the truth when Mustafi is doing the questioning."

The broad-shouldered thug approached Justin and swung a meaty fist in the direction of his jaw.

CHAPTER 22

Chantal and Gloria followed the old man's scribbled directions down the dusty main street. They crossed the large village square—it lay eerily vacant and childless at this early hour.

Past the square, the street narrowed between two rows of cheerless, gray block buildings. They came to a dry river and walked across a stone bridge. It was just wide enough for one car to cross it, and only one side had the suggestion of a sidewalk. Its walls were smeared with faded graffiti and ill-carved initials.

Gloria hugged her coat closer to her and felt the wind off the waterless riverbed blowing through her pant legs. She glanced at Chantal in the green coat she had loaned her. She too looked cold, and had sunk her hands deep in the pockets, shoulders hunched closer to her ears. Gloria found herself smugly noting that the coat looked better on herself than on Chantal. But she quickly chided herself for her pettiness.

At the bridge's end, more abandoned buildings stretched off to the right. Gloria glanced at the "forbidden" left bank and wondered just what was so terrible there. Though she did not really care to know, come to think of it. The bridge ended in a street that ran parallel to the river.

And right in front of the first house.

Chantal nodded her head and pointed with her eyes, "There is the door," she said quietly. As the old receptionist had said, it was a green double door. Or once green. A faded orange sign hung crookedly on the left door. The right one was ajar.

As they crossed the frost-slick street stones toward the building, they noticed that its roof had fallen in and the upper floor was crumbling. One tattered curtain the color of a thundercloud billowed out a glassless window.

"Don't sneeze. It will fall down," Chantal said, a wry twist to her mouth.

They hesitated a moment on the stoop and then cautiously stepped inside. Gloria went first, deciding to take some initiative. While she resented the way Chantal had almost gotten them abducted yesterday by her rash resistance, she also admired the drive and strength behind that resistance.

She went in far enough for Chantal to join her and then paused, looking around in the dim dankness. The space smelled of mold and urine. Something moved slightly in a dark corner. Chantal jumped when she saw a large gray rat crawl over a large bundle of rags.

"I don't see anyone," Chantal said, placing her hands on her hips and appearing angry that she had frightened so easily.

Gloria's stomach had just tied itself in a knot. She remembered Justin describing the Boy Scouts and the various knots they had learned as children. The one now clenching her insides together would be sturdy enough to pull down a tree. She tried to think of her baby and avoiding stress as it grew inside her. Avoiding stress? She sighed. "I think the old man was lying. We better get out of here." Her eyes had begun to adjust to the dark and the open doorway looked like a glaring beacon of sunny escape.

Chantal nodded. But as Gloria turned to leave, Chantal grabbed her arm and pointed at the bundle of rags the rat had run across.

It was not a bundle of rags.

Chantal moved toward it, but Gloria's attempts at heroism failed her, and she remained rooted in a half-turn—her feet pointing at the door, and her torso twisted to see a fallen human form. A man.

With a dark, red stain on his sweater.

★ ★ ★

Turk tired of playing with the ants. He went over to the warm stone wall, and squatted down with his back against it. He unbuttoned his shirt to let air hit his skin.

It was a sunny day and he wished he could close his eyes and go to sleep. He took out another cigarette and lit it, realizing he had been chain smoking since early this morning. He wished someone would bring him a good Turkish coffee.

For three hours he had been standing outside the building, and he still had six hours to go. Shit. And he had done the night shift.

At least he wasn't called to do the dirty work. There had been some action this morning, but he wasn't part of it. Someone had been shot just for asking questions. Someone was trying to find out about Zog Merkat and the Merkats didn't like it, so one of the Merkats went and shot the man. Ziginiglou was right. Just do your job and don't ask questions.

His legs started to go numb, so he stood up and began pacing back and forth. He needed to piss. He crossed the street and walked down a steep path descending to a dry riverbed. A dead tree stuck up from the cracked mud.

He opened his fly and began to relieve himself with one hand, the other on the tree, cigarette hanging from his mouth. He started to hum a Turkish song.

When he was just about finished he looked up at the old bridge spanning the riverbed and saw two women walking fast—very fast across it.

He squinted and wondered if he needed glasses. One of them was the Collins woman, the one they had taken in Barcelona.

He tried to stop urinating, shook himself, yanked his zipper shut and walked bowl-legged in their direction for a closer look.

The Collins woman had seen him. She said something to the other woman. Then they started to run. What were they doing here? Of course. The Collins women were with the evil ones. This was his chance for revenge.

Turk sprinted across the riverbed after them, slipped while clambering up the bank, and tore his pants at the knee. He quickly raised his large frame from the dirt, and scrambled up. At the top of the bank he saw the women bolting down the street.

Getting up to full speed in pursuit, he reached back with one hand to feel the gun stuck into his belt.

* * *

Glock pistol in hand, Laszlo waited in the men's room on the ground floor of Schubach's building. Armed with his preferred handgun, Czech made, Laszlo was ready.

Horst had found all the information they needed on Schubach's security team. Security was tight. Laszlo and Jordi had devised a risky plan that still managed to capitalize on weaknesses in the defense system.

It was now or never.

Laszlo squinted through a crack in the door into the hall and saw two men pass by walking side by side. One man was large and bulky. He had buzz-cut hair, massive neck muscles and muscular hands. He walked with a cocky gait as though he were ready to bulldoze anything in his path.

The man at his side was smaller and wore a perfectly fitted, pinstriped suit. He walked like the man in charge, though without any of the cockiness of the man obviously working for him. The smaller man was indeed the bigger one.

Klaus Schubach. Laszlo recognized his profile from the photos Horst had shown him.

As they passed by, Laszlo slipped into the hall and fell in behind them. He may as well have been barefoot, he made no noise in his rubber-soled shoes. With one forceful and fast movement, he crashed the butt of his gun into the larger man's neck—into a spot that would send the man to the floor with a thud. Weakness points were valuable things to know, indeed.

Schubach spun around to face a gun pointed at him. Taking in Laszlo, he asked slowly, "What do you want?"

"Move on, outside," Laszlo said, grabbing Schubach's arm, practically lifting him off the ground.

Schubach moved forward as Laszlo pulled him along, adding wrinkle lines to the stripes of Schubach's high-end suit. Jordi was waiting at the mailboxes in the entrance, a backup contingency plan in case things didn't go right. His gun was drawn and he joined in on the opposite side of Schubach.

"Do what we say," Laszlo commanded.

Laszlo held his gun to Schubach's head, pushed the front door open and walked right through. Two shiny black Mercedes were parked at the curb. A large man stood at the back door of the first car holding it open. A driver sat in the front. The two men seated in the second car turned their heads at the trio who were halfway to the first car before any of the guards took notice.

The man waiting by the open door jumped and began reaching inside his coat. Jordi pointed his gun at him and said, "Don't try or you and your boss are dead."

The man raised his hands in the air.

Jordi pointed his gun at the car in the back, where the two men were frantically reaching into their coat pockets and pulling out guns. Jordi shook his head back and forth while Laszlo shoved the gun at Schubach's head as a warning.

Schubach yelled out to the men, "Put the guns away."

Jordi approached the guard standing by the open back door, reached under his coat and pulled out a gun. With a pistol in each hand he pointed one at the driver of the first car and the other at the men in the car in the rear.

Laszlo said to the guard, "Walk into the building and don't turn around."

The guard did as instructed.

Laszlo shoved Schubach into the back seat, going in immediately after him while Jordi went to the driver's side, opened the door and pulled the driver out.

Jordi said, "Tell them that if they follow us, Schubach is dead. Do you understand?"

The driver nodded.

Jordi got in behind the wheel, started the car, put his foot to the accelerator and pulled out into the street.

Laszlo kept his gun at Schubach's head and in sight of the car behind them.

As instructed, it did not follow.

CHAPTER 23

Chantal flung open the door to their room and slammed it after them, "We need to get out of here."

Gloria was already stuffing her toiletry case and a shirt into her overnight bag. Chantal did the same, but after running most of the way back their hotel, every breath made her painfully aware of the wound to her lung. She channeled her breath into a question for Gloria, "Are you sure that was the man?"

"Yes. Didn't you see the way he reacted when he saw us?"

They heard footsteps down the hall. They stopped outside their room, and the brief silence ended with a hard knock on their door.

"Who is it?" Chantal asked, gesturing for Gloria to stay where she was near the doorway.

"I'm here to talk with you," Turk said.

"Come in," Chantal said grabbing her metal hair brush, then positioning herself where she would be hidden behind the door once it opened. But her heart was thudding so loudly, she wondered if he could hear it through the wall. And if he was alone or if had brought along backup.

Turk opened the door and stepped inside. He had a gun in his hand and took three steps toward Gloria. "What are you doing here?"

Chantal moved from her place behind him and said, "Turk, don't move or you're dead."

Turk froze, feeling metal pressure against his back. "How do you know my name?" he asked, raising his pistol in the air.

"Drop it now and take two steps forward," Chantal said.

He dropped the gun, stepped over it, raising his hands above his head.

"Don't turn around," Chantal said. She reached down and took his gun, now actually having one to threaten with. "If you have a knife, take it out and drop it."

Turk reached into his pocket and pulled out a long switchblade and dropped it to the floor.

"Now, kick it behind you, but move very slowly."

He did as told.

"Hands against the wall." Chantal was beginning to feel like an actress in one of those American TV series Justin had liked to watch dubbed in French.

He put his hands against the wall and Chantal said to Gloria, "Could you check him for other weapons? Be careful. I'll pull the trigger if he makes the slightest move."

Gloria moved her hands over Turk's body and retrieved a small gun tucked into his left sock. She cocked it and stepped back from him, aiming it at is chest.

Chantal continued to take charge, her breath having regulated itself in a surprisingly calm manner. "Now turn around and sit in that wooden chair over there."

Turk turned around and saw the two women holding his guns. He slumped more than sat into the chair. "Please don't let them kill me." All of his bravado fell from him and he looked like a petulant child afraid of punishment.

"What do you mean?" Chantal asked while Gloria began pulling a sheet off the bed and cutting it into long strips with Turk's knife.

He had dropped his head into his hands. Through his fingers he said, "The two men in Nice said they would kill me unless I left Europe."

Chantal narrowed her eyes, "Which two men?"

"The men with you. The muscular Spanish one, and the tall blond with the hard blue eyes."

"Oh yes," Chantal said, remembering the story of how Jordi and Laszlo had questioned the men who were running Jacques Tapic's office in Nice.

Turk lifted his head. "You mean they aren't here? When I saw her on the bridge," he pointed to Gloria, who was effectively shredding the sheet, "I thought they had tracked me down."

Chantal realized that Turk was speaking about Jordi and Laszlo, and he assumed they were here in Pec. "Yes, they are looking for you. That's how we know your name," she said.

"Oh no." Turk put his face in his hands. "They are evil men."

"They want to ask you questions," Chantal was beginning to almost enjoy this. But only almost.

"What for?" He was wining, now. "Please don't let them get me."

"Perhaps we can make a deal," Chantal suggested.

Gloria had made her way behind Turk. He was so intent on bargaining with Chantal, he even crossed his hands behind him as Gloria began tying them together with strips of bed sheet.

"If you give us information, then we will ask them not to kill you."

"Can you do that?"

"They are very violent and unforgiving, but they will listen to me. Give me information. First, why was that man killed in the building across the river."

"It wasn't me," Turk leaned forward in earnest. "It was one of the Albanians."

"Which Albanians?"

"We work for them. I don't like it, but it's the only work we can get."

"Why do you say we?"

"Ziginiglou. Ziginiglou and me. He's an accountant. I just do odd jobs."

Chantal remembered the name. Ziginiglou was running Tapic's office in Nice. "Why did they kill that man?"

"I don't know. He was asking questions about Zog Merkat. The Albanian group is ruthless. You don't ask questions about them, and you don't cross them. They just shot him. Life is cheap out here."

"Again, who are these 'Albanians' as you call them?"

"A group here in Kosovo that control the movement of things into Europe."

"Movement of things?"

"Smuggling."

"What do they smuggle, *Mister* Turk?"

"Lots of things."

"Like what?" She raised the gun in front of his face.

Gloria was bent over tying up his feet. Chantal was thankful that he was so distracted by the conversation that he was not taking an opportunity to break free.

"Like drugs. And…"

"And what?"

"People."

"People?" Chantal guessed where this was leading. The policeman in Gerona had been clear about the illegal smuggling of women into Europe, and the taxi driver had said the same.

"Yeah. Er, people who want work in Europe."

"Women?"

"Yes. Women."

"Does Zog work for this group?"

"Yes."

Gloria was now wrapping large strips of cloth around Turk's body, attaching him to the chair. He was beginning to resemble a mummy. But in a rather odd sarcophagus.

"Now, tell us where we can find Zog and why they took Justin Collins," Chantal commanded, steadying the gun. It was heavier than it looked on TV.

"Mustafi didn't tell me why they want Collins, but I think it has to do with Tapic's money. There was a lot of it, and they think Collins has it."

"Who is this Mustafi?"

"He runs parts of the Kosovo Albanian mafia in Europe. He is the one who gave us the jobs here. We had to get out of the European Union."

"How did Mustafi know where to find Justin Collins?"

Turk looked down at the floor and quietly said, "I helped find him. I was in Spain last summer." He looked in the direction of Gloria. "I knew where Collins lived. Mustafi said he would kill me and Ziginiglou unless we helped find Collins."

Gloria had now bound—or what looked like bandaged—all of Turk's body except for his neck and head.

"Then finding Zog is not so important. You must know where they are holding Justin Collins."

"Yes."

Chantal looked him in the eyes, gun pointed at his now white covered chest and said. "Tell us exactly where he is at and I will ask the two men not to kill you. Otherwise, I will turn those wrappings red."

For the first time, Turk started fidgeting. "If I tell you, then the Albanians will kill me."

"I wouldn't want to be in your shoes," Chantal said. Those shoes and the feet in them were now secured against the chairs legs. "Right now I wouldn't worry about the Albanians." She pointed the gun directly at his face. "Where is he?"

Turk locked eyes with the barrel and said, "Milan."

CHAPTER 24

Jordi sped at two hundred kilometers an hour for twenty minutes, took an off ramp south of Berlin, and pulled the car to a stop at the edge of a large forest. He turned around and pointed his gun directly at Schubach's chest where Laszlo's was still aimed.

"What do you want?" Schubach asked.

"An exchange," Laszlo answered.

"Exchange. What are you talking about?"

"A girl has been kidnapped in Brussels and we want her. The exchange is, you give her to us and we give you your life."

A brief look of recognition appeared on Schubach's face and then he said, "I don't know what you're talking about. I don't deal with thugs."

"You are a thug. Where is the girl?"

"What girl?"

"You know what I am talking about. Drug dealers took her. We want to know why, and where she is."

"I don't know anything about drug dealing. You have the wrong man."

"We doubt that," Laszlo said, his cold blue eyes staring at Schubach. "You are the head of a drug ring with supplies coming through Kosovo into Europe. You are also involved in the trafficking of women. Where is the girl?"

"Go to hell. You are speaking lies."

Laszlo turned to Jordi. "Would you help this man with his memory? Shoot him in the balls. That will help him remember trafficking of women."

Jordi moved the gun downward from Schubach's chest to his crotch and pulled the trigger. A loud boom echoed in the car, and the suffocating smell of sulfur filled the air.

* * *

Chantal and Gloria turned Turk and his chair on their side. Chantal knelt down beside him and said, "I would like to give you a word of advice. The two men from Nice are looking for you. While I will try to persuade them to give up their search, it is best for you to flee Kosovo. Do you understand?"

"You're not going to leave me like this, are you?" Turk asked, bobbing his head as vertically as he could.

"You are not listening, are you? Do you prefer to leave Kosovo and live or stay in Kosovo and die?"

"To get out of Kosovo, but don't leave me like this." He started to struggle at his bonds.

"Someone will find you." Chantal said, rising. "Until then you will have time to think."

Turk tried to move but was firmly attached to his chair. "I will leave Kosovo. Just untie me."

Gloria stood up in front of Turk. She had picked up the gun Chantal had set down. "Perhaps you recall forcing me into that van in Barcelona. *I* remember your wandering hands on my body." Her voice had gone soft and cold. The gun was fixed in her hand and her hand in the air. She barely breathed. Out of the corner of her eye, she saw Chantal looking at her. Gloria went on in an even lower voice, "I could kill you right here."

"No, it wasn't me," Turk gasped, his words pushing out of him as fast as he could make them, "It was Yass. He was the one who touched you."

Chantal shuddered at the mention of Yass.

"You helped him," Gloria felt a distance in her head. And a disconnect from the death grip she had on the gun.

"I didn't touch you. It was Yass," Turk continued. The roles were reversed, and he appeared to be trying to reason with a child. He looked at Gloria's green eyes and repeated, "I didn't do those kinds of things."

"I will tell you one thing," Chantal said, reaching for one last strip of cloth, "We never want to see you again."

"Don't worry. I will leave and go back to Turkahhhg…"

Chantal was tying a gag over Turk's mouth. She finished and Gloria stuffed the gun in her bag. Chantal took the knife and smaller gun and they left Turk to his thoughts.

"We better get moving," Gloria said. "Who knows what will happen if he gets free."

"Agreed," Chantal answered. "I think we got what we came for. We should get back to Montenegro as quick as possible." So much for dinner with the soldiers.

"I saw a taxi zone across the street earlier," Chantal said. "Let's get one to take us there."

Gloria nodded and they hurried through the door, crossing the street just in time to avoid being hit by two bicyclists zooming by. Other traffic moved at a slower pace.

Chantal went to the driver's window and panted, "Can you take us to Montenegro, to Podgorica?" Chantal asked.

"Hundred Euro," the taxi driver replied.

"Done."

They climbed in and slammed their doors in relief. As the driver pulled out into the street, Gloria, anticipating attack, noticed a black car cruising in their direction. She pointed it out to Chantal, who read aloud from its lettered sign, 'United Nations Agency for Trade Development.' In the back seat sat a man with graying hair.

When his face faded from view, Chantal turned to Gloria, "You won't believe this, but I think I have seen that man before."

★ ★ ★

Schubach jumped up in fright. "Noooo…" he screamed, holding his hands over his testicles. He looked down and breathed, "Ahhh."

In the car seat between Schubach's legs gaped a bullet hole.

"You missed," Laszlo said to Jordi. "Try again."

Immediately Schubach cried out, "No. Stop. She's not here."

"Where is she?"

"In Paris. The southern branch took her. Not me."

"Why?" Laszlo asked.

"We... they were not pleased with the progress being made by an international police team based in Brussels. Brussels is in the southern zone, so they wanted to handle it."

"And they killed the detective from California. Why did they take the girl?" Laszlo asked.

"They were stupid," Schubach said. "They should have killed her, except that someone saw her. She is very pretty and will command exceptional money." Schubach was making no attempt to hide his business now. "There are some clients who will pay a lot for a rare collection."

Laszlo could barely look at the man, he had narrowed his eyes so tightly in disgust. He had seen a lot in his life, but one of the things that repulsed him beyond the point of toleration was the abuse of women in this way. They were moved around from brothel to brothel, their passports confiscated by pimps and traffickers. Often they were young women lured from Eastern Europe under false and promising-sounding pretenses of work opportunities. Then they were smuggled into Germany, France, the Netherlands—wherever someone was willing to pay. Once no one wanted to pay for them any more, they were dumped off with no place to go. And left with only a shattered body and soul.

Laszlo raised the gun to Schubach's head. "This time it's not your balls. It's your brains. Where is the girl?"

Schubach looked at Laszlo and measured his intentions. After a moment of wise arithmetic, Schubach relented. "In Paris. The southern group operates on their turf. We operate on ours. Now let me go."

"No," Laszlo said, pressing the gun barrel against Schubach's temple. "Where is she?"

"Rue l'Argentine, not far from the Gare de Lyon. There is a center there. She will be held there until she is sold. But that's their business."

Laszlo heard gun fire from the direction of the forest. Immediately a 'tink' echoed off the side of the car, then another. In the forest he heard a voice cry out, "Mr. Schubach, are you there?"

"Yes. Help me," Schubach cried out, trying to get the window down to be heard.

Laszlo turned in the direction of the voice, and Schubach seized the chance to fling open the door and roll out on the ground.

More gunshot sounds. Glass shattered in the back window. Laszlo crouched down.

"Global positioning. This car has global positioning. They used it to find us," Jordi said, taking out a man in the underbrush from his open door, left-handed, while starting the car with his right.

He gunned the engine, sending mud spinning behind the tires. A volley of gunshots rang out, and Laszlo continued firing back as Jordi started for the autobahn. He heard a yell from nearby and saw Schubach go down to the ground holding his leg.

His own men had shot him.

CHAPTER 25

Gloria leaned forward and told the taxi driver, "It's better that we take a back road." He looked at her a second in his rear-view mirror, then nodded and turned off onto a dirt road.

Gloria then turned to Chantal, "Your face went white when we saw that man in the UN car. Do you know who he is?"

"I think I have seen him before," Chantal said quietly. She was trying to scan back in her memory. Before Tunisia, before Justin, in… "Geneva," she said, snapping her fingers and locking the location firmly in place. She closed her eyes and could see a circle of men in evening attire. She had approached the group behind one of the men who had his back in her direction. He had turned to shake her hand.

"Stefan von Portzer introduced us. It was shortly before I met Justin. Stefan had invited me to a large United Nations fundraiser. Several important artists were selling art and donating the proceeds to the UN Stefan thought I might be able to make some good contacts. Many political dignitaries were there, including the Secretary General of the United Nations and directors of various UN agencies." She looked Gloria squarely in the eye, "The man in that car is the director of a United Nations agency, something like the council or agency for trade. They also work with the World Trade Organization."

"You are sure it was him?" Gloria asked.

"I wouldn't forget that face." She remembered how the man's eyes had pierced through her. Through her dress, through her soul.

"I asked Stefan about him, and Stefan said he has a reputation."

Gloria lifted an eyebrow, "What kind of reputation?"

"Stefan didn't go into detail. He doesn't like to be too specific, but he did say that the man was known among women in Geneva. That was the last I ever saw him until today."

"Do you remember his name?"

Chantal sighed, but no name came to her tongue. "No."

"What do you think he's doing here, in Pec of all places?" Gloria asked.

"Who knows? The United Nations is involved quite heavily in Kosovo, and his organization is involved in trade, so maybe he is here in that capacity."

They bumped along yet another unpaved, pot-holed road. Eventually Gloria said, "I won't feel comfortable until we get out of Kosovo." She paused, watching a small animal run from the road into the bushes as they approached. "And until we can find Justin. Do you think Turk was telling the truth?"

"It's hard to know. When we were in Nice and they were interrogating the men in Tapic's offices, Justin said that one thing that motivates men like that is fear. Turk assumed Jordi and Laszlo were after him just because we were there. Irrational. He was afraid. So I guess we will have to assume that he is telling the truth." Chantal stifled a shiver that ran up her back.

She and Gloria each looked out their windows. Rocky brown hills covered in sagebrush were dotted with an occasional scrub oak tree.

Chantal realized that they had been extremely lucky with Turk. He had yielded his gun so easily, and then he had talked. Here in the taxi, without that adrenaline running through her veins, she wondered how he had been so controlled.

She tried to process what information they had gathered. Turk said this gang was working with Tapic and that Tapic owed them money. Did they think that Justin had their money? They were on the wrong track. Justin only had the assets he had made while working for Vine Industries. He even had to give back the million dollars from her life insurance. Curly Grady, the insurance investigator, had insisted on that. At least they had an address. Turk was either a good liar, or uninformed—his disclosure seemed genuine. Or were they being naïve?

The taxi wound up the dirt road into the hills. They were well away from any sign of human habitation.

Ahead in the distance sat a car parked in the middle of the road. Exactly like when they had encountered the bandits. Two men stood by the car.

"Who are they?" Gloria asked the taxi driver.

"My friends," he replied.

Chantal removed Turk's gun from her bag, held it against the back of the driver's head and said, "Keep driving and drive fast."

The man stiffened at the pressure of the metal to his scalp, but still slowed as he approached the car and the two men by it—one in a red shirt, the other bald. The same two men who had stopped them coming into Kosovo.

"Fast!" Chantal exclaimed, jamming the gun at the driver's head hard enough to buck it forward. "Do not stop or your driving career is over."

The driver put his foot to the accelerator and sped around the parked car. A look of recognition crossed the bandit's faces. In the side mirror, Chantal could see them scrambling into their car. In a moment they were following the taxi and gaining ground.

Gloria turned to face backward and yelled "Faster! They're catching us."

"Car not go faster," the driver cried out.

Gravel flew up behind the taxi as it gained speed down an incline, but the other car was faster, and soon its dusty shape seemed to be hovering next to the back window of the taxi. Its occupants did not look happy.

"How far is the border?" Chantal asked.

"Just ahead. Maybe one kilometer." He was fighting to keep the car on the road.

Chantal rolled down her window and leaned out it, aiming for any part of the car behind them. She pulled the trigger and her bullet lodged in the car's grill. She pulled again and the bandit's windshield shattered into an elaborate and opaque web. The bandit's car swerved right and into the ditch between the road and a low hill.

Chantal pulled herself back in the car and returned her pistol to the back of the driver's head. "Stop, and you are a dead man." The driver blinked.

Chantal turned to see Gloria looking at her, mouth slightly open.

CHAPTER 26

"What are you doing here like this?" Ziginiglou asked. He was yanking off the binding around Turk's mouth. The old receptionist, unfazed, stood beside him.

"They are coming to get us, to kill us," Turk spat and then gasped, taking in a supply of air.

"Who?" Ziginiglou asked.

"The men from Nice. The evil ones."

"You mean the large blond one and the Spaniard?"

"Yes. Untie me. We've got to leave. Quickly."

Ziginiglou lifted Turk upright in the chair and began unwrapping the long sheets from around his body.

A few minutes before, the old man had walked into the offices of the Merkat gang where Ziginiglou worked. He had said that someone must come the Balkans Hotel. A member of the gang had been captured. It didn't make any sense to Ziginiglou, but, since he was the only one in the office, he followed the man to the hotel and found Turk.

Ziginiglou held an end of the wrapping in his hand and turned to the old man. "Why didn't you untie him?"

The man shrugged, "I didn't know who he was. I though he was a member of the Merkat gang, but wasn't sure. I haven't seen him before. I wanted to check with you first."

"Who tied him up? Ziginiglou asked, unwinding Turk like a ball of yarn.

"Two women stayed in the room last night. They left this morning, not too long ago."

"What were their names?"

"They're in the registration book," he said, offering neither to look them up or assist with unwrapping Turk.

"Well go get the book!" Ziginiglou commanded.

The old man shuffled out of the room and Ziginiglou continued untying Turk. Turk began talking non-stop.

"It was the women, the Collins women. I recognized the one we took in Barcelona. They are here to find us, the two evil men, the evil ones, to kill us. They found us here. We must go, or we are dead."

Ziginiglou paused, a strip of ripped bedsheet in hand. "Are you sure you haven't sampled the shipment?"

"Listen, I'm clean and telling you the truth," Turk struggled, loosening the last bits of cloth. Ziginiglou undid the last knot binding Turk's hands, and Turk yanked them free, shaking them. His shirt was drenched in sweat.

"This doesn't make sense. I am an idiot to believe you," Ziginiglou pursed his lips. "How could they find us here?"

Turk stood up, "I don't know, but they did. The Collins women went to get the two evil ones. They are going to kill us. The women said we must get out of Pec."

"Out of Pec. How? If we do that then the Merkat gang will be after us."

"I don't care. I'm going." Turk knew that the Merkat gang would be after him anyway, because of the information he had give to the women, but Ziginiglou didn't need to know that.

"Where? Go where?" Ziginiglou flapped his hands around the room as if it offered no exit.

Turk had a thought, "Take a bus to Pristina, then to Macedonia, then to Turkey."

"That will take us a week."

"It's the only way. The bus for Pristina leaves soon. We can make it." Turk was already at the door, he opened it to find the old man standing there with a book in his hands like a serving tray.

"So, what are their names?" Ziginiglou asked, poking at the registration book.

"I only have the name of one of them. The one who signed in." He opened the book, slid his finger down a list of signatures and turned the page to Turk, "There. Her name was Gloria Collins."

Before he looked up, Turk and Ziginiglou were running past him out the door.

★ ★ ★

Gloria and Chantal entered the single waiting room of the Podgoriza airport. They had taken their conspiring taxi to Ivangrad, paid the driver—Gloria had insisted, Chantal looked like she would have rather shot him—and then had found another taxi to take them the remaining distance to the airport. With reason, they didn't want the taxi driver from Kosovo to know where they were going.

Before pulling up at the airport, Gloria had suggested they wipe any prints from Turk's two guns and knife. She then had put them in a grocery bag that had been stuck to the taxi floor. After exiting the vehicle, she slipped the bag in the first trash bin she saw.

The next flight out of Podgoriza left for Vienna in one hour. They bought two tickets and sat down on a small wooden bench close to the customs area, in the reassuring shadow of an armed policeman.

Gloria let her gaze wander over the people nearby, an odd sense of déjà vu passing through her as she remembered it was just a couple of days ago that she and Chantal had waited at the Girona station.

A woman garbed in long robes stood silently in a corner, clutching a worn leather handbag. Three men in business suits and freshly polished shoes stood with their backs to Gloria and Chantal, deep in conversation. A young couple kissed desperately, arms bound around each other.

One of the men in suits had turned around and was scanning the room. Gloria saw him look in their direction and then away. But he swung his eyes back to Chantal, a look of recognition lighting them. He paused a moment, then started in their direction.

Gloria had just enough time to nudge Chantal before the man was before them. In English, he asked Chantal, "Have we met?"

"I don't think so," she said, veiling her eyes.

Recognizing her French accent, the man switched to French. "Ah, *Français*. I saw you in Pec a couple of hours ago and I thought I knew your face. And I never forget a woman's face." He smiled to show off his even, white teeth. Chantal shifted under his gaze. He glanced over at Gloria and stared into her eyes until she looked away, then looked back at Chantal. "What are a French woman and her friend doing in Pec?" he asked with feigned surprise.

"Sight seeing," Chantal said, her eyes cold and lacking any hint of holidaying.

"It is a dangerous place for sight seeing." He smirked.

Neither woman responded, so he continued, "You're taking the next flight to Vienna? The connections there aren't very good. Why don't you just fly with me? My private jet is sitting on the runway, ready to leave immediately. I could take you to Paris."

"No thank you," Chantal replied. "We are going to Vienna."

"Then I'll take you to Vienna."

Gloria decided to speak, "We already bought our tickets."

He shrugged his shoulders. "It is up to you. My airplane is comfortable." He looked again at Gloria and then at Chantal. "Then I wish you a pleasant and safe journey. I trust we will have the pleasure to meet again soon."

He smiled and turned toward a side exit door, the two other men taking up places on either side of him.

Chantal shook herself. "That man gives me the creeps."

Gloria reached over and squeezed her shoulder, "We'll be out of here soon."

Chantal leaned back, then sat up straight again. "I just remembered." She turned to Gloria.

"What?"

"His name. It's Banneret."

* * *

Chantal walked over to the window that looked out on several planes. The three men were headed for a small business jet with 'UN' painted in blue on the tail.

Banneret followed his companions up the wheeled staircase, but before ducking into the entrance, he leaned toward one of the men on the ground, shouting over the roar of the engine. The man nodded and jogged back toward the building. He entered the waiting room and went straight to the airline counter where Chantal and Gloria had purchased their tickets. He said something quietly to the ticket agent, but the man shook his head. He leaned in closer, and the agent's face changed. He glanced furtively in Chantal and Gloria's direction, then typed something into his computer. Taking a piece of paper from a pad, he scribbled on it and passed it across the counter. Banneret's associate went back to the airplane and boarded.

After the UN airplane had taken off, Chantal walked across the room and approached the ticket agent.

"May I ask you something?" she said.

"Yes, what?" He fit a smile onto his face.

"You wrote something on a piece of paper and gave it to the man who boarded the UN airplane. Did it have anything to do with my friend and I?"

"I cannot tell you. Transactions with clients are confidential."

"He wasn't a client. He didn't buy a ticket."

"Nevertheless I can't say anything." He looked like he wanted to loosen his tie.

Chantal reached into her bag and pulled out a hundred Euro note, slapped it on the desk, and demanded, "Tell me."

The man surveyed the reception room and ducked his head a bit at

Chantal. Keeping his eyes on the lookout, he said in a low voice, "He wanted your names."

CHAPTER 27

The plane wheels contacted the ground with a jerk, and the plane slowed and taxied toward the gate.

When the seatbelt light had beeped off, they gathered their bags from the overhead compartment. Helping Chantal reach hers, Gloria mused aloud for a second time, "Why did Banneret want our names?"

"Do you think he would have us followed?"

"Who knows?" Chantal nodded to the flight attendant as they passed. "Why would a UN director be in Pec? And he said he was on his way to Paris."

"We ought to be even more careful to see if people are watching at us," Gloria said, looking around as she said this.

Chantal gave Gloria a look of weariness, "That's not easy. Have you seen the way all the men look at us?"

"They look, but we need to see if any follow." They merged with the passengers into the arrival gate. "Let's go look for a flight to Milan."

They found a departure monitor. The next flight to Milan left in six hours. Chantal brightened, "I have another idea. Why don't we take the next flight to Zurich, if we can get tickets? From there we can drive to Milan. I suppose it will take two or three hours. We will get to Milan faster, and it will be more difficult for anyone to track our movement."

Gloria nodded, "That sounds fine."

They made their way through the crowds to the Austrian Airlines ticket counter, and bought tickets for a flight to Zurich that was just boarding.

"It must have been fate," Chantal said with a smile. Gloria said nothing and handed Chantal's ticket to her.

Once in the plane and accelerating down the runway, Gloria turned to Chantal, "What of this so called 'fate'?"

Chantal looked at her, puzzled.

Gloria went on, "You said it was fate that got us the last two seats on this plane. Was it fate that brought *your* plane into the hands of hijackers? Fate that brought me and Justin together?"

Chantal said nothing. She focused on the laminated 'Emergency Procedures' card sticking up from the seat pocket in front of her. Gloria when on, in a soft voice that drew Chantal's eyes to her own, "And do I hate you because your fate was not to die?"

At that moment, the plane's wheels left the pavement, and both the women's stomachs lurched with a heavy gravity.

★ ★ ★

Laszlo and Jordi entered the offices of Louis Abdouelle on 25 rue Augustine in Paris. The offices were not far from rue l'Argentine, and they figured that their old 'friend' Abdouelle would know the exact address of the operation Schubach had described.

After steering clear of the gunfire in the forest, Jordi had driven Schubach's car to a small *Dorf* on the outskirts of Berlin. He and Laszlo had left the car there, taken a taxi into Berlin and then another to Tegel airport.

There, they hired a corporate jet to fly them to Paris. Sam Oliver, Anne Kent's grandfather, had told them that money was no object, and they were to spend at their own discretion. They were taking him at his word.

And now, here they were again at Abdouelle's office. The same heavyset secretary with chunks of dyed blond hair and fire-engine red lips sat on a too-small wheeled chair reading a scandal newspaper. She looked up and almost crumpled the paper when she recognized them.

"You two! What do you want?" she started to stand. Two hairsprayed strands of hair fell from their pinned elevation toward her cheek.

"Where is Abdouelle? We need to talk with him," Jordi said in French, heading for the door to Abdouelle's office.

"You can't go in there," she pointed after him. But she made no attempt to stop him.

Ignoring her, Jordi threw open the office door and stalked in with Laszlo following. Abdouelle sat behind his desk, his small frame and large belly almost hidden behind a tall stack of papers on the desk.

His head jerked up at the sound of the door. Seeing Laszlo and Jordi, he waved his hands at them and spluttered, "You... I didn't do anything."

"I know," Jordi said. "We are here for information." He grabbed a chair with one hand and set it squarely in front of Abdouelle's desk. He sat down, but the papers were stacked so high on the desk that they obstructed his view. Jordi stood up, wiped the papers off with one arm motion and let them fall to the floor in a flurry of white. "That's better. Now I can see you." He sat down again and adjusted his jacket.

Abdouelle eyed the papers on the floor and then looked at Jordi and Laszlo, who stood filling the doorframe. "What information?" Abdouelle asked.

Jordi surveyed him. He still wore the same uniform of wrinkled suit and faded white shirt. And to maintain the consistency, his tie still displayed grease spots from his last meal. Or one before. Jordi lifted his chin, "There is an organization near here, a couple of streets over, on rue l'Argentine. They are big players in drugs and prostitution. What's their exact address and what can you tell us about them?"

"Why do you think I would know anything?" Abdouelle answered. "I am just a struggling real estate agent." He lifted his eyebrows as far up as they would go in an attempt to display incredulous innocence.

"The way you were looking at those papers when I dropped them suggests you are something more than a real estate agent. Why don't we start going through them?"

Jordi reached down to grab a file that had landed at his feet, and Abdouelle cried out, "No. Wait. Let's talk." He straightened his tie and sat up in his chair. "As a real estate agent, I often have to know about buildings in the area and the people who inhabit them. Unfortunately there are some very shady people in this area of Paris. Now, granted, even though I am a poor man, I could act as a consultant to you… and consultants cost money."

"How much?" Jordi asked.

"Ten thousand Euro," Abdouelle said.

"Three hundred," Jordi replied.

"That's highway robbery," Abdouelle hollered, his eyebrows dropping into a scowl.

"Okay, ten Euro," Jordi calmly said. His eyes fell on a mark on Abdouelle's desk, a scar from where he had stuck Abdouelle's hunting knife some months before. Someone had attempted to repair the hole with an uneven layer of darker wood filler.

Jordi raised his eyes to Abdouelle, slowly running his thumb over the hole.

Abdouelle looked down and swallowed hard. "Okay, three hundred Euro. What do you want to know?"

CHAPTER 28

J ordi fixed Abdouelle with an unforgiving glare. "If you give us false information we will come back. And find you."

Abdouelle's business savvy returned to him. "My information is always dependable."

Jordi continued, "We are looking into large-scale drug trafficking and prostitution. Probably a Kosovo connection."

"Ah, yes, the Kosovo Albanians. I know about those people. They are a big problem. They control much of the drug trade in France. I would never deal directly with people like that," Abdouelle sniffed indignantly.

"I'm sure you wouldn't," Jordi said. "But as you said, you know the buildings in this area and the people."

Abdouelle looked around as if someone was hiding in a corner. He leaned forward and said in a low voice, "They are dangerous. Three hundred Euro is not enough."

Jordi leaned forward too, and in a lower voice said, "We may be more dangerous."

Abdouelle looked at Jordi and then at Laszlo who stood impassive by the door. "These men will kill me if they find out I gave you information."

Laszlo reached into his wallet, counted out three hundred Euro notes, and handed them to Jordi. Jordi stuck them in his shirt pocket. "Go on," Jordi said.

"376 rue l'Argentine, just a couple of streets from here. They are one of the most important gangs in Paris. The gangs from Africa, Italy, Russian, and of course local French compete against each other, and this gang is one of the strongest and most respected. At this address you will find the Kosovo Albanians. They were strong before the NATO bombing of Kosovo, but now they control over fifty percent of the drug dealing and prostitution in France, maybe more. There are even rumors that the UN protects them. The Kosovo gang has access to many women in the Balkans and Eastern Europe. They treat their women badly, and they are ruthless when other gangs try to compete with them. As I said. Dangerous."

"OK. So what do they do at 376 rue l'Argentine?" Jordi asked.

"Central command activities. Some distribution."

"Distribution?"

"Drugs and girls, but only some. Obviously they will use many centers. If the police bust one of them, the others can still function. In business terms we call it spreading the risk." Abdouelle relaxed back in his chair, proud of his definition.

Jordi was unimpressed. "Where do they hold the girls?"

"Why?" Abdouelle looked puzzled. "Aren't you going in there to get their money?"

"Answer my question," Jordi commanded. "Where do they keep the girls?"

"On the second floor."

"Can you give us a floor plan?"

"Yes. Sure." For the next few minutes, Abdouelle drew out the floor plan, explaining where people would be. At this time of the day, many of the men would be gone, out covering operations out in the field, taking care of drug distributions and payments, and visiting the pimps in the city.

Armed with the floor plan, Jordi turned to Laszlo and Laszlo nodded.

Jordi said, "That's all we need. Now, you don't leave this office, or use the telephone or talk to anyone for the next few hours. Understood?" He threw his eyes to the knife mark then reached in his shirt pocket, took out the three hundred Euros and tossed them on the desk. Abdouelle swiped them into the top drawer.

Jordi added. "If you hear anything that might be of interest to us, you call this number." He handed him a card with only a telephone number on it, to a throwaway phone so it couln't be traced back to any location. "You will be paid for any useful information." He leaned far forward onto the desk, his nose nearing Abdouelle's. "But if we ever hear you are using information against us in any way, you will receive another kind of payment."

"I would never ever say anything against you to anyone," Abdouelle said to the face far too close to his own for comfort.

"We are absolutely sure you will not," Jordi said, backing away. "Now, if you will excuse us."

Laszlo walked across the room, picked up the telephone near Abdouelle's elbow and ripped the cord from the wall.

"Remember, no telephone calls," Jordi reminded him.

They left and walked through the front office. Abdouelle's secretary was giggling into the telephone which she had wedged between shoulder and ear, leaving her hands free for gesturing. Laszlo slipped the receiver from her then lifted the cradle and ripped the wire from the wall.

"What are you doing?" she cried.

"You are wasting too much company time talking on the telephone," Laszlo said as he walked out the front door after Jordi.

★ ★ ★

The door to Justin's room opened with a loud clunk. Before he had counted them, four men entered. Three flew on top of him and pinned him to the wall. He struggled out of instinct, but the force of the men was too much. He decided it was best to not resist.

They twisted his arms behind him and secured his hands with a plastic cord. "Come," the questioner from yesterday said. He had remained by the door. "Mustafi will now continue our question session. I do suggest that you come willingly." The three men pulled Justin forward and forced him through the door, following the fourth man down the hall and into the same room as the day before. Once tied in the same chair, Justin was told by one of the thugs to simply, "Wait."

Justin said nothing.

Several minutes later a man walked through the door. He filled the frame. Though he was only of medium height, he was stocky and wide with muscular hands. One of these—covered in gold rings—was smoothing his large, black mustache.

Justin thought he looked Mediterranean. But if his name was Mustafi... possibly Turkish.

"What do you want?" Justin asked. "And why have you brought me here?"

The man smiled. "That is strange," he said. "We meet and immediately you ask questions. Is that polite?"

"Why am I here?" Justin repeated.

"More questions. And so aggressive. You are not very civilized," the man made tisking sounds and wagged his finger at Justin. He looked around for a chair, and one of the thugs brought him one. He sat down heavily, facing Justin. "I also have some questions. If I answer yours, then you will answer mine. Is that an agreement?"

"Who knows?" Justin shrugged, noting that his shoulder hurt from the thug tousle.

"I shall answer your questions, and then you will answer mine," the man repeated, pausing for a moment. "You will answer my questions one way or the other, either the easy way or the hard way."

He waited for these implications to sink in. "My name is Mustafi and I manage business affairs."

"What kind of business?"

"International trade, but it really doesn't matter." He flicked at the air with the other ringed hand. "That is really irrelevant to our main topic."

"Which is?" Justin asked.

"We need some truthful answers," Mustafi said. "You were already questioned by my friend here, and you failed. You were not honest with us. I know. I double checked."

"I answered his questions."

"Now, now, Mr. Collins, you answered the questions, but with the wrong answers."

"What do you want to know?" Justin asked. He had given up struggling against the cording around his hands. They were firmly bound. Besides, in addition to Mustafi, there were four other men in the room. Though he felt distantly flattered by such precaution, it did dampen any enthusiasm he may have had for an escape attempt.

"We need information about a businessman in France, Jacques Tapic. Among many things, Mr. Tapic had business relationships with one of my principles. Now my principle, the man I work for, wants to know what happened."

"Like I said yesterday, I only know that he was killed. At least that's what I read in the newspapers."

"I think you know more than that," Mustafi said. "I just got back from Monaco where I visited the firm of Féret and Jaccoud. They were financial advisers to Mr. Tapic. After some discussions with them, they were... persuaded to reveal information. It seems some men visited their office and extorted Mr. Tapic's money, which was under the custodianship of Féret and Jaccoud. It was a considerable sum."

Justin kept his gaze steady. "I wasn't there. I don't know anything about it."

"I have to be honest with you Mr. Collins. We have been informed that Mr. Féret and Mr. Jaccoud have met an unfortunate end. My principle was also displeased with what they had done and desired that they be taught a lesson. Such a lesson is also conveniently an example. You don't want to follow their example, do you? Tell me what happened."

"I don't know." Justin wished he knew how much Mustafi did know.

"Besides the money, Mr. Tapic had offices in Nice where he held his information. What happened there?" Mustafi's eyes were rooted to

Justin's face. "What happened to the equipment in that office?"

"I don't know anything about the office."

"Mr. Collins. You keep telling me lies." He turned to one of the men, "show him what we do with liars."

The questioner from yesterday crossed the room, looking pleased to be doing the dirty work today. He raised his fist and struck Justin under the eye.

Justin rocked backwards in his chair. Three months before, a car had run him over a cliff and his head had come into enough contact with a rock to lay him up with a conclusion for days. More recently, in the farmhouse with Tapic, he had banged his head against a stone wall and passed out. This was not helping the healing process.

"I don't know," Justin said, tasting blood on his tongue as he articulated. He wondered how much he could divulge without harming Chantal and Gloria. Would they go after them as well, searching for the money?

Mustafi came forward to stand by his muscle man. "We have witnesses. Two of our associates, now under our employment, were in that office, a Mr. Ziginiglou and Mr. Turk. They are reliable men and said that your team evicted them from that office. When we checked, the office was empty."

"They don't know what they are talking about," Justin stated bracing himself for another blow.

"Ah, so you acknowledge that you know Ziginiglou and Turk."

"No." Justin swallowed blood and wished he could have swallowed his words. "Who are they?"

"As I said, reliable men." Over his shoulder, he said, "Teach him to tell the truth."

The man raised his fist again and struck Justin on the side of the head.

Justin passed out before his chair fell to the floor.

CHAPTER 29

Now into the 400's, the building numbers on Rue l'Argentine were slowly descending. The last marked building they had seen was 452. They had to be getting close to 376, Laszlo was thinking. Just then Jordi elbowed him. "There it is."

The cracked structure matched Abdouelle's description. It was begging for a wrecking ball.

Their plan being frontal assault, they moved immediately forward. Having no time to stake out the place, they could not isolate people individually to extract information. In all likelihood, Schubach had called his counterparts in France. He would be angry with his pride and leg injured. And he would want revenge.

Plus, Abdouelle would sell information to the highest bidder. Laszlo doubted that the containment at his office would last long.

They walked across the street and went inside the entrance that lead directly to the stairs. Both pulled handguns from under their coats and went down a narrow dark hallway and up to the second floor. The building was quiet. From Abdouelle's description, they knew that the few men in the building were likely to be on the third floor.

The second floor appeared to be a sort of dormitory, with doors on both sides of the hall. Laszlo tried the door handle of the first room and it opened. It was empty except for two simple metal bed frames and a small wooden table between them. Laszlo and Jordi began checking all the doors. Each had a variation of beds and night stand.

One door was at the end of the hall was locked. Laszlo put his ear up against it and listened. He could make out at least two female voices speaking quietly. He nodded to Jordi and Jordi turned and faced down the hall, holding his gun.

Laszlo kicked the door at the point of the door handle and the door flew open. He went inside, gun first.

Two young women cowered next to each other on one of the beds.

"Do you speak English?" Laszlo said.

"A little," one of the girls said, shaking her head.

"Spanish, German, French?"

"French more than English. We are Romanian."

Laszlo switched into Romanian. "What are you doing here?" he asked.

The sound of their native language from a man who appeared more inclined to protect than abuse them set both their tongues loose at once.

"Wait," Laszlo said, raising his hand. "One at a time."

The brunette, the smaller of the two went first, "We were promised jobs, and now they keep us locked up. We are scared. They say we owe them money. We must give it back."

"Have you seen an American girl here?"

"Brown hair? Her name is Anne." The slightly larger, darker one replied.

He pulled out the photo and showed it to the girls. They looked to be seventeen or eighteen years old, timid and innocent.

They looked at the photo. "Yes, that's her," the first girl said. "She was here with us. She said they shot her uncle and took her."

"What else did she say?"

The darker girl seemed less inclined to speak, so her friend went on, "Our English is not good and she knows some French, so we couldn't communicate very much. She is strong."

"Strong, what do you mean?"

"One of the men came to her and said he wanted her. She kicked him in the groin and he doubled over in pain. She kept kicking him until other men came to his rescue."

It sounded like Anne Kent wouldn't give in to her captors too easily. Laszlo found himself almost smiling but then righted his face. These men were used to getting their way immediately and would not tolerate much resistance. More than likely it would motivate them to find new ways to break her resolve and force her to submit to them, and they wouldn't hesitate to use violence and perversity. They had to find her fast. He asked, "Where is she?"

"They were talking in French and said an order had been made. We were just talking about it. We think she was sold. She almost escape out of building, but they caught her. They drugged her and took her away."

"Where did they take her?" Laszlo was itching to get going.

"They said to Italy, to Milan. We were there before they brought us to Paris. That seems to be one of their centers, at least from girls they bring from Eastern Europe."

"When did they take her?"

"Yesterday," said the second girl, a faraway look in her eyes.

Laszlo pressed on, "Would you know how to find the place in Milan?"

The smaller girl looked at the other who nodded. "We think so. They took us out of the place by car. It is not far from the Milan train station, so we know the area of the city and what the street looks like. I think we could find it."

"Will you help us?" Laszlo asked.

"Yes, *please* take us from here." The desperation in the darker girl's voice bled through her words. She looked to be on the verge of tears or a break down.

Jordi stuck his head through the door and said, "*Hombre*. Trouble. We've got to move."

"Let's go," Laszlo commanded. The girls were off the bed before he'd closed his mouth.

Laszlo placed an arm around each of the two girls and rushed into the hallway. Footsteps pounded on the stairs. Jordi ran ahead and saw two men starting to descend. He fired. One of the men yelled and fell to the ground while the other men retreated.

Laszlo led the girls down the stairs while Jordi covered the rear. When they got to the street they ran half a block, ducked into an alley and kept running.

The two girls were running so fast that Jordi and Laszlo had to keep up with them.

★ ★ ★

After Gloria had been driving the maze of Milan streets for two hours—dodging erratic pedestrians and careening Italian drivers—she and Chantal finally found 23 Garabaldi Street.

Not far from the Milan train station, this was the address Turk had given them. The buildings in this neighborhood were stained black by engine smoke, their facades cracked and crumbling from the continual rattle of train cars along the tracks.

Gloria slowed down as they passed number 23, but a high concrete wall with razor wire curled around the top and hid the building from view. On the wall, some protesting artist had graffiti'd a large red flag emblazoned with a yellow hammer and sickle and a black swastika. The word *Assassini* curved below it.

"Do you think Turk was telling the truth?" Gloria asked.

Chantal sighed, "I told you before that we just have to take the risk."

"I'm just asking," Gloria said, color coming into her cheeks. She was not in the mood to be trifled with. She had been willing to drive to distract herself from the morning sickness that had been toying with her insides all day.

Just as Gloria thought Chantal would leave the issue, Chantal spat out, "You get on my nerves. I have to think about everything, to do everything."

Gloria slowly turned her head from the windshield to the passenger seat. Offended incredulity seared across the green of her pupils, "I just drove here from Zurich, three hundred and five kilometers in two and a half hours. And I have been navigating through this death-trap of a city for the last two. *Who* does everything?"

Chantal closed her eyes. She took a deep breath and said "I'm sorry" without meeting Gloria's eyes.

Gloria didn't reply. At the end of the street she turned the car to the left, went two blocks, found a free space and parked the car. As the engine ticked to stillness, Gloria watched the keys swing to a stop in the ignition. Their tiny movement after hours of driving made her dizzy.

After a full minute of silence, she turned to Chantal and reached for her hand. Chantal was faintly taken aback, but did not pull away. Gloria finally spoke. "Let's try to get through this. I'm just as frightened as you." She squeezed Chantal's hand and then returned hers to the keys, pulling them from the ignition and dropping them into her purse.

"Did you get a good look at the building?" Chantal asked.

"No. I was driving. What was your impression?"

"Turk must have been telling at least part of the truth. It was exactly as Turk described it. Graffiti and wire and all."

"Shall we go to the police?" Gloria asked.

Chantal noticed how tentatively Gloria asked this, knowing her opinion of how they should operate. But she tried her best to answer positively, "That's certainly an option, but what we would tell them? That some thug in Kosovo gave us a suspicious address and could they please go knock on the door and arrest all the people?"

A smile twitched at Gloria's lips, "I see what you mean. Shall we try to get a better look at the place first?"

"OK. How?" Chantal asked.

"Well, first we could walk by. Figure out the layout as best we can."

Chantal nodded, "But what if Turk told his gang in Kosovo about us, and they telephoned here and are waiting for two women?"

"Then only one of us should walk by. What would Justin call it… a 'stakeout'?" The word fell stiffly on her Spanish tongue.

Chantal reached for the door handle with a smile. "I guess I'd better do some of that everything I said I was doing."

CHAPTER 30

Lionel Banneret headed for a reserved dining room at the European Union headquarters in Brussels. Three large round tables were each set with eight places.

A committee of twelve high-ranking UN and EU officials had been meeting throughout the day. The topic was the involvement of the European Union in activities of the UN in the developing world and how the EU might better assist in these efforts. The dinner was a chance for additional people to join in—for networking and quiet negotiations.

Banneret looked around the room. The thickly-plated silverware of each place setting pointed perfectly toward the small bouquets of red roses centered at every table.

Waiters wearing white tuxedo jackets and black ties stood by the long sideboard, bedding champagne in ice, lighting the warmers under waiting appetizers, and bringing in special requests from those already present.

One of the men spotted Banneret when he entered and raised a manicured hand at him. He excused himself from a small circle of men and came to Banneret. They smiled at each other and shook hands.

"Lionel. I wasn't sure you would make it." The man pumped his hand, his gold cufflinks reflecting in the candlelight.

"I had to stop in Paris, but with the private jet comes flexibility," Banneret replied.

"It is a pleasure to have you here."

"And it is my pleasure to be here." He smiled at his old friend Jean-Marie Villepin, a member of the European Parliament and the head of several committees. Together, they had been involved in French politics for years and then had moved on to the United Nations and the European Union, each taking high-ranking positions.

Well-managed rumor was starting to circulate that Villepin was on the list to be the next president of the EU. A significant political appointment. The current president was under pressure to resign for failing to resolve a scandal involving the mysterious misplacement of several billion Euros. With Villepin as president of the EU and with other political leverages both men possessed, the necessary influence would be in place to ensure Banneret's appointment as Secretary-

General of the United Nations.

"How are things in Kosovo?" Villepin asked, cocking his head to the side and sending a whiff of expensive aftershave in Banneret's direction.

"The situation is stabilizing and our local representatives are gaining political advantage. Most importantly, international trade is increasing. The presence of our peace keeping force has been of great assistance." Banneret looked Villepin in the eye.

"Excellent news," Villepin responded, his own eyes glinting. "I am sure we will continue to see the fruits of our efforts begin to materialize."

"Things are progressing," Banneret said. But he paused. In a low voice he said, "We must talk about Jacques Tapic."

* * *

Chantal left the car, thought of something, and headed toward Garabaldi Street. One street over, she found a row of small shops, ending with a small corner grocery store.

Inside, she selected two bottles of water, crackers and a couple of apples. She bagged her own purchases in two bags though they would have fit in one and went back to the car.

Gloria raised one eyebrow at her quick return and the other at the grocery bags. Surprise turned to a stomach growl Chantal could hear before she had even climbed into her seat.

"Good idea. I am hungry and thirsty," Gloria said, reaching inside for an apple.

"That's not the only reason." Chantal said, ripping open a package of crackers and popping two in her mouth. Barely chewing, she swallowed and said, "Carrying a bag from a local shop makes us appear to belong here. More like women who went shopping, not women trying to break into an evil prostitution ring."

Each woman took a swig from a water bottle and they divided the things into the two bags. Bag in lap, Chantal spoke, "I was thinking you could come to the corner of Garabaldi street. There is a phone booth you can pretend to call someone on. You can see me from there. If anything happens to me, then go to the police."

"This is the first time I will not want to go to them," Gloria said, her face drawn tight.

Gloria left the car and went to the phone booth. A few minutes later,

Chantal walked past without looking at her.

This section of the street was lined with derelict buildings from what looked to be an abandoned industrial zone. Chantal walked on the sidewalk opposite from number 23. She walked slowly, occasionally looking across the street for any clues about the place. All she saw was the high block wall they had drive past and a bit of the upper floor of the building.

The wall was about three times her height. Razor wire rolled its way across the top. The double-door metal gate was almost as high as the wall with one tight strand of razor wire running across each door.

Chantal bent over to adjust her shoe. She was standing in front of a building that looked just as rundown as the rest on the street. She continued down Garibaldi, turned left at the intersection, and circled around the block. She came to the phone booth where Gloria returned the receiver to its hook.

"What did you find out?" Gloria asked.

"Not much. A high wall with a metal gate that a large truck could drive through, but I couldn't see inside."

"That's all?" Gloria looked disappointed.

Chantal too. She pursed her lips. "We need to see inside."

"How are we going to get inside?" Gloria reached inside her grocery bag for her water bottle.

"No, *see* inside. I have another idea. There is an abandoned building across the street, about six stories high. We might try and find a way into the building, perhaps away from Garabaldi Street. If we can get inside, then we can look over the wall."

Gloria made a small toasting gesture at Chantal with her water bottle, "Good thinking. Let's go."

★ ★ ★

They found the opposite side of the abandoned building in the alley. After some poking around, they discovered a hole that once had been a door and was now boarded over with wide wooden planks.

Her queasiness having left her, Gloria felt doubly energized. She pulled at a nailed plank, found it loose, and yanked it away. She squeezed through and Chantal followed.

They waited a moment until their eyes adjusted to the darkness. Gloria took deep, steadying breaths and told herself they would not find a dead body here.

As the darkness lightened to dimness, Gloria saw that they stood in a hallway with a flight of stairs rising up at the opposite end. Chantal had already headed for them. Enough light came through the opaque windows that they could see where they were going as they began climbing.

Door frames, bare of doors, gaped into rooms of trash, the occasional mattress, and small heaps of cloth and clothing. Like the Pec building, everything reeked of damp and urine.

Arriving on the seventh floor, they stopped to catch their breath. They stepped over a long, rusted pipe into a large room. A stained brown curtain hung from half a window near the stairs. A slight breeze disturbed the filthy fabric and it shifted stiffly.

They had a fine view of number 23 Garabaldi.

Gloria stood behind the cover of the curtain, and Chantal at the edge of the bare window frame. They peeked from their cover to look at their target building.

Beyond the wall lay a parking area big enough for three or four trucks to park. The building itself resembled an office building with a warehouse or small factory to the left with a loading dock. One dark car was in the parking area.

"We wait?" Gloria asked.

"We wait." Chantal answered.

They spent the afternoon and evening taking turns watching the compound. One watched while the other one rested. From one of the rooms downstairs, they brought up a rickety metal stool and set it in front of the window.

During one of Gloria's shifts, Chantal returned to the several stores around the corner to pick up a few blankets and more food.

Gloria had kept her eyes on the building until, like a computer monitor with a document left open too long, her retinas were etched with the building's outline. When she closed her eyes, she could still see a faintly red afterimage of the place she prayed would lead them to Justin.

Them. She had thought in the plural despite wanting to find Justin for herself. She was beginning to be able to tolerate Chantal, but she certainly did not want to share her husband with the woman.

Chantal came back just then, holding blankets high. Gloria resisted thinking the English phrase Justin had told her once: *speak of the devil.* Instead, she smiled at Chantal and accepted a pink checkered blanket. Synthetic but warm.

"Go and rest," Chantal told her, taking Gloria's shoulder in her hand and gently pushing her away from the window. "You've been there a long while."

"I am starting to stiffen like an old woman when I sit too long in any position," Gloria said, putting her hands to her lower spine and bending backwards in a stretch. She crossed to a corner of the room and lay down on a low, wide shelf that looked relatively sturdy. It also had far less likelihood of insect infestation or worse that did the soggy mattresses they had seen on the lower floors. Night fell, and she dozed.

At eight o'clock, Chantal whispered from the window, "Come here."

Gloria joined her at the window and looked across the street into the courtyard of number 23. There was still only one car parked there, and a man was opening the trunk and putting something inside.

Gloria yawned. Not all that exciting, but more than she'd seen during her last watch. Just as she was getting ready to back away from the 'action,' a white truck rolled down the street and stopped at the metal gate.

Gloria's yawn turned into a sharp intake of breath. The side of the truck wore two large letters printed in light blue, *UN*. And underneath that, *Agency for International Development*.

The man inside the courtyard closed his trunk and went to the gate to open it. As the gate slid to a width large enough to accommodate the van, the man motioned for the driver to enter. The van backed up to the loading dock, and its driver got out and yanked open the back doors.

Five young women climbed out into the yard spotlight. The man who had opened the gate said something to them, and they headed inside the building.

Even from the seventh story window across the street, Gloria could see that blue bruises blossomed across the pale forearms and face of one of the girls.

CHAPTER 31

Villepin looked right and left as if readying to cross a street. In a low voice, he said to Banneret, "It was a shock. We were at dinner with Jacques in his home one evening, and the next day he is dead. Will we ever really know who did it?"

"I am investigating and will update you at a more appropriate time."

Villepin looked again across the room and said, "I understand. We should speak privately."

Banneret nodded. "We had better circulate. Is there any specific objective for the evening?"

"Yes," Villepin whispered like a ventriloquist through a large smile, rolling his head toward a corner of the room, "The two men at the end of the table over there need some convincing about my candidacy." He returned his gaze to Banneret, "Especially the German."

"Leave it to me," Banneret nodded.

They parted to mingle. Banneret shook hands through a cluster of various dignitaries on his way to the sideboard. Several bottles of chilled white wine from different countries in the EU were diplomatically presented. He passed up the French Bordeaux and went for a German vintner he did not know.

Eying the German now alone at the other end of the sideboard and actively engaged with several selections of appetizers, Banneret approached him, glass in hand. "Ah, Dr. Becker. It is so nice to meet you again."

The German politician took a small bow. "Mr. Banneret, How do you do?"

"Excellent." Banneret lifted his glass and took a small sip and swirling it in his mouth like a taster. He swallowed and smiled, "By the way, this German white wine is also excellent."

The German beamed. "As good as the French?"

"It has a lovely bouquet," Banneret answered. He would not even use it as cooking wine.

"Our wines are improving," Dr. Becker replied. "Maybe some day they will be as renowned as our beers."

"With German attentiveness to quality and production I have no doubt," Banneret agreed, carefully not looking at Becker's hefty beer belly.

"How are things in your UN agency?" Becker asked, popping two pickles in his mouth.

"Moving forward nicely." Banneret selected an olive with a toothpick and twirled it in his fingers. "We are helping with the development of trade into the EU. We are very grateful for the support we are receiving from EU members. Particularly the German contingent." He pulled the olive into his mouth with his teeth. After two quick bites he gave Becker a long look, "May I ask you one thing, of course off the record, but just to see what you are thinking? I know you have so much influence over your Germen colleagues, and I would be most interested to know your views if I may sound you out."

"On what topic?" Becker asked, trying to pull a shrimp from its shell while keeping his small plate horizontal.

"It's just curiosity, but there are rumors that the current president of the EU may be resigning due to various reasons. I am wondering in which way you are leaning in support of the candidacy of a new president."

Becker grabbed a small sausage off the table, having evidently given up on the shrimp. He pointed the squat sausage at Banneret, "Off the record, I am not decided. But I have been thinking for some time that it would be appropriate to have a German as president. After all, Germany is the largest economy in the EU. I think it is time to recognize this contribution and leadership by appointing a German." He finalized this by popping the sausage of his homeland into his mouth.

"So interesting," Banneret nodded. "Your reasoning makes sense of course, but there are a number of extremely qualified individuals to consider. Does it not seem right to appoint someone on the basis of their merit rather than nationality?"

"Like who?" Becker asked.

"Look around the room," Banneret said, doing so and landing his glance on Villepin. "For instance, Mr. Villepin would be an excellent candidate, and it seems there is growing momentum in support of his candidacy."

"I will go with my own line of reasoning," the German said, forking a canapés onto his plate.

"I understand, but the world of politics is a strange place and self preservation is a primary drive for any politician." Banneret smiled with no light in his eyes.

Becker left the canapés to absorb pickle juice. "I don't understand."

Banneret left his smile in place and explained, "Politicians are elected to make the best decisions on behalf of the people, but there can be flexibility in those decisions. Especially where survival is concerned."

"Survival? What..."

"Let me present a hypothetical situation." Banneret interrupted. "Say that it was discovered that a politician like yourself had been involved in illicit affairs. More specifically, active pedophilia."

Becker appeared to be on the brink of choking up his sausage.

Banneret went on, "And say this news was made known to the press, supported by evidence in the form of photos and audio recordings. Say these had been gathered at a house in the north of Brussels two months ago. That would be quite damaging would it not?"

Becker stared at Banneret with his mouth open. A bit of green stuck between his eye teeth.

"You see what I mean—that self preservation of the politician determines his decisions. But of course, unpleasant disclosure is rarely necessary. I am confident you will make the right decision regarding the appointment of Mr. Villepin."

A waiter passed by with a collection of used glasses on his tray. Banneret set his unfinished wine on it and, said to a rather purpling Becker, "I am afraid I have to retract my earlier statement. The German wines still pale beside the French."

CHAPTER 32

Without any proof that Justin was in the building, or that anything illegal was taking place, it made little sense to go to the police. Gloria was the first to say this after they had watched the five women being herded from the truck.

Chantal had glanced at her, wondering if Gloria anticipated that she would say something about not involving the authorities. But Gloria was not acting defensive, so Chantal merely nodded. Nothing further happened by midnight, and they decided that there must be other entrances they could not see from where they were.

With no better option presenting itself, the two women decided to spend the night where they were. Chantal insisted that Gloria take the broad shelf for a bed, and she herself curled up on the hardwood floor. After being decidedly catty earlier that day, Chantal felt the need to redeem herself.

She stretched out near the shelf and before she finished wondering what they would to in the morning, bright dawn light woke her. Sore from her neck to her heels, she slowly moved her muscles and extended her limbs. Twisting sideways in a stretch, she glanced up at Gloria, half a meter above her. Her long red hair hung down the shelf and caught the early sun. *Again, that angelic face,* Chantal thought. It was both disturbing and peaceful to look at this woman.

When circulation returned to the parts of her that had been pressed against the floor, Chantal quietly rose and went to the bag of food she had brought back yesterday evening. She pulled out a bottle of water and drank half of it. She then took her sketchpad from her own bag.

Bringing water and pad to the window, Chantal sat on the stool and looked into the courtyard across the street. The UN truck was still parked where it had been last night. Everything looked still, so she started to sketch Gloria's face without looking back at her. She wanted to preserve that peacefulness.

But it did not come. After rubbing out several charcoal lines and trying again, she managed for a solid resemblance, but nothing more.

She lay the sketchpad on her knees.

The street below was slowly coming to life. Vespas and small cars roared down the dirty pavement, and honking from larger streets nearby echoed through the valley of Garabaldi street's industrial monoliths.

An older couple crossed from one sidewalk to the other, their hands speaking as much as their mouths. A man let his dog piss under the *Assassini* graffiti and continued on his way. Yet beyond the wall, the courtyard remained completely still.

Chantal found herself mouthing a prayer of protection she remembered from childhood. It was for Justin and the trafficked women she had great sympathy for. She closed her eyes and tried to block out what her imagination told her was happening or going to happen to them.

When she raised her head to look back at Gloria, she almost jumped to see two green eyes at her shoulder, focused on the sketch pad.

Gloria was smiling, "It looks like me. You are very good."

Chantal appraised her work and started to shake her head, but out of the corner of her eye, she saw a movement out the window and leaned in that direction. Gloria did the same.

A man came through a door next to the loading dock. The driver from yesterday. He descended the several steps, when to the cab of the truck and removed an object.

"A gun," Gloria said.

The man stuck the weapon in his belt, walked across the loading dock and opened the doors of the truck before heading back into the building.

Moments later he reappeared with three women behind him and two men bringing up the rear. One of the women was slower than the others and a man behind her pushed her forward. She lost her balance, stumbled and fell. The man laughed and turned to the other man and said something. As he turned they had a good look at his face.

"Zog," Chantal breathed.

Gloria nodded. "The man on the identity papers."

They kept their eyes locked on the scene below them. As the three women entered the van, another man left the building. Hands tied and his head bowed, he was 'escorted' by two broad-shouldered men on either side of him. His face bore thick bruises and caked blood down one side.

"*Justin,*" both women said in unison, his name sounding like a prayer of desire on their lips. They both forgot themselves and pressed close to the open window, leaning out for a better look.

Behind Justin a woman emerged, hands also bound. She shuffled along, supported by yet another thick-necked man. Their captors loaded Justin and the woman into the back of the truck with the other three women. The doors shut.

As the truck began to move toward the metal gate, Zog looked up. As the truck passed through the gate and began turning right, he saw the two women. He raised his hand to their window, drawing the attention of one of the men standing beside him.

Zog's dark eyes managed to bore through both Chantal's and Gloria's in the same, single glare.

CHAPTER 33

"Run!" Chantal yelled, clutching at her sketch pad and taking only enough time to grab the small satchel with her passport as she leapt for the door. Gloria snatched her purse and bolted for the stairwell after Chantal.

They jumped down the stairs two at a time, having barely enough light to avoid stepping on the debris lurking at every landing. Reaching the bottom floor, they ran to the door with the wooden panels they had entered by, and slid through out on the street. Men's voices were already audible from somewhere in the building. The women pelted down the street toward their car.

Gloria stole a quick glance back and saw a man sticking his leg through the opening between the boards, but he got stuck and pulled his leg back in. Two pairs of hands began to pull on the nailed panels.

They made it to the end of the block before Chantal turned around and saw Zog half-way through the opening. He saw them. The other man had already made it through was sprinting toward them.

"Get the keys out. Hurry!" Chantal called to her.

Gloria had gotten ahead of Chantal. She found the keys in her purse as they took a corner so fast they had to lean into the turn.

Half a block to their rental car.

Gloria's middle was clenching with queasiness, side splits and fear. She almost fell onto the car when she got to it. With shaking hands, she managed to cram the key in the lock, open the door, and release the lock for Chantal. They dove into their seats and Gloria had the ignition on by the time Zog and his thug had turned the corner.

Heedless of oncoming traffic, Gloria backed out into the street, cutting off another driver who laid on his horn.

Zog reached the women's car. He got his hand on Chantal's door handle, opened it and made a grab for her. Gloria put her foot to the accelerator, passed a car in front of them by swerving into the oncoming traffic, and then jerked the car back into the right lane. She missed a head-on collision by inches.

Zog was still holing onto the swinging door. His body cracked into a parked car they were passing. He lost his grip and fell rolling to the ground. The car behind them came to a screeching halt. Several cars were honking while Gloria gunned the car through an open space, ran a red light, and sped down the street.

"Turn right," Chantal said.

"Why?" Gloria asked.

"The truck. It left the courtyard. Justin's inside."

Gloria heaved the car to the right and circled back to Garibaldi Street in the direction the truck had turned.

No truck in sight.

"It's gone already." Gloria said, body slumping slightly forward toward the steering wheel. Her grip on it was numbing her fingers.

Chantal said in a voice steadier than Gloria's would have been, "Just drive down the street."

At the end of the first block they scanned the street. Just cars.

"Could it have gone in the other direction?" Gloria asked.

"The truck turned right. It had to come down this street."

The traffic moved swiftly, and at the end of the third block Chantal jerked forward and pointed through the windshield, "It's there, turning left. There it is."

A small break in traffic gave Gloria the chance she needed, and she wrenched the steering wheel hard to the left and accelerated.

"Not too close," Chantal said. "Don't let them know they are being followed."

Gloria bit her lip. She knew to stay out of sight, but she did not want to add any tension to their situation by saying so.

She followed the truck from several blocks behind. It headed north through Milan, took an expressway leading out of the city, and after a few kilometers merged onto the *Autostrada*, the west-bound freeway.

Gloria drove the car to the toll gate, took a ticket and stayed several kilometers behind the truck. She lost sight of it occasionally, but it was important to not let driver know he was being followed. After half an hour the truck turned north onto another *Autostrada*.

The women's rental was soon on the same road. Chantal read from the exit sign that announced, 'Mt. Blanc, Chamonix, Ginebra'.

For over two hours they followed their quarry through the northern plains of Italy as the highway began to curve its way up through small mountains. Finally, they saw the snow-peaked Alps looming high above in the distance.

"Do you know where this road leads?" Gloria asked, realizing they had been silent since Chantal had read the signs.

"Through the Mt. Blanc Tunnel into France."

Gloria thought a moment then asked, "Do you have any ideas why they are going there?"

Chantal shrugged, "*Je ne sais pas*. We only know that Justin is inside the truck with some women." She turned to look out the window.

Gloria hesitated to continue. Chantal seemed to be in a dark mood. But they needed to organize themselves somehow. "What are we going to do, realistically? We are two against who knows who many dangerous men. We have no weapons. We have to come up with a plan." Gloria tried to keep her voice earnest and honest.

Chantal turned from the countryside to look at Gloria's profile. "I am thinking." She said nothing further.

The *Autostrada* wound its way into the Alps. Rocky cliffs rose into jagged peaks on either side of the road, and they passed the occasional waterfall rushing down from invisible glaciers above.

The traffic narrowed to a single line as they approached a custom's guard house. In the past every passport had been checked, but with the advent of the European Union, borders had opened. The UN truck rolled right through and went on ahead to the toll booth to pay for traversing the tunnel.

When Gloria approached the customs agent, he looked into their window and flagged them to stop.

"*Passeporto,*" he snapped, hand open.

Gloria and Chantal pulled out their passports and handed them to the agent. He opened Gloria's, looked at the picture and then its original. He took his time to compare face and hair. Then he put his face closer to the open window and let his eyes rest on her bosom.

He smiled. He took Chantal's passport and did the same. "*Francais.* Where are you going?" He asked, speaking French with a strong Italian accent."

"We need your help," Chantal said. "The truck up there, the one going into the tunnel. There is a problem."

"A problem?" the man responded. "With a UN truck?"

"There are people inside," Chantal said, raising her voice.

"Of course there are people inside. Someone has to drive it."

But Gloria persisted, "No. I mean people in the back. They are trafficking people. Kidnapped people."

The customs agent smiled, "What do you mean?"

Gloria noticed that he seemed to be taking the delay as an opportunity to continue ogling them. Annoyed but determined, she clarified, "I mean that you must call the French police and ask them to stop that truck on the other side of the tunnel."

"A UN truck? You are kidding. No one would do this."

"You must stop that truck. Our husband is inside."

"Your husband?" He looked at each of them in turn.

Gloria ignored his incredulity and went on, "Kidnappers are holding him in the back of that truck."

The customs agent laughed, "Well, he is a lucky man to have such beautiful women for wives, but your names are different on the passports. One says Collins and the other says Montalvo. This is a great joke." Handed Gloria back the passports.

Gloria had not changed the name on her passport and still had her maiden name.

"Please, I am serious."

The agent looked behind their car where a long line of cars was waiting. "Good joke," he said, bringing his attention back to them. "Do you know what kind of incident we would have if we demanded a UN truck to stop and be inspected? Neither Italians nor the French would do that. Move ahead." He waved his hand forward in the direction of the tunnel.

"No," Gloria said, pounding her fist on the car door. "You *must* stop that truck."

"No. You *must* go now," he said, pointing a stiff finger toward the tunnel. "Any more of this foolishness and I will have you detained." His humor had left him, and the uniform he wore began to look more authoritative.

"Let's go," Chantal said softly to Gloria.

"Two women. One husband," he said, tapping the side of his head with his index finger. "You think I'm crazy?"

Gloria looked in the rearview mirror as she pulled away. He was still watching them even as another driver pulled up to his booth and handed a passport out his window.

★ ★ ★

It felt like lifting heavy weights just to open his eyelids. Justin looked around and saw a dark furry haze. A haze in motion. He sensed the vibration of road passing beneath wheels. But then he stopped thinking about movement—it made him dizzy.

He remembered. Just before entering the truck, one of his captors had pushed the needle of a syringe into his arm. After that, everything went black.

Testing his head, he turned it slowly and looked around him. Other people swayed in the truck. Or was he swaying, or the truck…?

He tried again. The people were women. He began counting them but could not tell if there were four or six. They shifted and separated and blended together, their mouths moving. He tried to talk, but slurry sounds came out of his mouth, and his head turned inside, making his stomach feel nauseous.

Mattress. He seemed to be lying on a mattress. The impossible mass of his body was anchored to it.

He turned over and saw a woman lying next to him. Gloria. So glad to have Gloria there. Or was it Chantal? She was speaking English with an American accent. Someone else, then. Her words hit his skin and sent him spinning.

He put his head back down on the mattress.

The weights won and his eyes fell shut.

CHAPTER 34

Daylight was swallowed by darkness. The tunnel went for eleven kilometers through the mass of Mont Blanc, Europe's highest mountain. After ten kilometers of darkness, broken only by artificial light from their headlights and the fixtures along the walls, Chantal remembered a story about a train that had entered a tunnel, as it did daily. Instead of coming out on the other side as usual, the train continued in the darkness. It went faster and faster, and just before it reached the speed at which it could no longer hold together, one of the passengers realized in terror what was happening. They were plunging into the center of the earth.

"I wish those cars would move faster," Gloria said, snapping Chantal from her plummet. Gloria had her chin out past the steering wheel, trying to see ahead.

"We'll be out soon enough," Chantal said, adding, "I hope. And I hope we didn't lose the truck." What they had lost was lost valuable time with the customs.

"There. Light ahead," Gloria said.

In a minute they passed into daylight that illuminated the green forests on the French side of the mountain. The rains from the north emptied themselves on this northwest side of the Alps. The Italian side to the south where they had come from was drier.

"Can you see the truck?" Gloria asked.

"It's got to be ahead," Chantal had her seatbelt in a death grip, the flat black of it now a clenched cylinder in her fist.

Gloria went across a double line, passed two cars and sped down the mountain, racing around curves. After five kilometers they came to a larger four-lane road where they had to make a choice to turn right to Chamonix, or to go left in the direction of Geneva.

"What's your guess?" Gloria asked.

"The truck had a Swiss diplomatic license plate," Chantal said. "Why don't we head toward Geneva. We can go a few kilometers. If we don't see the truck, then we go back to Chamonix."

Gloria accelerated down a long straight grade in the direction of Geneva.

"There it is." Chantal let the mangled seat belt go and used the hand—now imprinted with its weave—to point, "Over there."

The truck was stopped in the parking lot of a small restaurant.

A hand-written sign above the establishment read, *'Steaks, Frits, Sandwichs'*. Gloria sped to the next exit, turned around and went back to the parking lot. They drove by the vehicle. Its cab was empty.

"Stop. Let's get him out of there," Chantal had her door open before Gloria brought the car to a full stop next to the truck.

At the rear loading door of the truck, Chantal grabbed at the padlock that hung there. "*Merde.*" Gloria was just getting out of the car. Chantal turned to her and said, "Open the trunk."

Gloria reached back down for the small lever by her seat and popped open the trunk. She went to it and pulled out the jack handle, bringing it to where Chantal was pounding on the door. "Justin! Justin are you in there?"

Gloria wedged the jack handle into the loop of the pad lock and began to pull. She gave it her full weight, but nothing happened. Again, not even significant scratching. She joined Chantal in calling out, whacking the jack handle on the door.

Muffled noises made it through their noise. Female voices called, "Help us!"

"Is Justin inside?" Chantal yelled.

"Help," a voice repeated, more clearly this time.

"Maybe two of us can break it," Gloria said, positioning the jack again and nodding for Chantal to join her. They pulled together. It didn't budge.

Chantal kicked the tire in frustration. She had just noticed that the truck had Swiss license plates, with CD-GVA on them, when she heard Gloria give a quiet cry, "Go. Go. In the car, *now.*"

Chantal looked up to see two men emerging from the restaurant. The driver and rider. Two more men were behind them. Unfortunately, all men looked up in unison. They broke into a sprint toward the truck.

The two women flew into their seats, having left their doors open. Gloria put her foot to the floor, spinning tires and sending gravel into orbit. The driver and the rider ran to the back of the truck and saw the jack handle sticking through the padlock loop.

The other two men ran to a blue car, jumped in, and in a few moments were only several hundred meters behind the rental car and closing the gap.

"They are faster than us," Gloria said through gritted teeth, gaining speed down the long incline.

The other car continued to loom larger in their rearview mirrors.

"Try a side road," Chantal said. "We won't be able to lose them here."

After one kilometer Gloria spotted a paved road off to the right heading through a forest. She took it at high speed, almost losing control of the car. Moments later the blue car made the same turn. The rental emerged from the forest where the road curved along the side of a steep mountain. On their left, a steep gorge ended far below in a distant, rushing river.

The blue was now directly behind them. It bumped them from behind. "Faster," Chantal screamed.

"I can't." Gloria yelled back, "I'll lose control if we go any faster."

The other car rubbed into them again, bending metal. Chantal heard a squeaking noise. "What now?" she asked more of the car than Gloria.

"I think they bent the car into the tire," Gloria said, as she swung onto a dirt road.

They sped for several kilometers, the blue car still on their tail. But when the road widened again, the blue car gained speed and started to overtake them, bashing into the side of their car this time.

Chantal looked through Gloria's window and saw the faces of the two men. The man on the rider's side was grinning back at her.

When the blue car was just about nose to nose with the rental, Gloria jerked the steering wheel to the left. Somehow their car gained leverage, pushing the blue car off the side of the road.

And over a ravine. It flipped several times and landed in a rocky stream below. Gloria pulled into a small meadow, turned the car around and drove slowly past the overturned blue car. A man was pulling himself out of the window on the rider's side, something in his hand. He looked up in their direction and shook his fist.

Gloria gunned the car, the left back wheel making a screeching noise, the tire smoking and the acrid odor of rubber filling the car. They made it back to the paved road before the rubber tire broke off, leaving the car to roll on its metal wheel.

Chantal found herself clutching the sides of the seat, her neck muscles still strained as they had been when looking over the ravine at their pursuers. She could not swallow.

"We can't go long like this," Gloria said. "I'm pulling off." She drove off the next side road, stopped the car and turned to Chantal, "We should get the rubber tire so they don't suspect we have a problem."

They went back to the tire, hoisted it off, and together threw the smelly, heavy thing into the bushes that lined the road. Back at the rental, they got out a bottle of water—one thankfully left from before their stakeout—and took a swig each, then washed off the filth from the tire.

Chantal handed Gloria the water bottle for another swallow and stood looking at the wheel.

Gloria capped the bottle and asked, "Can we put the spare tire on it?"

"It will be pretty hard without a jack handle." Chantal flicked her hand at the bare wheel to show it her annoyance.

Gloria sighed, "Then let's get it out of sight. They got in the car and drove it further down the dirt road and then into the forest.

Gloria cut the engine and said to the steering wheel, "We lost Justin."

"I know," Chantal said in a soft voice of longing.

"Shall we go back to the paved road down there and try to hitch a ride?"

"It looks like the only option we have, but we have to be careful." Chantal rubbed her fingers into her throbbing temples, noting that the fingers themselves ached too.

"Because of the man crawling out of the blue car."

"Yes. And did you see what he had in his hand?" Chantal asked, turning to look at Gloria.

"No, I was driving."

"He had a cell phone." Chantal pulled at her door handle and pulled it open. "He might be calling for help."

CHAPTER 35

From the seventh floor window, Laszlo had a good view into the courtyard across the street.

He and Jordi had chartered a corporate jet from Paris to Milan the previous evening, spent the night in a hotel near the airport, and drove around half the day searching for this place.

The two Romanian girls knew the area but not the exact address, and the tangle of narrow alleys and dead-end streets in Milan certainly didn't make their task any easier. Finally, somewhere in the middle of the afternoon, the taller, reticent girl—Corina—recognized the concrete wall topped by razor wire on Garabaldi Street. For the first time since her rescue, she had looked animated.

This old abandoned building provided a perfect vantage point for observing number 23. But entering the top floor, both men had been surprised to find a couple of blankets with price tags attached, fresh food from a deli they had passed a street over, and two travel bags with well-made women's clothing. Jordi had gone through the things, but found no identity papers.

Laszlo wondered what women had been doing in this room and why they left their things. And, would they be coming back?

Jordi handed Corina and Nicoleta the remaining cheese and bread from the abandoned provisions. The bread was still soft. While the girls tore into the food, Jordi joined Laszlo near the tattered brown curtain. They stood watching the courtyard over the wall Corina had sworn surrounded the building where they had been kept. She remembered the graffiti.

Nicoleta came to the window. As if sensing Laszlo's doubts, she pointed with her stub of *ciabatta* at the gate, "That is where we drove in. They parked over by those steps. And then we went in the door over there," she said, still pointing with the bread. "We stayed there for three days, and then they took us to Paris." She bit into the crust.

"Do you know what they were going to do with you?" Laszlo asked.

She swallowed, and softly said, "Yes, we found out when other girls told us. It was terrible. We were promised something different. But then, we couldn't escape."

Corina remained over on the blankets, rocking faintly with her hands clasped about her knees. Laszlo looked at the two girls. Eighteen or nineteen years old. He resisted a shudder at the 'job' intended for them. To Nicoleta, he asked, "Do you know the layout in that building and how many men are in there?"

"I only know about the rooms were they kept us. There must be four or five men, maybe more inside. New ones kept coming and going. Their leader is a man named Mustafi. He is very cold."

Mustafi… no, Laszlo did not recall having heard of him. But then, Mustafi was a popular Albanian name.

Laszlo turned to Jordi and asked, "Have you got any ideas?"

Jordi jerked his chin in the direction of the *Assassini* and what lay inside. "I say we 'meet' this Mustafi." He met Laszlo's eyes, "Why talk to the little people when we can talk to the man at the top?"

★ ★ ★

Gloria and Chantal sat behind a large, dead-brown bush, looking out on the paved road. Gloria swatted at a fly. "We have to be careful. If we walk out there and try to hitch a ride, those men or men working with them might come along. We know that at least one of them is capable of getting out of the car, and he had a cell phone." She swatted at the fly again and narrowly missed Chantal. "Sorry. Should we wait?"

"It is a risk. Yet we can't spend the day and night here. And we need to get away from our rental car."

"Let's start walking," Gloria said, rising and beginning to do so. "Whenever we hear a car in the distance, we try and find cover. If we can see far enough, we can tell if it's the blue car and stay hidden. If not, we hope for a ride." Chantal hefted herself from the rock she had been going numb on.

They were about four or five kilometers from the main expressway. For forty-five minutes they walked without hearing or seeing any cars, the noise from the rushing river obscuring any sound of an approaching automobile.

A dark storm cloud had caught on the mountaintops. With it, the temperature had begun to descend rapidly as daylight faded.

Gloria released the hug she had been giving herself for warmth and stopped. "I think I hear something." She leapt over the embankment with Chantal at her heels. Moments later a black car sped by.

The first into the ditch, Gloria had a split second to glance back and get a glimpse of the license plate. 'CD-GE'. She nudged Chantal before they stood back up. "That car must be with them. What other diplomatic car would be out here in the middle of nowhere in France? Let's move. They may be coming back this way."

They walked briskly for ten minutes, and the road broke off from the deafening river into a forest. Gloria exhaled, relieved to be able to hear sounds again, her own breath included. Even though they could hear if a car approached, they were hyper-alert and ended up jumping into undergrowth on false alarms. Gloria had a fine collection of scratches up her arm.

Gloria was picking green out of one red puncture when Chantal called out "Car!" They ran for a screen of low pines.

A black car moved slowly down the road and approached their position. Chantal and Gloria kept their heads low, not looking up. Without seeing it, they heard the car disappear down the road.

"What are they thinking?" Chantal asked.

"They may have thought that we drove away from here, or that we hitched a ride and got out of here," Gloria said. "I would certainly like that." She stood up.

Chantal dusted off her pants, "Or, that we are on foot and are still in the area."

"We don't have to be so pessimistic," began Gloria, not paying attention to road noise until the sounds of another approaching car were quite close. She and Chantal started to head back for cover, but too late.

A small white utility van zoomed around the corner and then slowed when he saw them. A young man was driving. Chantal flung out her hand in a quick hitching gesture, and the van stopped several meters ahead of them.

Chantal ran over to the passenger door and opened it. In French she asked, "Can you help us? Our car broke down."

The young man leaned back in his seat and got a full look at both of them. He shrugged, "Sure, get in."

They both climbed up into the front seat. Gloria looked into the back of the van and saw that it was full of boxes. A strong smell emanated from them.

"What are you doing out here?" the man asked Chantal who was sitting in the middle, very close to his gear shift.

"We got lost," Chantal told him. "Then we went off on a side road and had a flat tire. There was no jack handle. We couldn't fix it."

"No jack handle?" the young man asked.

"Yeah, poor planning."

"I was thinking that."

"Where are you headed?" Gloria asked.

The man turned and looked at her. "You from Spain?"

"Yes I am."

"I love going on holiday there."

"It's a great place for that," she smiled, "but you didn't tell us where you are going."

"I'm making a delivery at Creymere and then I need to get back to Arveyes."

"If we pay you, could you take us to Geneva?" Chantal asked. "We will give you two hundred Euro."

"I would like to, but I need to get back to my cows and goats. They need to be milked."

"You are a farmer?"

"Among many things." He made a small, encompassing arc with his left hand. "One needs many jobs to survive. Right now I'm delivering my cheese. But you can smell that."

Goat cheese. That was it. Gloria tried not to wrinkle her nose.

"How could we get to Geneva?" Chantal asked.

"We can call a taxi when we get to Creymere," the driver said.

Gloria wondered if a taxi company would tell someone they had picked up two women—especially if the price was right. She spoke before Chantal had a chance to, "We have had bad experiences with taxis."

"Really," he said, looking at them. Chantal looked at her too.

"Is there another way?" Gloria asked him.

"I have a friend in Creymere. I think we can figure something out." He reached for the radio and found a station playing soft chansons. "My name is Luc. What are your names?"

The van had just reached the main road to Chamonix where, in a parking area off to the right, sat three black cars close together. Seven men stood around them.

One of the men was talking on his cell phone.

Neither Gloria nor Chantal offered Luc their names at that moment.

The man on his cell was the man who had climbed out of the overturned blue car.

CHAPTER 36

The truck ground to another halt and sounds of passing traffic increased. A car honked somewhere outside and then another.

When he opened his eyes this time, Justin could see distinct forms in the dim light. Three women sat in a huddle, swaying to keep their balance when the truck started forward again. They were whispering in a language Justin did not understand. They looked younger than twenty.

He turned and looked behind him and saw someone else. A young woman lay next to him on a long mattress. The one he had mistaken for Gloria or Chantal. Her eyes were closed, and he assumed she had been drugged like he had.

He raised his head and spoke to the young women. "Do you speak English?"

One of the women said to him, "Yes, a little." She did not look surprised that he finally spoke.

"Do you know what's going on," Justin asked. "Why are you here?"

"We are looking for work," she answered. "They said they give us jobs."

"Jobs?"

"Yes, in German factory. But we are afraid. They said they put us in the truck to get us through borders, but the men no are nice with us. They beat her." She pointed to the girl next to her who sat with her head down. At her mention, the girl raised a bruised face to Justin and then let it drop back into her knees.

The truck lurched to a stop, angled downwards and in a moment stopped again. Just as the girls had retrieved their balance, the back doors of the truck opened.

Justin found himself looking into a dark space. Several black cars were parked along one wall. An underground garage?

Immediately four men jumped into the truck, grabbed him and hauled him to his feet.

Justin asked, "Where are we?"

They offered no answer, but dragged him down from the truck into the dark garage. He did not even have time to look back to see what they were doing with the women. Justin scanned every door, wall and corner for possible escape routes, but he was in the hard grip of men who meant business.

They brought him to an elevator. After ascending, the elevator opened and Justin was brought down a hall to a restroom. One of the men said, "Go." They watched him as he relieved himself, and when he was finished they led him to a room.

Justin saw one of the men pull out a syringe. Just as he registered the man's intent, the needle entered his arm.

Once again, everything went black.

★ ★ ★

They followed the road to Geneva for half an hour. As they descended out of the mountains, the alpine forest gradually gave way to rolling meadows and eventually to broad pastures and fields.

The storm broke, and patches of rain hit the van whose battered windshield wipers left a muddy blur across the glass. Before they reached the outskirts of Geneva, the driver turned off the main road onto a small rural one.

Through the rainy haze, small white stucco and dark timbered farmhouses dotted the landscape. Luc turned off and went half a kilometer down a small road just wide enough for one vehicle. Chantal felt at home amongst the cozy French countryside, despite being far more Parisian than rural. She had spent enough time in small villages like this one to include them in her comfort zone.

"Jean-Robert lives there," Luc said, gesturing at a building. 'Maybe he will take you to Geneva."

He drove the van around the main farmhouse to a building in the back. Next to the barn was parked a small truck with 'Jean-Robert Dordeau, Fromages, Vins' painted on the side.

Luc turned his van around and backed it next to a door on the side of the barn. He opened the van door and began to unload the boxes of cheese, taking them inside the barn and putting them in a large refrigerator. Gloria and Chantal climbed out and joined him in the barn, out of the drizzle.

"Jean-Robert sells cheese and wine and other produce coming from this region, my cheese included. He goes to Geneva three times a week for deliveries. Maybe you can ride with him." Luc thumped down another box and went for another. Chantal decided against offering to help. The boxes were large and she had no energy left. And Gloria should not be lifting anything too heavy.

"When does he go?" Gloria asked as Luc turned back to them with a final box of the heavy smelling goat product.

"I'm not sure. Ask him," and he nodded at a man who had just stepped out of the farmhouse and was heading towards the barn. Roughly in his late sixties, he was dressed in a brown shirt, stained blue canvas pants and muddied boots. He wore his age and his work clothes with ease and a felt beret. Smoke from his hand-rolled cigarette dissipated in the cold, muggy air. He approached Luc who had just slammed shut the van door, and they shook hands.

"Jean-Robert. Let me introduce you to Chantal and Gloria." Luc pulled his hand out of the shake and used to indicate the two women.

The farmer looked at them through creased eyes and stuck out his hand, shaking Gloria's and Chantal's in turn.

Chantal felt her hand enveloped in the rough muscle of the farmer's calloused one. She smiled at him, but his face and cigarette did not change position. Drizzle changed to rain, which he stood in, just out of the barn, and ignored.

Luc addressed him, "These ladies need to get to Geneva. Had car troubles. Do you think you could take them?"

The farmer looked at Chantal and Gloria and said, "Maybe." The cigarette, almost down to a butt, bobbed on his lower lip. He had shoved his hands in his pockets.

"When do you go?" Gloria asked.

"Tomorrow," he said.

Chantal looked at Gloria and back at him, "Could you take us now?"

"No."

Chantal persisted, "We will pay you."

"I have to milk the cows now. Then tomorrow they get milked again at five o'clock in the morning. We will leave at six thirty. Be ready or you will be left behind." He turned to go.

Gloria stepped forward, "I'm sorry, but we don't have a place to stay."

Profile to them, he spoke in the direction of a fence, "I have a cabin in the forest behind the barn. I rent it to vacationers in the summer. You can stay there tonight for fifty Euros." He graced them with a curt glance, "And an additional fifty Euros for the trip to Geneva."

"That's fine," Gloria said. "As long as we can get to Geneva."

"Come with me then," the farmer said, moving off in the direction of the forest.

Chantal turned to Luc, "Thank you so much for the ride and for setting us up with Mr. Dordeau. You were extremely helpful."

"My pleasure. And I wish you luck." He waved at them and climbed into the van.

Gloria and Chantal hurried to catch up with the long-strided farmer who seemed unhappy with delays or interruptions of routine. They were clearly an interruption.

The three crossed the farmyard and followed a narrow path through the forest up to the door of a tiny wooden chalet. A stream murmured in the trees behind the house, and a pewter chime near the door made music of the increasing wind.

Chantal imagined coming here in summer—walks in the woods hand-in-hand with Justin, Sophie running ahead and collecting wildflowers. In the evenings, they would eat fresh cheese from the farm and sit on the porch watching dusk gather into the trees.

But right now, the November rain was falling fast and she was here with Justin's second wife, no clothes, and no food. How lovely.

The farmer took out a large key, opened the door and motioned for them to step inside. The cabin was simple and homey, a far cry from their lodging in Rome or Pec. A plaid couch sat low and soft in front of a fireplace. Off in a corner, a tiny kitchen was hung with copper pans and dried herbs. In the middle sprawled a thick-planked, rustic wooden table and chairs.

"The bedroom is in there," Dordeau pointed, "And the bathroom. Make a fire if you want. It is the only heating. Wood's outside. My wife will bring you some food. There is wine in the cupboard there if you want."

He shut the door and left.

CHAPTER 37

Gloria and Chantal stood still, listening to the rain on the roof. Chantal was afraid to say how glad she was to be here away from hardwood floors, speeding cars, and chasing thugs. If she voiced her appreciation of this moment, it would disappear into the world of fairy tales and leave them cold and hungry in a thunderstorm.

Aloud, she did say, "Heaven. Or haven. Maybe both."

"I'm cold." Was Gloria's response. "I'll get some wood to make a fire."

Chantal joined her. They walked around the cabin and found a large pile of evenly stacked split logs under a shallow covering. They each took an armload inside and went back for more.

Standing over the filled firewood box, Gloria said, "Now we don't have to worry about getting up in the middle of the night for wood." She looked at Chantal. "And yes, this is a heavenly haven."

Chantal smiled and looked at the wood they were supposed to turn to fire.

A box of matches lay on top of some old newspapers next to the fireplace. Gloria crumpled up the paper into loose balls, and made a teepee of kindling she then topped with logs. Soon yellow and orange flames were filling the room with warmth.

"You start a fire like an expert," Chantal said.

Gloria rose from her crouch by the snapping flames. "My family has a small summer house on the Costa Brava just north of Barcelona. We often had barbeques when we went there. My father taught my brother, sister and I how to start the fire. Did you ever barbeque?"

"No." Chantal pulled an armchair close to the fireplace and curled her legs under her in it. "I didn't have much opportunity growing up in Paris. We rarely had money for holidays. My vacations were mainly visiting the art museums along with my younger sister. That's how I became interested in painting."

They heard the noise of an engine outside and Gloria pulled aside the checkered curtain from the large window. They could see an older woman getting out of a rusted jeep. Gloria opened the door and went outside, followed by Chantal.

"*Bonsoir,*" the woman said with a crooked and genuine smile, "Brought you food."

She turned to the back of the jeep where two cardboard boxes with several covered pots inside rested amidst a snarl of farming equipment and rope.

Both Gloria and Chantal said thank you and each took a box. The woman stepped back into the jeep.

"Don't worry about doing the dishes. Just put everything back into the boxes, and I'll take care of it tomorrow." She nodded more to herself than to them, then changed to nod to a shake, "Oh yes. I forgot this." She reached across to the passenger seat, grabbed something and in her hand, and gave it to Gloria.

An alarm clock. The woman continued, "Be ready by six thirty. Otherwise he will leave without you. He's like that," she laughed. "He will forget that you are here. He gets into his routines and forgets about things."

She drove away without introducing herself. Chantal had the feeling that if the woman knew she was the farmer's wife, then it would be redundant to bother informing anyone else.

They carried the boxes inside to the table, took the pots out and lifted the lids. A lamb stew with boiled potatoes, onions and peas, salad, fresh country bread, several pieces of different kinds of cheeses and a rhubarb pie for desert.

The two women stood looking at each other across the box of food. Such a small and large blessing. For a second, Chantal was not sure whether she was thinking of the dinner in front of her or the woman on the other side of it.

Chantal found herself seeing Gloria for the first time as an 'ordinary' woman. Not as Justin's other wife. Would she have befriended Gloria under other circumstances? Unable to answer her question, she said, "Let's open that wine."

She found several bottles in the cupboard, chose a Bordeaux, and found a corkscrew to open it. Gloria put two more logs on the fire, and the cabin corners began to warm up.

They ate the meal at the table, both facing the fire and saying little, they were so hungry. When finished, they did as the woman had instructed, and set the pans back in their boxes.

Gloria had only one glass of the wine, being careful of her pregnancy. Chantal, on the other hand, went to put the wine bottle away and realized that it was empty.

"I'm exhausted," she said, going to the couch and flopping down on one side of it. Gloria took the other end and stared at the fire.

Chantal glanced at Gloria. She must be just as tired. And carrying a baby. "How are you feeling?" She asked, glancing at Gloria's belly. "With the baby, I mean. Still have morning sickness?"

Gloria looked down at her waist. "I feel as good as can be while chasing down kidnappers and being chased by them in turn. Sometimes I feel a bit nauseated in the morning, but it goes away."

"I had it during the second and third months when I was pregnant with Sophie, but after that it went away. But, during the entire nine months I had a craving for salty things like shrimp, pickles and cheese."

"Shrimp sounds good. You know, my mother said she never felt better than when she was pregnant," Gloria said.

Chantal had the sense that Gloria was made to be a mother. Before she had thought, she said, "I wish you many children."

But not with my husband, she added in her head.

Gloria turned and looked at her, her green eyes reading the expression that fell across Chantal's face as soon as the wish was out of her mouth. "We said we would be friends."

"I can't share him," Chantal said to the fire.

"Neither can I." Gloria shifted to face Chantal, "Does the question have less to do with Justin and more with us? If our goal is love, then the solution must have to do with love."

"I'm not sure I follow you."

"I'm not sure I follow myself," Gloria smiled. "It's just that I have been thinking about the basis of our motivations. We both want the same man. That's true. We both love Justin and I sense that he loves both of us. We are competing for him. But does competition originate from love? I don't think so, so I don't want to compete with you. It doesn't seem to be a healthy starting point." She pulled a strand of her hair and began to circle it around her finger. It caught firelight and shown like a ruby. "If we start from the wrong basis, we won't make the right decision.

"I agree. But we can't even start unless we have Justin."

Gloria let her curl drop, "It may not be Justin's decision."

"What do you mean?" Chantal asked.

"If you know Justin, you know that his morals are tied to his commitments. He made commitments to both of us and he will strive to fulfill them, even though it might end up destroying him. Can you imagine what it will do to him? Having to navigate between two women competing against each other? We will hurt him badly and I don't what to do that. I don't think you want to either. Because Justin is what he is, it seems to me the decision is on our side. Do we put him in the middle, or do we make a decision?"

They remained quiet watching the fire for several minutes and Chantal said, "We are different."

"Yes?"

"Well, not so different" Chantal was loosing her train of thought. She watched a flame snap and send glowing sparks to the hearth. Instead of differences, she found herself thinking of her similarities with Gloria. "We both believe."

"Believe?"

"In a God of love."

Gloria nodded.

"But, out personalities are different. I am headstrong. You are restrained. Both tendencies can be good and bad."

Gloria was looking at her with a furrowed brow.

Chantal tried to clarify what was completely unclear in her own head, "We talked about friendship. Do we have to have that—friendship, love—for each other before we can decide how best to love Justin?"

Gloria said nothing for a long while. The fire was low in the grate by the time she spoke. "I think we are both afraid of losing Justin. Fear is the enemy of love. If we continue in fear, we will never resolve anything." It was Chantal's turn to say nothing.

When flames had turned to reddened coals, Gloria stood and added two more logs to the dying fire. She straightened and faced Chantal. "I am going to bed. We are too tired to resolve anything tonight." She left the room.

Chantal lost track of time, her head a gentle fuzz that seemed to match the color of the firelight across the floor.

Gloria walked into the living room in a towel, carrying her washed bra and panties. She placed them on a metal coat hanger and hung them on a chair close to the fire.

Chantal heaved herself from the soft folds of the couch and went into the bathroom, following Gloria's example by washing her under things. As it was, they had only the clothes on their backs.

Looks like she too would be sleeping with nothing on tonight. She hoped there were plenty of blankets.

There were. She crawled in to the bed. For once comfortable, solid and clean. Gloria was already sound asleep, her breath steady. Chantal watched her.

Gloria was lying on her back, her eyes closed, lips softly open. She wondered how Justin felt when he kissed those lips. A shiver tingled up her spine—from the cold or something else, she did not know.

She turned out the light.

CHAPTER 38

Handling the wire cutters with the ease of scissors, Jordi snipped the razor wire on the top of the wall. French Foreign Legion training came in handy. After a few minutes, he had a hole big enough to slip through. He dropped down three meters into the courtyard.

Laszlo followed a few seconds later, landing beside him with a soft thud. Jordi had already crouched down in position, gun ready in his right hand.

Laszlo glanced at his watch. Five a.m. They had spent the previous afternoon and evening crystallizing a plan and purchasing the necessary supplies before the shops closed. They had also questioned the two Romanian girls about every detail of the interior of the building, the number of men inside, and the physical characteristics of Mustafi.

Then they took Corina and Nicoleta back to the hotel and told them that if they didn't return by ten o'clock the following day, the girls should do their best to get back to Romania. Laszlo had left them an envelope with enough money to buy train tickets and to pay off customs agents if needed, since the girls did not have passports.

Inside the courtyard, Laszlo looked around. Earlier, from the seventh story of the building across the street, they had not seen any surveillance cameras, but he wanted to double-check from a closer perspective. If there were cameras, they would find out just about now.

The darkness remained unbroken by light or gunfire. Laszlo and Jordi waited for two minutes, letting their eyes adjust and looking for details. They silently moved around the edge of the courtyard, concealed in the shadows. Jordi took the lead, sliding around a couple of cars before coming to the loading dock. Jordi went up the steps and inside, Laszlo covering him and following a moment later.

They crept down a hall until they came to the third door on the left. Just like Corina had told them. It was a solid metal door with a bolt lock above the door handle. A key protruded from the lock just below the door handle.

Laszlo slowly twisted the key in the lock and felt it snap open. He pushed the bolt lock to the right, turned the door handle and opened the door just wide enough for him to slip inside. Jordi waited in the hall, gun in hand. In the dusky glow of the street light coming through the bare window, Laszlo counted five humans forms on mattresses on the floor. From their size, he guessed they were women.

Laszlo moved over to the closest one, kneeled down, and gently put his hand on her mouth.

She stirred and blinked, then tried to sit up, twisting away from his hand. He put his index finger to his lips and whispered, "Shush, I'm a friend. Do you speak English?"

She nodded her head.

"We're here to help you. Do you want to get out of here?"

She started to sit up again, "Yes. Oh please, yes."

One of the other girls shifted on her mattress and muttered in her sleep.

"Quiet," Laszlo whispered to the first girl. "I need to find Mustafi. Do you know how to get to his room?"

The girl hesitated, and said, "Two floors up. End of hall."

"Are there other men here? Where do they stay?"

"Next floor up," she answered. " Men stay on next floor. Mustafi has all of third floor."

"Wait here and please be quiet. I will come back and get you," Laszlo said

Laszlo slipped back into the hall, tapped Jordi on the shoulder, motioned with his hand toward the stairs and pointed up.

Jordi gave a nod of acknowledgement.

They went to the end of the hall and up the stairs. On the next floor they stopped and listened. The sound of men's voices talking and laughing wafted through an open door down the hall.

Jordi led the way up to the next floor. A single door stood at the top. He tried to open it. Locked. He took out a small pen flashlight and pointed the light into the hole. "We are in luck," he whispered. "The key is not in the hole."

He took out a set of special tools that he had found in a shop in Milan, inserted a thin metal blade in the keyhole and then a second one, and began to jiggle them back and forth. In a moment they heard a click, the lock opened, and he pressed down on the door lever.

Jordi walked in, Laszlo directly behind him, both with their guns raised. This floor appeared to be more of an apartment. Teak tables and fine leather couches crowned an elaborate Persian rug. Mahogany bookcases filled with artifacts and books lined the walls. A door on the left opened into a modern silver and black kitchen. The door next to it was shut.

Jordi opened it and went inside. In the middle of a massive double bed topped with overstuffed silk pillows and a silk comforter, lay a man. A large man.

Laszlo walked soundlessly over to the man. In one quick movement he took his massive left hand put it on the man's mouth and pinned the man's head to the bed.

The man's eyes jerked open and he flailed his arms and legs, struggling to free himself.

His iron grip firmly holding the man down, Laszlo looked at him and said without preliminary, "Mustafi, we need information."

Mustafi raised his hands, grabbed Laszlo's arm and tried to move the hand from his mouth. Laszlo pinned his head onto the bed even harder, thinking that while he'd like to break Mustafi' jaw, that would make questioning him difficult. Mustafi relaxed his hands. His eyes remained wide open.

"Now I am going to take my hand off your mouth," Laszlo said, "and you will talk. Do you understand?

Mustafi tried to move his head up and down but it didn't go very far. Laszlo released his left hand and put the barrel of his gun to Mustafi's head. "Now, sit up slowly," Laszlo commended.

Mustafi sat up and Laszlo grabbed him by his t-shirt, pulled him up from the bed, and sat him in a chair. Rolls of soft fat hung over the top of his boxer shorts, and skinny legs stuck out their bottoms.

"What do you want?" Mustafi asked.

"Information." Laszlo said. "There is an American girl here. Where is she?"

"No American girl here. We have no girls here."

Laszlo slapped him across the face. "Downstairs there are girls. We saw them. One more lie and you're dead. Where is the American girl?"

"No American girl."

Laszlo turned to Jordi and said, "Shoot him. One of the other men downstairs will tell us."

Jordi raised his gun and pushed the barrel against Mustafi's head.

"No. Wait. She's not here," Mustafi cried.

"Where is she?"

"Gone."

Laszlo heard noise behind them, and he turned around. Two men stood there, one with an automatic handgun, the other with a shotgun pointed at them.

"Drop the gun," one of them said.

CHAPTER 39

A booming crack reverberated through the cabin. Chantal shot up from a deep sleep and pulled the sheets close to her chin.

Gloria did not move. She whispered, "What was that?"

The room flashed bright as day and another explosion followed.

"Thunderstorm," they both said, sighing in relief. Gloria watched Chantal fall back to a lying position. Her impact with the soft bedding was inaudible with the rain pounding against the window and roof.

Moments later, thunder shook the cabin at the same instant a natural strobe light shot bright white into their room, leaving them seconds later in eerie shadow.

Chantal shuddered and clutched the sheets tighter and stared at the ceiling. "It's silly, but I hate thunder."

"I was scared of storms when I was little," Gloria said, "But my mother told me a Native American myth about two sisters and their brother thunder. They were dancing in a village, and a young warrior fell in love with one of them. But he had to ask her brother for permission to marry her. He followed the sisters along the river to their cave where the brother arrived in a loud clap of thunder. I don't remember the rest of the story, because I started laughing when my mother got to that part. Here I thought the world was breaking open, and it was just one man. Somehow that story made the thunder seem human, and I stopped fearing it." Gloria yawned.

Gloria watched Chantal's profile as another bolt of lightening lit her skin to a ghostly white and then faded to leave her in darkness. Gloria had the feeling her story had not helped much.

Chantal said nothing, and Gloria wondered if she missed Sophie, missed telling her daughter soothing bedtime stories. Was comforting a child also a comfort to the mother? Gloria shifted up into her pillows and reached over to Chantal, encircling her shoulders with her arm.

Gloria felt the tension in Chantal's neck release into the crook of her elbow.

★ ★ ★

After several minutes Gloria's arm relaxed and Chantal felt her fall into sleep.

As the lighting subsided and the thunder settled into pounding rain, Chantal tried to remember how she has comforted Justin. Failed mergers, lost jackets, mild winter depressions. Had she been enough for him? Pillowed in the warmth of Gloria's arm, skin on skin, she wondered if Justin had been attracted to Gloria for the things that she, Chantal lacked.

Instead of making her bristle with anger, this worry saddened her. And with the sadness came a small, silent fear. That Justin did not love her as much as he had loved Gloria.

Gloria was right. Until she could release her fear, she could not love Justin.

Chantal fell asleep with the new and itching thought that she did not know a selfless love.

★ ★ ★

Laszlo and Jordi slowly put their guns to the floor.

"Are you the men who were in Berlin?" Mustafi asked. He stood up, and, with as much dignity as he could gather back to himself, reached for a robe lying across a chair near his bed. He went on, "Schubach sent out news. For some reason he does not like you and wants to see you back in Berlin. We will arrange that. But first, I think we had better teach you a lesson."

Laszlo and Jordi stood with their backs against a wall. The two men standing in front of them had their guns trained at them.

Mustafi sat down on his bed, stroking his chin. "It interests me how you got in here," he mused. "I must strengthen the security." He stopped stroking his chin and pointed his finger at them with a look of recognition, "I know you two."

"We don't know you," Laszlo said.

Mustafi shook a finger at him and walked over to his desk in a corner of the room. He rummaged through some papers and brought one back and handed it to Laszlo, returning to his perch on the bed.

Laszlo was looking at a grainy photo of Jordi and himself standing in front of a desk with a knife stuck in the desk. It had been taken months before in Abdouelle's office. Laszlo handed it to Jordi who looked at it and then tossed it on the floor. It glided sideways through the air, landing at Mustafi's feet.

"So what?" Laszlo said.

"Someone was looking for you at the time. Your photo was being distributed," he nodded at the page that had landed face up.

"Who cares. Where is the American girl?" Laszlo asked.

"Why are you so concerned about her?" Mustafi asked, looking genuinely puzzled. "Although I must say she is a real prize."

"Is she here?"

"No. She has been sold to the highest bidder, a considerable sum." Mustafi's eyes lit up at that.

"Where?"

Mustafi shrugged, "It wouldn't hurt to tell. Geneva. A rich patron, a connoisseur of fine merchandise placed the order. She will be delivered to him soon."

"*Loco,*" Jordi said through clenched teeth.

"Where in Geneva?" Laszlo persisted, "Who is this man?"

"None of your business. Confidential information. Anyway, you should be more concerned about yourselves right now. I think we will start by cutting something off, a finger, a toe, or… something else, and then we turn you over to Schubach." Mustafi smiled.

"Where is she?" Laszlo said.

"Now, I don't think we have anything more to talk about. I would teach you a lesson right here, but I don't like blood on my things." He stood up, eyes narrowing, "And I promise you, things will get bloody." He nodded at the men, "Take them downstairs."

CHAPTER 40

The alarm rattled through Gloria's dream. She ignored it, or tried to. It was on Chantal's night stand.

Head under the covers, Gloria heard it switch off and felt Chantal's hand on her back. She turned over, eyes still closed, "What time?"

"Six. The farmer leaves in half an hour."

Gloria's eyes popped open and she remembered why she could not remain curled in the soft bed. "We need to go to Geneva to find Justin."

Chantal was climbing out of bed, "We should get dressed and go."

In ten minutes they had dressed and straightened up the cabin. As they stepped outside, streaks of light were just beginning to stroke the sky. Their shoes sunk into the ground, soft and muddy from the night's rain.

They saw a light burning in the farm window. As they neared the front of the house, they saw the farmer loading boxes into his truck.

"*Bonjour,*" he said. "Sleep okay?"

"Yes, great, except for the storm," Gloria said.

"We get those around here. They form in the mountains and then explode over us. More bark than bite, but they can be pretty wild. Knocks down some big trees from time to time. Just this one box and we are ready to go." He lifted a box and headed for the truck. "Did you eat anything?"

"No, it's quite early," Chantal said.

"There's a container with fresh coffee and some mugs," He said, motioning to the workbench along the wall. "Help yourselves." The women took mugs and filled them from the container. They gladly wrapped their hands around the warm mugs, sipping the steaming country coffee.

Slamming the tailgate shut, the farmer asked, "Are you ready? You can bring the container along."

The doors slammed the fresh morning air out of the truck cab, locking in the sour scent of cheese. Jean-Robert started the engine and headed toward the freeway toward Geneva.

Chantal sat in the middle and asked the man questions about farming and what it was like to sell products in the region. Jean-Robert described the difficulties of being a farmer in France, where the small landholders barely scraped by and often had to find alternative jobs to make ends meet.

Gloria watched the cars in front of them. One was from Great Britain. Having to ferry a car must be such a pain, she thought, noticing its license plates.

Something triggered in the back of her mind. The UN truck's from yesterday was Swiss. It had a 'CD' and 'GE'. If she remembered right, all the different Swiss cantons had a two-letter code on their car licenses. 'GE' must mean for Geneva. And all diplomats had CD on their license.

The truck must be based in Geneva. And the United Nations Agency for Trade Development must have designated parking somewhere.

Chantal was saying something to her, "How do rural farmers deal with that in Spain?"

"Sorry?" Gloria left the license plates to the recesses of her mind, "Deal with what?"

★ ★ ★

Mustafi's men motioned with their guns toward the door.

Laszlo and Jordi held their position against the wall. Laszlo guessed that the downstairs rooms were better suited for spilling blood. Mustafi did not look like the kind of man who would tolerate stains on his carpet.

The men took a step toward the wall. The man with the shotgun approached Jordi and pushed the barrel of the gun into his ribs and then motioned to the door.

Jordi seized the moment and the barrel of the shotgun. While pushing the gun away from Laszlo and himself, he pulled his barber's razor from his pocket.

With a quick snap of his wrist it was open. And with a quicker reverse motion, he sliced had the sharp blade across the man's neck. The man jerked backward and the shotgun went off, spraying pellets in the direction of the bed.

The other man was startled by the shotgun blast and jumped. Laszlo grabbed the man's wrist with his left hand and with one straight blow smashed his fist into the man's jaw. Bone cracked, and the man fell to the floor.

Jordi picked up the shotgun and his own handgun. Laszlo picked up his Glock. They looked at Mustafi. He was lying backward on the bed groaning. A large cherry-colored hole spread across his shirt.

Laszlo went over to the bed, "So much for keeping blood off your things. Where is the girl?"

"Geneva… Confidential…"

Laszlo grabbed him, "Who bought her?

"Arab, Ri-i-ch," he slurred. His eyes fluttered shut.

Running feet pounded down the hall.

"Let's go," Jordi said, heading toward the door. Laszlo followed, quickly looking at Mustafi and the man who had held the shotgun. Both lay in blood.

Jordi took a quick look into the hall and fired the shotgun. A man went down and he fired again, hitting a second man.

They ran by the fallen man and out to the stairway, looked for a moment, and continued down to the next floor. Men were staggering out of their rooms, awakened from their sleep. Jordi fired the shotgun again and the men woke up, beating a hasty retreat into their rooms.

Laszlo and Jordi made it to the ground floor and ran to the room with five girls. When Laszlo yanked open the door, he saw that the girls were all awake, dressed and ready.

"Come," Laszlo said.

Laszlo ran in front, the girls following behind him. Jordi took up the rear, shotgun in hand. They ran down the stairs next to the loading dock, and Laszlo sprinted across the courtyard to open the metal gates. The girls ran through the opening.

Two men appeared on the loading dock and began firing guns. Laszlo raised his Glock and fired twice, and the two men hit the ground. Jordi gave him a brief smile.

More men appeared and Jordi ran through the opening. Laszlo turned and followed. The girls were already well down the street, their liberators behind them.

CHAPTER 41

The truck clattered along the cobblestones and came to a halt in front of a tiny *Fromagerie* in the old town of Geneva. The smell of fresh bread wafted through the open door of the bakery across the street. Chantal glanced up at the date above the door of the cheese shop. 1782. Rows of stone and plaster structures lined both sides of the street.

Gloria handed Jean-Robert two hundred Euros—twice as much as he had asked—and thanked him. He nodded and began to carry boxes into the shop.

"Do you know Geneva?" Gloria asked Chantal.

"A little bit. I came here with Justin several times when we visited Stefan von Portzer. And I was here once to visit Stefan before I met Justin."

"Was he your lover?" Gloria asked.

Chantal was surprised at her directness. She did not meet Gloria's eyes. "Stefan took an interest in my art after visiting an exhibition of mine at a small Parisian gallery. He bought some of my paintings and invited me to an important art show in Geneva. He had a girlfriend at the time." She gave Gloria an indecipherable smile. "He always has a woman on his arm." Chantal pointed at the bakery, "Let's get a *pain au chocolat.*"

As the woman wrapped their pastries in paper with the bakery logo, Chantal smiled at how good Stefan had been to her. Gallery contacts, buyers—he had introduced her to enough of the right people that she had been able to live off her art. No small feat. That art show in Geneva had put her name on the lips of wealthy and important people. Including Banneret, the director of the UN Agency for Trade Development. She frowned. They were out on the sidewalk now, savoring their breakfasts directly from their wrappers.

"Yours isn't good?" Gloria asked.

Chantal shook her head, sending flakes into the morning breeze. "*Au contraire.* I was just thinking of Banneret.

Now Gloria frowned, "Then we should contact Stefan."

"Yes. He lives about fifteen minutes from here." Chantal led Gloria out of the old town, crossing the shopping street Rue du Rhone. Clothing and jewelry boutiques tempted buyers with their wares.

The women walked over to the edge of the lake where a fountain shot water out of the lake several hundred meters into the air.

"That's called the *jet-d'eau,*" Chantal pointed out. "It's a famous landmark in Geneva. You can see it from the balcony of Stefan's apartment." They walked past the *jet-d'eau* until they came to a stately building. The front door was locked. An electronic code pad set in brass gleamed on the wall next to the door.

"I forgot. We need the code. We can't just go up and knock on his door." Chantal jutted out her lower lip. "We should call first anyway."

They walked back down the street and found a small brasserie, where several people were sitting outside on rattan chairs, sipping coffee and perusing various newspapers. Chantal didn't have any Swiss Francs to pay for the call, so the waiter changed ten euros for her. She went to the phone, inserted her coins, and made the call.

The phone rang. And rang. But there was no answer. She hung up and turned to Gloria, "Maybe we should call later. He sleeps late and may have the telephone off the hook. Or, we can wait until nine o'clock, go to his office and talk with his secretary."

"That's fine," Gloria replied. "I'm still hungry," she grinned and put her hand on her womb, "Can we order something and pass the time here?"

"Of course." Chantal pointed out a free table. The helpful waiter took their order of tea and croissants. They lingered over these until Chantal tried again to call Stefan. Again, no success. They left the brasserie and walked to Stefan's office, near the central banking sector of Geneva. Every building seemed to be a bank.

"I've heard about this, but I can't believe it," Gloria said, running her fingers over a shiny plaque embedded in a marble façade. "So many banks. I am a banker, and I have not heard of most of these."

"Yes, this is the land of money," Chantal said. "More banks per square meter here than almost any other place in the world."

"And Stefan has an office among them?"

"Yes, over there." Chantal pointed to a tall building along the lake. The ornate window moldings and peaked roof contrasted with the square glass and metal buildings around it. "He owns the building and has an office on the top floor. Overlooking the lake, of course."

Gloria shook here head, "What does he do?"

"I don't really know. Many business-related things—investing, finance. And people like Laszlo Vartek and Doby the computer programmer work for him. Very much out-of-the-office kind of work. He attends concerts and dinners, and has constant, trophy women. But to be honest, I don't know much about his business affairs. The Swiss are very reserved and less prone to flash their wealth around than some wealthy Germans, French or Italians do."

Gloria said, "I would like to know him better. He was one of the only people to stay close to Justin after Justin came to Spain. He remained a real friend to him. I only met him once, at our wedding. But I recognized him as a very articulate and cultured man."

They had reached the building's entrance. Shiny brass nameplates announced the presence of financial firms and investment companies.

Inside, under a glistening chandelier, Gloria asked, "Does Stefan own all those companies?"

"No. I think they just rent space from him here."

They rode the mirrored elevator to the top floor and went to a large double oak door with ornate knobs. Next to the door was mounted a yet another brass nameplate. This one read, 'Stefan von Portzer'. Chantal rang the doorbell. They waited and she rang again. After waiting several minutes she said, "I guess we should try later."

Chantal stared at the door as if willing Stefan and his inevitable solutions to be on the other side. But she knew how late he slept. He had probably been out till the early hours mingling, maintaining business contacts, or establishing female ones. She was surprised at how disappointed his absence made her.

Gloria placed a hand on Chantal's arm and said, "I know something that can cheer us up."

Chantal gave her a wan smile and raised her eyebrows in question.

"We only have the clothes we're wearing. Let's go shopping."

CHAPTER 42

Returning to the Rue du Rhone, Chantal and Gloria joined the mid-morning throngs of shoppers surging in and out of the boutiques.

Gloria pointed to a glassy department store, its windows lined with mannequins in full winter fashion. "I like the English word 'splurge,'" she said to Chantal as they pushed open the doors. "Justin taught it to me." Oops. She had not wanted to mention anything that might bring back tensions today. But when she glanced at Chantal, Gloria saw that she was heading off sideways toward a pair of wide-legged, red wool pants, a smile of anticipatory ownership on her lips.

She had been right, a little shopping would distract them. Heading toward another section of the store, Gloria found a quieter pair of black wool pants. Well, she found several, but limited herself to one pair. Then she selected a tailored but casual shirt, a lambswool shawl that could double as small blanket in a pinch, and a thickly knit cardigan.

Arms filling, she found the accessories and lost herself amidst the striped scarves and leather gloves. Reaching for a furlined hat from the vertical display rack, she almost jumped when a lacy camisole materialized under the hat.

"Isn't it delicious?" Chantal asked, turning the undergarment over for Gloria to see the tiny stitching on the back. "I got sidetracked in lingerie."

And in other departments, thought Gloria, eying stack of clothing Chantal had set at her feet. Aloud she said, "It's lovely. But for, er… chasing down criminals in November, don't you think…?"

Chantal laughed. "Oh, I'm not buying it. Yet. I just like to see what's in fashion. And to have things on hand for special occasions."

Gloria wondered just what special occasion Chantal might be thinking of. But she did not have to wonder who Chantal was thinking of sharing it with. She wished again she had not let Justin's name slip out of earlier.

Chantal tossed the camisole into a bin of gloves and looked at Gloria's neutral-hued choices. "Practical," she said. Then she reached down for her load of reds, greens, plaids, and what looked to be a shiny, golden scarf. "You were right," she said to Gloria over her burden. "Shopping does cheer a girl up."

Not so sure now, Gloria watched Chantal's scarf trailing behind her in a filmy, reflective banner.

★ ★ ★

A tissue lined shopping bag swinging in time with her stride, Chantal tried to feel as good as she was pretending to. She regretting alluding to a 'special occasion' with—as Gloria had undoubtedly guessed—Justin. She had not even felt the desire to be spiteful, but it had happened before she had time to stop herself.

She and Gloria strolled across the Pont du Mont Blanc, the bridge that spanned the Rhone River, and made their way toward the train station where many middle-class hotels catered to the hoards of conference attendees who came to meetings at the UN and other international organizations.

Close to the train station on Rue de Lausanne, they found several banks. Gloria went inside one and withdrew three hundred Swiss Francs on her cash card, the maximum allowed for any one withdrawal. She tried again for the same amount, and the machine accepted the second transaction.

Leaving the station on the Rue de Lausanne, Chantal pointed ahead, "I know of a good hotel near the United Nations." Gloria merely nodded and followed Chantal inside to the reception desk.

The desk clerk watched them cross the lobby. Chantal kept eye contact with him as she approached the desk. When she and Gloria set down their shopping bags, he said, "Hello, may I help you?"

"Do you have a free room?" Chantal asked, leaning a hip into the counter.

"Yes. You are lucky. There wasn't a single room in the entire city last night. Several large conferences were taking place at the same time," He clicked the computer mouse and glanced at the monitor, "But today we have a few."

"Non smoking please," Gloria told him.

"Did you say one room or two?" He looked up at the women.

"One," Gloria answered. While passing time at the brasserie, Chantal had suggested that it might be better for security if they shared a room.

"One bed or two?"

"Doesn't matter," Chantal said this time, "Just a quiet nonsmoking room off the main street."

The desk clerk looked up at her, paused a moment and said, "Can I have your credit card?"

"We prefer to pay cash," Gloria answered.

"How many nights?" He asked.

"Just one." Chantal replied.

"Then could you fill in the form and we are all set." He slid a form across the counter at neither one of them in particular. Chantal reached for it and filled it out with a fictitious name and address. She handed it back to the clerk."

He took it and set it next to his computer. "Since you are paying cash, I will need to see some identification."

Gloria reached into her purse and handed the clerk fifty Swiss Francs. Without moving a facial muscle, he took the bill. He slid it in a drawer, reached in another drawer and took out a small hotel envelope with two electronic keycards in it. Only then did he break out his receptionist smile, "You are in Room 401 on the fourth floor. The elevator is over there." He pointed to a wall on the side of the lobby.

They took the elevator to the fourth floor and entered their room. There was one queen-sized bed.

"Well, now we know what he was thinking," Gloria said, smiling and setting down her bag and purse on a chair.

Chantal followed her in, closing the door. "Better he thinks we are two women who want to stay incognito in order to be together, than two women incognito for other reasons."

"I guess so far so good," Gloria said, peeking through the curtains at their view and then checking out the bathroom. Chantal was pulling her purchases from their bag and snipping off the price tags with her nail clipper.

Gloria stuck her head out of the bathroom, "I'd like to take a shower and then put on some fresh clothing. Mind if I go first?"

"Go right ahead." Chantal lay her new things on the bed and looked at them. If she had bought them with Justin, she would have given him a fashion show. And she would have changed in front of him. Slowly.

She closed her eyes and wished she had the gift of ESP. Why had Justin's kidnappers brought him here to Geneva? And why did they think he had Tapic's fortune? Unanswerable questions for now.

She preferred to think of Justin lying on the bed, watching her pull on the lacy, impractical panties she had bought. One leg at a time.

CHAPTER 43

Laszlo watched out the window of the small corporate jet as they entered a mass of gray clouds. Five minutes ago, he had been looking at a majestic view of the Alps, their snow-covered peaks glinting in the sunlight not so far below.

Anticipating the turbulence that soon began to toss the plane, he reached down to buckle his seatbelt and motioned for the others to do the same. Corina and Nicoleta rested peacefully, but the wide-eyes and white knuckles of the girls from Milan betrayed that they had never flown before.

Jordi turned to Laszlo, "Geneva is a big city. We don't have much of a lead."

"Not so big," Laszlo replied, referring to the city, not the lead. "Four hundred thousand people, maybe." He gave Jordi the faintest suggestion of a smile, "But we know that most of them do not concern us."

Jordi sniffed, "Pity we did not have more time with Mustafi." He turned his pearl-handled barber's razor over in his hand, gently running his index finger along the engraved words *Por Honor*.

"I know. Things happened fast. Too fast." Laszlo took a deep breath, adding, "We were lucky."

"Tell me about Geneva," Jordi jerked his chin in the direction the plane was going. "I have never been there. What are we looking for?"

"I go there often, because Stefan is there," Laszlo said. "It is a quiet and clean city, full of banks and insurance companies. A number of important multinational companies have their headquarters there. And, of course the United Nations is there."

"And we are looking for a rich Arab." Jordi, shook his head.

"Wealth is easy to find." Laszlo said, "And much of it from the Middle East. Most are upright citizens. But the press has been reporting stories of Middle-Eastern diplomats and sheiks who hire domestic help from countries like India and the Philippines. When the workers arrive, their bosses take away their passports. The people become slaves. Not paid. Not able to go home." He looked at the sleeping Romanian girls. "There are also stories of girls being held against their will, drugged and sexually abused. Once they are taken it is hard to find them."

Laszlo paused and looked out at the mountains. "That's why we need to find Anne Kent as soon as possible before she gets lost in this system." He turned back to Jordi. "I would like to call Stefan in Berlin. He knows Geneva and might know where we can start asking questions."

Jordi took in the seven girls seated in the plane with them. "What about them?" They looked to be less than twenty years old.

Laszlo shook his head, "I don't know. Since Switzerland is not a part of the European Union, they still check passports at the border." Like the sheiks' domestic help, these girls had been relieved of their identification papers.

Jordi rose, "I have an idea." He spoke in hushed tones to Laszlo who went up to talk to the pilot.

Twenty minutes later the airplane landed at the Geneva airport and taxied to the parking area for corporate jets.

Jordi turned to the girls, "We are in Geneva. Customs here is strict. They will not let anyone in the country without a passport."

The girls exchanged worried looks, and some of them started to speak.

Jorid held up a hand, "Don't worry. I have an idea, if you are willing. The pilot can fly you to Spain. You will land in a small international airport in Girona near the Costa Brava. I will call ahead, and two of my friends, Pascual and Sanchez will be there to meet you. They will speak to the chief of customs. His name is Manuel Espinosa and he knows me. Pascual and Sanchez will take you to a guesthouse run by a Senora Pascual, Pascual's mother. You will be safe there. She will watch out for you until I get there, and then we can decide what you want to do. Perhaps you can find real jobs in Spain, or you can return to your home countries. But you will have to be patient and wait." He paused. "I promise you Sanchez and Pascual will treat you with honor."

Some of the girls looked at each other. Nicoleta spoke for them, eyes on Jordi, "We trust you. We will to go to Spain."

* * *

"Do you think the truck is in there?" Gloria asked, "I do not see a parking lot."

They stood in the brown grass in front of the Place des Nations, a large oval traffic island circled by a drive that split off in five different directions. The Place was used for demonstrations of all kinds, and in its middle rose an immense sculpture of a wooden chair, tall as a house, with one of its legs broken in half. A monument set up to protest against land mines.

"I don't see one either," Chantal replied, looking at the United Nations building directly in front of them. A long, blocky structure, it was built on a hill overlooking Lake Geneva. A large metal gate stood at the front entrance. Barricades occupied strategic points along the sturdy fence that stretched from it.

Gloria turned to Chantal, "Maybe we should start by finding the UN Agency for Trade Development. Let's go ask the guard."

Ignoring the other international organizations surrounding the Place des Nations—the World Intellectual Property Organization, United Nations High Commissioner for Refugees, International Red Cross, World Trade Organization and World Health Organization, to name a few—they crossed the circular street to the entrance of the United Nations.

Approaching the guard at the front gate Gloria smiled. He looked at her with a stony face. Gloria said, "Excuse me, We're looking for an organization called the United Nations Agency for Trade Development. Are they in this building?"

"No, they are down the street over there." He pointed in the direction of the High Commissioner for refugees building. "Just turn right at the HCR and go two blocks. It's there on the left."

They thanked him and began walking in the direction he'd indicated.

"Do we just walk into the place?" Gloria asked.

Chantal thought a second. "Let's walk around it first, just to see if we see anything."

They walked two blocks and saw the building on their left. It was new and glass-faced, five stories high. A sign in front of it read 'United Nations Agency for Trade Development'.

They walked around behind the building. In the back, they found a parking lot surrounded by a high chain-link fence. The gate was locked.

Gloria's heart jumped. She grabbed Chantal's arm with both hands and turned her to the direction she was looking, "There. There it is."

Chantal looked down a row of dark cars with UN diplomatic license plates. Next to them was parked a medium-sized white truck.

On its side was printed 'UN Agency for Trade Development.'

CHAPTER 44

The revolving glass doors spun around, releasing Chantal and Gloria into the lobby of the UN Agency for Trade Development. High heels and hard-soled dress shoes clicked in staccato across the marble floor as women and men in dark suits entered and exited in silent trajectories.

A low murmur of voices and porcelain cups clinking down on saucers rose from a sleek coffee bar off to the left. People sat alone in comfortable leather chairs or in small groups around low tables. A reception desk stood against one of the walls in the lobby. A well-preserved woman was seated behind the desk reading a newspaper.

Slightly self-conscious in their casual street wear, Chantal and Gloria approached the desk. The woman finished the last line of her article before she looked up.

"Would it be possible to obtain information about your organization?" Chantal asked.

"What kind of information?" she asked, turning the page of her newspaper and laying it down just enough to see who was asking. She kept her hand in the section she has been reading.

Chantal used her ingratiating smile, "Is there someone here who schedules the movement of your trucks?"

"I never heard that one asked before. Why do you want to know?"

"We would just like to talk to that person." Chantal was at a loss of what to say.

Gloria added, "We are interested to know about the movement of merchandise. We are working on methods for helping non-profit transportation become more effective. We would just like to ask a couple of questions, if possible. We won't take much of anyone's time. Can you help us?"

"I suppose." The woman let the newspaper close regretfully. She lifted the telephone in an elaborate manner, tapped in several numbers with her manicured hand and said to the receiver, "Claudio, There are two women here to see you." She waited. "No, they don't have an appointment. They just want to ask a couple of questions."

She listened for a moment, returned the receiver to its cradle and said, "He will be here in a minute. Please wait over there." She pointed to a waiting area with several chairs and a low glass table with magazines and brochures on it.

Chantal and Gloria seated themselves and waited as instructed. The receptionist went back to reading her newspaper.

Five minutes later a thin, mid-sized man with black curly hair walked out of the elevator and strode toward them.

Without appearing to do so, he took close note of the women. Chantal gave him a look.

He stuck out his hand. "My name is Claudio Firenze," he said. "I understand you have some questions for me."

"My name is Gloria Montalvo and this is Chantal Travers," Gloria said, shaking his hand. Chantal took his as well, but said nothing, letting Gloria do the talking.

Gloria continued with her spiel, "We are doing a study on shipments and trucking requirements in non-profit organizations, and we have some ideas on how to make things more efficient. We are wondering if you might help us. We apologize for not making an appointment." She smiled. *Far more warmly than I am in the mood to pretend,* Chantal thought.

Gloria cocked her head and flashed her green eyes, "But could we ask you a couple of questions?" Chantal was impressed. Gloria was rarely willing to affect the flirtatious female.

This time, Claudio was less ambiguous when looking at Gloria. He smiled and said, "Why don't you come to my office?"

"Why thank you," Gloria said. "That is quite kind."

He led the way to the elevator and pressed the button for the third floor. They followed him down the hall of closed doors. Half way down, a door opened and two men exited. Chantal made an abrupt stop.

One of them was Banneret.

His eyes met hers. For a split second, he looked surprised. Quickly regaining his composure he said, "I see that Vienna didn't please you. How interesting to find you here in our office in Geneva." He turned to Firenze and said, "Claudio, how are you helping these ladies?"

Firenze looked flustered and said, "They asked for information about shipping information in non-profit organizations, and I thought I might help them."

"How very interesting," Banneret said, looking at the two women and then back at Firenze with a twinge of a knowing smile. Firenze shifted on his feet, not meeting Banneret's eyes.

Banneret continued, "I believe I made a brief contact with these ladies during my last trip, so perhaps I can help. I would be pleased to help them from here."

Firenze nodded his head and scurried down the hall.

Banneret looked at Chantal and Gloria and extended his arm toward the hall, "Why don't you come to my office. It is my honor to help you. After all, you made the effort to come all the way from Kosovo on holiday to visit this office." He barely made an attempt to conceal the facetiousness in his suave voice.

He led them into the elevator. They rode it to the top floor where a door opened into a large office. They passed a woman dwarfed behind a massive oak desk and continued through another door. They entered an even larger office in the top corner of the building. The room's floor-to-ceiling glass windows faced the lake. An even larger desk than the receptionists stood in one part of the room and barely seemed to fill it. Only a few papers lay neatly stacked on the desk. There was no computer.

"Why don't we sit over here?" He said, motioning to a long, green leather couch with matching lounge chairs. "Would you like a coffee, or something to drink."

Both women declined as they sat down.

"I think I remember you," Banneret said, seating himself in one of the chairs and looking at Chantal. "Some years ago you were at an art show here in Geneva."

"I don't remember," she said. Keeping her face blank.

Banneret acted as if he had not heard her. "That is why I thought it was strange to see you in Pec. It kept haunting me—where I had seen you. It took me some time to recollect." He smiled and crossed his legs. "It is strange that you are here, Miss, ah, I am sorry, but I don't know your name."

"My name is Chantal Chevalier," Chantal said, and this is "Gloria Montalvo." Chantal remembered that one of his men had gotten their names from the airline ticket agent at the airport in Podgorica.

"How may I help you?"

Chantal sat up straight, warming to her native language and Gloria's story. "We are conducting a study and have taken an interest in various population's migrations within Europe. We have become particularly focused on the increase in the illegal trafficking of people from Eastern Europe into Western Europe. We are contacting UN and non-governmental organizations to see what is being done."

"Ah, yes. This is a difficult problem," Banneret said, shaking his head with a commiserating frown. "But, why do you contact this agency. We focus on trade development." He kept his eyes wide and curious.

"That's just it. In some countries human trafficking is thought of as the development of trade—illegal—but money-generating."

"But illegal," he repeated.

"Yes, but growing nonetheless. We are concerned," Gloria leaned forward and took her knee in her hands to emphasize her concern, "And are looking for support to bring awareness to this problem."

Banneret continued to play the sympathetic listener, "A very noble cause. There are many people who share the same concern, and governments are discussing this. I happen to know of committees examining this issue even as we speak, and I am convinced that solutions will be forthcoming. But as I mentioned, this topic is well out of the charter of my organization."

"It may be," Chantal said, "but we have been doing some investigating."

"Investigating?" Banneret lowered his chin and kept a smile in his eyes. Chantal did not like being made to feel like a child playing a game. Control, she told herself. Control.

Gloria broke in, "We have reason to believe that someone in this organization may be involved in trafficking."

"You what?" Banneret raised his eyebrows and uncrossed his knees. "That is impossible."

"As I said, we have reason to believe that vehicles from this organization are being used to traffic women into Western Europe.

We followed one of your trucks, the same one that is parked outside in your parking lot."

"Impossible," Banneret repeated.

Chantal gave up on all pretense. "We followed that truck from Milan to Geneva. We heard women inside crying for help. If we could know the exact moment that truck arrived in Geneva, then we could prove or disprove our assumption. Could we talk to the driver of the truck, and inspect inside?"

"That's improbable and ridiculous," Banneret said, now clearly annoyed. "We have an excellent reputation as an international organization. Do you know what would happen if journalists found out that actual investigations were going on by... by two persons with no credentials. I am afraid I cannot allow this. You have to understand my position."

Gloria added, "And there was a man in the truck with the women. What happened to him?"

The condescending smile back in place, Banneret said, "Now this is absurd."

"We are asking you to help us," Gloria said.

Banneret looked at both women. "I would be pleased to help you on other matters, but there is nothing I can do for you on this one. Now if you will excuse me. I have an appointment and I must ask you to leave." Banneret stood up, crossed to the door of his office, opened it and motioned for them to go outside. Chantal and Gloria got up to leave.

As they passed by, Banneret said in a low voice. "Your game is dangerous. Be careful when you set out to defame an excellent organization such as this."

* * *

Banneret closed the door and turned on his heels, heading for his desk and grabbing the phone. "Get up here immediately."

Minutes later two men walked into Banneret's office.

"Two women were here and they are just leaving." Banneret said. "Find them and bring them to me at our secret location. Do you understand? Zog, your boss Mustafi has made too many mistakes. Don't follow his example." Zog clenched his jaw.

To the other man Banneret said, "Yesterday you crashed a car and ended up in a ditch. Luckily you survived. If you fail this time, I'll make sure that you end up in a ditch. Permanently. Now, go get them." He flung his arm at the door.

The two men moved hurried from the office, descended in the elevator to the reception area and ran out onto the street.

No women in sight. Zog swore, turning to the other man, "Take the left, I'll take the right." Before Zog's instructions had followed up his curse, both men had begun running in opposite directions.

At the end of the street, Zog came to a halt. On the other side of the street, the two women getting into a taxi. One less mistake.

CHAPTER 45

Back on the street, Chantal and Gloria flagged down a taxi and jumped inside, slamming the doors shut beside them. "To the train station. Quickly please," Chantal panted.

Neither woman said anything as they kept their heads turned to keep a close watch on the traffic behind. The silence did not last long.

Gloria spotted it first. "Look. The taxi behind us. It's following us." She turned to the driver. "Can you lose that other taxi?"

He nodded his head, accelerated down several blocks, went through small alley and the taxi behind disappeared. Several minutes later they were at the train station. Gloria paid the driver with a generous tip and they ran inside. They found a small coffee bar and went to a table in the farthest back corner. A waiter came and they ordered two *café au laits*.

They let their pounding hearts slow down while they waited for their coffee. When it came, Gloria took a sip of the rich dark liquid, wishing it were white tea. Caffeine was not going to help her nerves.

Chantal asked her, "Do you think he knows?"

"Banneret? There's something strange about him." She ripped open a raw sugar packet and sprinkled some of its crystals into the milky foam in her cup. "At first he seemed smooth and diplomatic. But his demeanor changed when you became more specific. Now that he knows what we're after, what do we do? I am the first to admit that no police officer would believe us at this point."

Chantal gave a humorless laugh, "*Non*. I can imagine us going to police and telling them the director in United Nations was involved in a kidnapping."

"I have no ideas." Gloria admitted, sticking her finger in the milk foam and licking it. She leaned back in her chair.

"I wish we had help," Chantal said, "I'm going to try and get a hold of Stefan von Portzer again." She went over to a telephone on the wall, inserted several coins and dialed von Portzer's number. The telephone rang for thirty seconds. No answer. No voice mail. She came back to the table and simply shrugged, chugging half her coffee and pushing it away.

Gloria asked, "Do you know anyone else in Geneva?"

"No. I haven't been to Geneva that often. When Justin and I came here we usually came to visit Stefan."

Gloria pressed her fingers to her temples. Fragments of names were circling through her head. She lowered one hand and snapped its fingers, "I thought of two people. When we were in Nice three weeks ago—while you were in the hospital—Stefan brought a lawyer from Geneva to orchestrate the press conference. Dr. Chevrolet. He might help, but…" she waved as if to clear space for another person, "… there is someone else."

"Well? Don't keep me in suspense." Chantal smiled.

"You mentioned Doby. The computer programmer who works for Stefan. Justin said he does research for Stefan and that he found interesting information about the Eurotech company. If we can find him, then maybe he can help in some way."

"Hmm. It's about our only possibility. Let's start with Doby and then try Dr. Chevrolet. Do you know where he works or lives?" Chantal looked hopeful.

"All I remember is that he lives in farmhouse somewhere up in the Jura Mountains."

"There must be hundreds of villages in those mountains," Chantal said, hope slipping from her face.

Gloria hurried to reassure her, "I think he has a web site, and I think I remember it. Let's go find a cyber-café and look it up. Maybe we can find something." She caught the eye of their waiter who came with his change purse.

They paid their bill and asked the waiter where they might find a cyber-café. He suggested some small computer shops a couple blocks away. They walked in the direction he indicated and eventually found a shop that sold notebook computers. Inside, a young man sat in a chair bent over a desk. What looked to have been a laptop computer lay scattered in pieces across the desk. He held a screwdriver in deep concentration on some tiny black fragment. He finished removing the microscopic screw and then looked up.

"Excuse me," Chantal said, "Is there a cyber-café around here? We need to look something up on the Internet."

He glanced up, then let his gaze rest on the two women. Grinning, he said, "Go ahead and use the PC over there. We're not a cyber-café, but I've got a broadband connection on that computer that I'm not using right now."

"Thank you," Chantal said.

Gloria took a chair in front of it the computer and selected a browser. She typed in the hyperlink she remembered and immediately Doby's site popped up. It seemed to be a hodge-podge of different things, none of them in a traditional layout. Gloria began to click through the different pages. No contact information.

"Anything that might tell us how to find him?" Chantal asked, leaning over the monitor.

"Not really. He seems to value his anonymity." Gloria clicked on a link and photos appeared. Swiss farms and villages floated by long with a streaming video of rural scenery.

"I don't recognize anything," Chantal said of the photos.

"Why would he put this here?" Gloria asked.

Chantal stood up straight, "Maybe he is into photography." She found another chair and rolled it next to Gloria's, sitting down.

They watched the streaming video again, searching for anything that might give them a clue as to Doby's whereabouts. The video showed an entrance to a village. On the second viewing, Chantal made out a sign that said 'Arzier'. Afterward a picture of a farmhouse came up.

Gloria pointed at the image, "I think that's it. Justin told me he had visited Doby at his farmhouse, and he said the name of the village. I'm pretty sure it was Arzier."

The video ended again, and they looked at the still photos of different farms. One of them was the same as the one on the video.

"Can I make a printout?" Gloria leaned back and asked the young man, who was still engaged in taking apart the computer.

"Sure, all you want," he replied, looking up from his work.

Gloria pushed the print button and the printer started to whir. She went over to him, "Sorry to bother you, but is there a place called Arzier around here?"

"Yeah. It's a small village about 25 kilometers from here." He pointed with his screwdriver, "Up in the Jura Mountains. It has a great view of the lake and the Alps." He went back to his parts.

Chantal looked at Gloria. Gloria said, "That must be it. If we go to Arzier, perhaps someone would know of him."

"Let's get a taxi," Chantal said, grabbing the photo printout.

They offered to pay the men for the use of his computer, but he refused. The women walked back to the train station where a line of taxis waited for fares. They took the first in line, got in, and asked the driver to take them to Arzier.

As the taxi pulled away from the curb, Chantal looked up and cried, "*Merde!*"

"What?" Gloria asked, looking where Chantal had seen a man running toward them.

"It's Zog."

CHAPTER 46

Having lost Zog at the station, the taxi took the motorway in the direction of Lausanne. After twenty kilometers, the road headed to the west and began winding into the mountains.

Small suburban villages of modern houses stood amid the forests and far enough from Geneva for their occupants to enjoy the countryside. Eventually the taxi came to Arzier. In the town square, Chantal saw the village mayor's office. She stopped the driver and went inside.

Passing a rack of brochures on local attractions and accommodations, she headed straight for the counter and smiled at the woman sitting below the high counter. The woman stood up. "Can I help you?"

Chantal handed the printout to her. "I am looking for this farm. It was in my uncle's family several generations back, and I am trying to find out if anyone I am related to still lives there." The woman smiled in recognition and assistance. "Why yes, I know this place. It's about kilometer out of town off the main road near a forest." She mentioned a road and fenced pasture to turn left after. "I do hope you find it and..."

Chantal was already out the door.

She jumped into the taxi and instructed the driver where to go.

A ways down a tree-lined, country road, Chantal saw a farmhouse emerge from the ever-greens. The same one as in the photo. But to reinforce it, she held up the paper, and Gloria nodded. Chantal smiled and said to her, "Looks like I've found great uncle Gilbert." To the driver she said, "You can turn in here."

Before the wheels had completely stopped on the gravel drive, Chantal and Gloria had their doors open. Over her shoulder, Gloria asked the driver to wait for them. They went straight to the front door.

Both of them raised their fists to knock at the same time. Two minutes later a man appeared. Dressed in a band t-shirt and jeans, he was about Gloria's and Chantal's age with a wiry build and short, spiky hair. He looked out his vintage, black-rimmed glasses at the two women on his doorstep. The look was neither friendly nor unfriendly.

Chantal spoke. "Excuse us, but we are looking for someone by the name of Doby. Does he live here?"

"Why do you want to know?" he asked, his hand still on the door.

"My name is Chantal Collins, and this is Gloria Collins. We believe that Doby can help us." She looked hard at him. "Are you Doby?"

"Yes, I am," Doby said. "Please come inside."

Gloria went back to pay the taxi driver. When all three were in the foyer, Doby invited them into the kitchen.

"It's a surprise to see you here," he said, not acting at all surprised. "I'll make some coffee." He started to fill the electric kettle with water. "Tell me what's going on."

★ ★ ★

By the time their cups were empty, Chantal and Gloria had finished their story. Chantal added, "We thought that Stefan might be able to help us, but we can't find him. He's not at his apartment, nor his office."

"He's been in Brussels," Doby reached for the French press pot and gestured at the women with it. They shook their heads and he filled his own mug.

"Brussels?" Gloria asked. "What is he doing there?"

"There was a kidnapping. Actually a murder and the kidnapping. A police detective from California was murdered. He was working on an international task force to break an illegal drug syndicate. He was the brother of Paul Kent the CEO of Unipac. Paul Kent's daughter, Anne, was there and she went missing. Since Stefan is doing some work for Unipac, Paul Kent and Sam Oliver asked him to help. I guess you know that Sam Oliver is the chairman of Unipac and also Anne

Kent's grandfather."

"How can we contact Stefan?" Chantal asked.

"I think you'll have to wait." Doby took a large swallow of his black coffee. "He called me yesterday on his way to Berlin to follow up on something that the big guy had found out."

"The big guy?" Chantal asked.

He smiled, "Yeah. Laszlo Vartek. I call him the big guy. They were in Berlin, he and the dude from Spain."

"Jordi?" Gloria asked.

"Yep. Laszlo and Jordi are working together to try and find Anne Kent. That's about all I know."

Gloria drummed her fingers on the polished wood of the table. "Doby, do you have any idea why someone would want to take Justin? When we were in Kosovo, Turk said something about Jacques Tapic's money. Do you know what he was talking about?"

Doby looked down at his lap and shrugged his shoulders. The band logo on his t-shirt shifted. "I don't know the entire story, and it was complicated. But there was something like one hundred and fifty million dollars of cash in Tapic's bank accounts. Stefan managed to have them transferred into bank accounts in Geneva. Shares in Eurotech and Unipac were also reallocated to people."

"Shares reallocated?"

"Yeah. About two billion dollars worth of shares."

"Two billion dollars? Reallocated how?" Gloria asked, her banking instincts whirring.

"You don't know?" Doby asked.

"Know what?"

Doby sighed and pushed his glasses up the bridge of his nose. "I'm not sure I should tell you. I don't know all the details myself." He took a breath. "I understand the cash was given to different people and the shares were split fifty-fifty. They gave me some."

"What does that mean?"

"Like I told you, I don't know all the details, so don't quote me. Something like fifty million dollars of cash went to Justin with half the shares. One billion dollars worth of shares in Unipac, give or take. Dora Vine decided on this since the money was technically hers. I thought you would know about all of this." He looked unsure as to whether he should have revealed anything.

Chantal and Gloria looked at each other. Gloria started reworking motives in her mind. Money made a big difference in figuring out why Justin had been abducted. Someone must know about the money.

"Someone must know about the money," Chantal said. For a second, Gloria wondered if there had been an echo in the room.

Chantal went on, "No one told us. Neither Justin nor Dora Vine. We had no idea why anyone would take Justin."

"Well," Doby began, pushing back his chair. "Do you need any help?"

"We can take all the help we can get," Gloria said.

CHAPTER 47

Two men pushed Justin through a door into an office. The office was large and modern Swedish. A blond bookshelf ran along one wall, and geometric chairs clustered around the curved computer desk that matched the shelves. Ceiling-to-floor curtains of thick white gauze let an opaque light through the windows behind them that made the red carpet on the floor glow.

A man sat behind a desk. He looked to be in his fifties, with black wavy hair graying at the temples. He wore a dark suit over a white shirt. A red silk tie hung straight from his collar, overlaid in gold paisley.

"Sit," one of Justin's escorts commanded.

Justin took the chair closest to him. It happened to be in the middle of the room and in front of the desk. Justin waited, looking at the man in front of him.

The silk-tied man was reading a packet of papers and kept his eyes down for a good minute. Finally he looked up and said, "Mr. Collins, I will get straight to the point. I just need some simple information, and I can guarantee that I will get it one way or another. Until now you have been most uncooperative, but we have numerous methods to extract what we need. I trust the drugs have now worn off and you have a clear mind?"

"Who are you?"

"Who I am is of no significance." The man waved himself off with his right hand. "What I want is to know is what happened to Jacques Tapic's assets—the money and the objects that were in his offices in Nice. Where are they?"

"I don't know a Jacques Tapic"

"Stop this," the man said, shaking his head wearily and leaning forward. "We have enough evidence that you were in those offices before they were vacated. We have spoken to eyewitnesses, a Mr. Ziginiglou and Mr. Turk, and also to two computer engineers who worked in the office. We have not been able to interview a handful of accountants who worked there. It seems they have disappeared, left Europe. Everyone we have spoken with said that you were in that office and that you had some leadership role. Now, please explain."

The only thing Justin could seem to do at this moment was wonder how long he had been wearing this filthy shirt and pair of pants. How many places had he awakened, groggy and beaten, since that morning at the monastery? He wanted, almost more than anything at this moment, to submerge himself in the sea and let it wash him clean.

That not being an immediate option, he considered what he should do. If he gave them information, he would be of no use to them. But if he did not give them information, they would torture him until he did. And then have no use for him. But more importantly, he had to think of Gloria and Chantal and Sophie. He would give the money back in a heart beat if it would end this. But would they track down his family and kill them because they knew too much? He needed to buy some time.

"What exactly are you after?" Justin asked.

"Exactly what I said." The man repeated exactly with emphasis. "What happened to the money and the information that was in that office."

"Why do you need the information?"

"That is none of your business," the man answered.

"I don't know what happened to the money."

"That is a bad lie. My people visited Féret and Jaccoud in Monaco and they said they transferred Tapic's money, as well as the registration of companies and subsequent shares in Unipac, to a gentleman from Geneva, a certain Stefan von Portzer. And his lawyer, Dr. Chevrolet. I assume that von Portzer and Chevrolet were working on your behalf. You see, Féret and Jaccoud became most helpful toward the end of our, er, interview. Before they were killed. We are now looking for von Portzer and Chevrolet and when we find them we will interview them in the same way."

Well, the lawyer's deaths answered Justin's worry about what would happen to him either way. Should he just avoid the torture and get on with it? *No, stall a bit longer,* something in him said.

"I don't know what you are talking about," Justin maintained. He had the feeling that this was not going to be well-received.

"Mr. Collins. My patience is running out." The man stood up and leaned over the desk toward Justin. "For the last time, what happened to the information that was in the offices in Nice. The paper files and the computers?"

"You seem to be making a big fuss over a few papers. If I were you, I'd be more interested in whatever money you were talking about."

The man stood up straight, folding his arms. He regarded Justin with a pained smile that indicated Justin would be the one in true pain soon. "I told you we have many methods to gain information from you. But I think you will share with me once you give this some consideration." He turned his head toward the men in the room. "Gentlemen. Please take him away."

Justin looked down at the floor as he was led out. He wondered if his blood would be the same color as the carpet if it spilled there. If it would stain at all.

CHAPTER 48

Doby pulled the curtains across the small wood-framed window to block the glare of the late afternoon sun. Chantal and Gloria's empty stomachs announced their audible pleasure at the things Doby had just pulled from the antique ice box. He started to open a bottle of wine while they filled their plates with fresh brown bread, hard raw milk cheese, and rounds of farmer's sausage.

Chantal let the bread and cheese she had lain on top of it sink in to her teeth and tongue. Her whole body seemed to be thankful for the relative safety of this remote farm.

The events of the past ten hours had held enough excitement for ten days. Leaving the French farm at six o'clock, trucking to Geneva, finding the UN Agency for Trade Development and the van that had carried Justin, speaking with Banneret, and seeing Zog.

Finding Doby was some relief, but real relief would only come when they found Justin.

"Do you think Justin was taken to get the money back?" Chantal asked of the room.

"I can't think of any other reason," Gloria replied. "Remember what

Turk said about someone wanting to find out about Tapic's money? It all makes sense."

"It seems that way," Doby said, filling the last of everyone's glasses with Swiss red wine. "I thought it was a lot of money to be holding in cash when I first saw the bank accounts."

"How did you see the bank accounts?" Gloria asked, setting down her piece of sausage. "Were they in the Nice office?"

Doby stopped halfway through reaching for another piece of bread. "I've said more than I should have. I can't divulge all the details, but it started before Nice. It actually started last July when Justin came through here. He had done an audit in Amsterdam and came across information about Chantal's air crash, or should I say the simulated air crash, and he asked me to start some research. Stefan referred him to me." He paused, swirled the wine in his glass, as though he were looking for the right words. "In my research I discovered the bank accounts, through their data bases."

"You saw their bank accounts?" This time, Gloria dropped her sausage. "How did you do that?"

"It was technical," he said, sipping his wine.

Gloria kept after him, "But you went into their systems?"

"Technical stuff. That information plus research confirmed that Justin should be looking for you in Nice. He had come to that same conclusion through his own discoveries. Things added up. I put it in a report that I gave to Justin."

"What report?" Gloria asked.

"Where did I put that?" Doby asked himself, rising and disappearing into another room. In a few minutes he returned with several sheets of paper stapled together. He handed the sheaf to Gloria.

Giving up on her lunch, she glanced through the pages. Chantal continued eating, admiring the way Gloria was asking all the right questions and assimilating the situation. Chantal realized she had been taking charge in many of their recent adventures. But if she sat back and let Gloria go at something, she saw that this woman was diligent and resourceful.

After returning to the front page, Gloria stared at it for several seconds. "This is incredible. Tapic was stealing money from Eurotech and putting it in his own accounts."

"He was going to do the same thing with Unipac, as part of the merger between Eurotech and Unipac."

Gloria flipped back to a flowchart in the report and asked, "What's this?" She leaned toward Doby.

"It's just a pictorial map of relationships. In this case, where most of the telephone traffic was going, particularly from an office in Amsterdam, but also from the office in Nice. That is how we tracked down Tapic, or at least how he was implicated in the office."

Gloria looked at the flowchart. "There are two links from Tapic, one going to a telephone number in the European Union offices and another to the UN. Do you know what these are?"

Doby and Chantal looked at the report.

Doby pursed his lips and then explained, "I was never able to identify who owned those numbers in Brussels and Geneva. Tapic was a politician and it was logical that he talked with people in Strasbourg and Brussels, but also plausible that he would be communicating with people in the UN—both in Geneva and New York."

Chantal asked, "Do you think he was talking with Banneret?"

"Maybe, but I couldn't trace the number to a person." Doby took the report, made an "oh well" gesture with it by flipping his wrist, and then tossed it out of the way of their luncheon.

"What *did* happen at that office in Nice?" Chantal asked. "We never got all the details."

"Stefan asked me to come down to Nice to help. They were staking out an office that seemed to be important for clarifying what Tapic was doing. The office had some accountants and programmers, and Stefan brought me in to help with the computers. Storming the office and obtaining the information housed there allowed Stefan to recover the money. Sam Oliver said it should all go to Dora Vine because of all the suffering she went through, and Dora decided on a distribution. A good portion of it went to Justin, and both of you."

CHAPTER 49

Chantal and Gloria looked at each other.

Chantal spoke first, "So if the kidnappers took Justin to get back the money, how did they know about it? Were they aware of the office in Nice?"

"Who knows? It seems that Tapic had some minor partners." Doby smiled and dusted his hands of bread crumbs over his plate. "I have an idea. We cleaned out the office. They had some state-of-the-art things—high-speed computers and servers and such. I loaded it all into a truck and brought it back here. It's still in my workshop. To be honest, I haven't even plugged anything in. it's just sitting in there." He pointed in the direction of a door at the end of the room.

"Could we see?" Gloria asked, already pushing back from the table.

"Sure. Come on."

Doby led them through a door into what was probably once a bedroom but was now a workshop. Inside were tables lined with electronic equipment, computer parts, test and measurement equipment, and numerous piles of wires.

"This is where I keep my parts. In a way it's a decoy. I do my real work elsewhere. In a bomb shelter underground. That's where my operational equipment is." He went to flick on additional lights. "You may already know, but many houses in Switzerland are built with bomb shelters. This farmhouse" he turned around with his arms out, "is a couple of hundred years old. But the bomb shelter was built around twenty years ago. It's an ideal place to do my work."

"Where is the equipment from Nice?" Gloria asked.

"In the corner. All that stuff over there." He broke off and turned to face the corner of the workshop where a large stack of computers, monitors and servers were stacked. "Like I said, I haven't even gotten around to those things. I was going to strip them for parts."

Gloria walked over the tower of plastic and metal. "Do you think you could find further information in these?"

"For sure. Let me get working on it." He stopped, looked at the equipment and said, "I just thought of something else."

"What's that?" Chantal asked.

"The two computer guys in Nice. I could give them a call. They were scared as hell when Laszlo and Jordi questioned them." He smiled, remembering. "If I mention them, they might tell me if there is anything special to look for."

"Everything helps," Chantal said. "Can you think of anything else we might do?"

"You may want to find out more about Banneret," Doby said, beginning to pull down some cords that were strangling a hard drive. "I can do some research on the Internet to find out more about his background, who he talks with, and maybe some other things."

"How do you do that?" Gloria asked.

"Public information, too difficult to explain. Anybody could do it, if you know how." Doby extracted a hard drive from the stack, dusted it off and heaved it toward a table.

Chantal wondered. It was obvious that Doby was going beyond public information, but she didn't want to ask. As long as they could find information that would lead them to Justin.

"Any suggestions for what we should do now?" Gloria asked.

"Maybe stay out of the way until I can find further details. Sounds like you have got some pretty bad guys out there looking for you." He paused, the cables in his hand swinging.

Chantal felt the urge to do something now. Sitting back—for Gloria or this whole mess was not sitting well with her. "No. I think we should try and watch Banneret, to see where he lives and see who visits him. At least we can do that while you are doing your research."

"It's risky," Doby said, "But it might give you some information. Do you know where he lives?"

"No." Chantal smiled, "But I bet you can find out."

Doby returned the smile. "Give me a minute."

He walked over to his computer, clicked a few times, made two printouts and handed them to Chantal.

"He lives in Champel, one of the best parts of Geneva. His telephone number and address are unlisted, but I know where to go to get that information. Wait a minute."

Doby clicked away some more, made another printout and handed it to Chantal. Gloria came to her shoulder and looked at it with her. Doby was shaking his head, "I should be able to tell who is neighbors are, but this is strange. It looks like he is the only one in the entire apartment building. A company called Regie Trading owns the building, but who knows what that is. I'll look around and try to find out."

"Tomorrow is Saturday," Chantal said to Gloria, "and he may not go to the office. Why don't we at least watch where he lives just to see who comes and goes? I can't think of anything else to do, but you've got to be careful."

Doby drove them back to their hotel in Geneva as they continually looked for Zog or anyone else that might be following them.

CHAPTER 50

Gloria awoke before Chantal and slipped out of bed. She dressed and went down through the quiet lobby to the street. She had seen a park around the corner, and for some reason she felt the desire to sit under a tree and pretend that her biggest worry of the moment was what to eat for breakfast.

The plan was to meet up with Doby for lunch at a brasserie near Banneret's building. But before the day truly began, Gloria was going to find some peace if it killed her.

She looked up into the leaves where the early morning sun was dappling them. It was too cold to sit still for long, and she hugged her new cardigan close, enjoying the fabric in her fingers. A mother walked her small boy through the park. She held his hand that he had lifted high to reach hers. Gloria tried to calculate how long it would be before the child in her womb would be that age. Would be old enough to walk by her side.

And then she thought about other things. Sophie and her mother, now sleeping nearby. Justin sleeping or… No. She would remain positive.

She reached for the cross that hung from her neck and sent a prayer up through the leaves, trusting that they would be no impediment to the journey of her request.

★ ★ ★

The address Doby had given Gloria and Chantal yesterday proved easier to find than 23 Garibaldi Street in Milan.

This was an upscale neighborhood in Geneva. Across the street from the address stretched a row of high-end commercial shops. But the women were more thrilled with the brasserie and a tea room than the jeweler's or designer boutique.

Chantal clapped her hands together as much for warmth as to get things going. "So where do we conduct this stake-out?" She decided she like that word, and this juncture in her life was likely, and hopefully the only time she would get to practice it.

"I don't know about you, but I'd freeze outside." Gloria said, hugging her shoulders to emphasize the weather. "I vote for the tea shop." She stopped. "But then, we can't stay there all day." A car drove slowly past and began parallel parking across from them. Gloria turned to Chantal, eyes bright, "Maybe we could rent a car and move it to different parking spots now and then.

"Not a bad idea," Chantal said. "And then we can still go in and out of the tea shop."

Just when Chantal was thinking she'd perish if she had to go hunt down a rental agency before eating something, Gloria suggested that Chantal stay and eat breakfast. "I had a croissant after before I came back up to the room this morning," she said.

Chantal smiled. "You're sure you don't mind?"

* * *

Gloria pulled up in front of the tea shop with a small, gray car that looked similar to the other cars on the street. She had chosen something as nondescript as the rental agency offered.

She closed the door and spotted Chantal through the tearoom window. She waved at Gloria and then made a "nothing" gesture with her hands and shoulders. So no Banneret yet.

They sat for an hour. Nothing moved in or out of the building. It was an eight-story, white structure. Like many others in Geneva, the building was understated and tasteful. Its front door was solid metal as opposed to those of its neighbors with glass doors, and a large garage gate occupied the lower right side of it.

Having nursed their tea and pastries long enough, the women moved to the car. They watched mid-morning shoppers hurry by out of the cold. Now and then, Gloria turned on the engine for the heat. Other than that, they kept still and in their own thoughts.

Noon. And nothing had come in or out of Banneret's building.

They went to the brasserie as planned. At twelve fifteen Doby came in and joined them at their table which had a view of the building under observation. He kept pulling or pushing his glasses and did not take his coat off.

He said nothing until Chantal asked, "Did you find out anything?"

"A couple of things." He cracked his knuckles. "First, I tried to call the two computer guys from the office in Nice. I got hold of the girlfriend of one of them. Several nights ago they both disappeared," he swallowed. "Their bodies were found yesterday. So I looked at the websites of the local newspapers in the south of France, and there were several articles on the story. The newspapers said that the bodies bore signs of torture—badly beaten, cigarette burns, all that James Bond stuff. One of them had two fingers cut off." He looked down at his own fingers. "The police are investigating, but it sounds pretty brutal."

Gloria asked him, "And you still think this is linked to Tapic and the money?"

"It's the only thing we can go on. And someone else must think so to have done this."

Chantal leaned forward over her placemat. "You mentioned a couple of things. What else did you find out?"

A waitress finally stopped by their table for their order. Chantal and Gloria gave her their selection and Doby absentmindedly pointed to an item on the menu. He returned his focus to Chantal. "I did some quick research on Banneret. He has been the director of this agency for six years. Before that he was a French politician. He has significant contacts in the French government and in the European Union. He gets a lot of positive press because of his agency's efforts to help developing countries build up their export trade. He and his people work closely with the World Trade Organization, but somehow his agency has managed to avoid most of the negative pressure coming from the anti-globalization movements, unlike the WTO."

Doby finally took off his jacket and leaned back in his chair, the majority of his information divulged. But Gloria thought of something else to ask. "Do you know what he does personally?"

"You mean his interests?"

"Yes, how he spends his time—with whom, on what."

Doby shook his head slowly, thinking. "He travels a lot and visits refugee camps."

"On personal time?" Gloria wrinkled her brow. "Even if those trips are work-related, what do refugee camps have to do with trade development?"

The waitress returned with their beverages, and Doby reached for his beer. "Interviews quote him as saying that his organization is trying to help people migrate to places where they can find jobs. Something like that."

"Is there anything negative ever published about him?" Chantal asked, tasting her red wine. She grimaced and muttered, "*Suisse*," under her breath.

"Yes." Doby tapped his forehead to dislodge the memory of it. He snapped his fingers. "A couple of years ago there was some negative press about the UN Sex for Food Program."

"The what?" both women exclaimed at the same time. Gloria almost dropped her mineral water. A sizable spill hit the table and spread toward her napkin. She ignored it.

Doby smiled in acknowledgement of the grim ridiculousness of such a program. "A group of journalists found out that UN workers were obtaining sexual favors from people in refugee camps. They demanded that young boys and girls have sex with them before the refugees could get any food. It was claimed to be widespread not only with UN organizations, but also some non-governmental organizations. If you don't believe me, check it out online. It's all there."

Gloria finally mopped up her water and asked, "What happened?"

Doby held his beer aloft. "The UN appointed an independent committee to investigate, but it went hush-hush and nothing ever came of it." He took a swig. "No one was incriminated."

"How did Banneret fit in?" Chantal asked.

"His name appeared as one of the UN officials involved, but he had witnesses that he wasn't at the camp where that particular accusation took place. But you have to understand that this so called 'program' was not an isolated event. It was all over the place. Africa. And other countries with a UN presence."

"That's disgusting," Chantal said. "Whitewashing the truth all in the name of helping humanity."

"It looks that way," Doby replied. "The UN is good at that."

The food arrived, and the three diners let their own thoughts rattle around in their heads. After downing his noodle dish, Doby excused himself. "I need to get back to work. You two be careful. If I find anything I will call you at your hotel this evening." He put on his coat and left the brasserie.

Gloria watched him take off down the sidewalk in quick strides. He did not look like any of the shoppers slowly poking their heads in shops and toting bags of purchases.

She and Chantal finished their coffees and then reluctantly returned to their rental which was parked across the street. They spent the rest of the afternoon wishing they were not in the rental.

When a nearby church clock chimed six o'clock, it was Gloria's turn to get out and stretch. The sky had turned dark and the streetlights were on. She walked past the closing stores. When she nodded *bon soir* to a proprietor turning the key in his shop's lock, she felt a twinge of envy at the man's ability to go home for the evening.

Gloria returned to the car where Chantal was staring listlessly out the windshield at their seemingly vacant building. She climbed in and slammed the door. "I don't think we are going to see anything. Perhaps we should go back to the hotel."

"*Oui.* Yes." Chantal pulled on her seatbelt and was leaning over to say something to Gloria, when she froze. Gloria followed her look of surprise out her window.

A small white truck had pulled up in front of the garage doors of Banneret's building. The doors opened automatically.

The side of the truck read 'UN Agency for Trade Development'.

And the driver was the same man who drove it from Milan to Geneva.

CHAPTER 51

Laszlo and Jordi walked across the Pont du Mont Blanc, the bridge that spanned Lake Geneva at the point where it became the Rhone River. They found a small bistro and practically collapsed in their chairs, wordless with exhaustion.

They had spent the day visiting contacts that Laszlo had made over the years during his visits to Stefan von Portzer.

Laszlo sometimes stayed in one of the guest rooms of Stefan's six-bedroom apartment. And sometimes he stayed at a local hotel if Stefan was entertaining female friends. For all his nights in Geneva, Laszlo had been at hotels far more than at Stefan's. Earlier that day, he and Jordi had checked into a hotel.

It had been a long day, starting with several personal protection companies, lunching with an ex-policeman who had become a private detective and taking dinner with a Non Governmental Organization that was working to stop the trafficking of people. During all these visits, they had managed to gather bits of useful information.

But at the end of the day, they knew little more than they had at the beginning.

The two men had been keeping a lookout for any Schubach's thugs. Laszlo half-regretted this. With a little questioning, they might have been able to reveal Anne Kent's location.

They did learn that Geneva was a prime location for the trafficking of women, especially beautiful women who would command high prices. They also learned that illegal drugs were increasingly becoming a problem. Much of this was attributed to an influx of Kosovo Albanian gangs. But no one seemed able to pinpoint the leaders of this trade. The groups behind it were fragmented—rival gangs competing for territory.

Wealthy Saudi sheiks were prime clients for expensive high class call girls, and some of the Saudis had been known to forcibly take these girls back home with them. The detective they talked to had worked on a case where a girl had been taken against her own will by a Saudi sheik, and he knew of several similar cases.

To get the girl back, the detective had to find politicians willing to demand that the Saudi government get involved. This had resulted in threats of preventing Saudis from entering Geneva and not allowing them to purchase property. Finally the Saudi government told their wayward sheik to give her up.

The detective didn't have any direct leads for Laszlo and Jordi, but he said he heard of girls being sold to Saudis.

Laszlo looked down at what appeared to be a coffee in front of him. Had he ordered something? He shook his head, trying to keep awake after a night without sleep followed by a day of work that had turned out to be nothing.

"*Nada* after all that trying," Jordi said, speaking aloud what Laszlo was too tired to.

"No. Well, background information yes. But we are not even sure that Geneva is the right place to look. Mustafi seemed truthful, but can we trust a lifetime liar like him?" Laszlo asked.

"Hard to know," Jordi reflected. "Geneva has wealthy people. Some of them would probably make this kind of transaction. But there are many other places where this could happen. Paris, Berlin and London."

"I know. This could be the wrong place."

Laszlo sighed and pulled out his cell phone, "I think I'll give Doby a call."

* * *

"Are you thinking what I'm thinking" Chantal asked Gloria, her eyes on the garage door the UN truck had just passed through.

"Justin might be in that building," Gloria breathed. Chantal realized that their level of desire and frustration must be equal, and for the first time, she did not find herself annoyed that Gloria would want Justin as badly as herself. If Gloria felt what she did...

Her thought was interrupted by a sleek black car that eased in front of Banneret's building. At the same moment, two men emerged from the building's metal door, supporting a young woman between them. She stumbled and dragged her feet. Her head lolled to the side with each step.

Chantal straightened forward against the seatbelt. "That's Anne Kent. Doby showed us her photo."

The men lifted Anne into the back seat of their car and climbed in on either side of her. As soon as they shut their doors, the car roared away.

"Quick. Let's follow them," Chantal said, eyes on the car but hand waving in the air at Gloria.

Gloria shoved the car in gear and followed. The black car drove down to the lake on the road past Stefan von Portzer's apartment. It continued on for ten minutes, climbing to a hill above the lake. Large expensive homes dotted the manicured hillside.

"I think I know this area," Chantal said. "Stefan told us about it. Many bankers, business people and rich Saudi sheiks live here."

The black car pulled into a driveway. A guard left his watch house and opened the gate for the car to pull inside.

Gloria drove by and Chantal took note of the address. "We need to find a telephone," Chantal said.

A kilometer further, they found a small square where a public telephone booth shed its fluorescent light into the dark street. Gloria parked the car while Chantal opened the clear doors and stepped inside. She dialed Doby's number and he answered on the second ring.

"Doby? It's Chantal."

"I just walked in," he said. She heard the clatter of keys hitting a solid surface. "What's going on?"

"We saw Anne Kent being led out of Banneret's building. We followed the car she was transported in to a mansion here above the lake."

"What…?" He interrupted her, "I think you should get out of there. Let me take care of this. And I would stay away from Banneret's building."

"There's a chance Justin is in there. We have to keep watch."

There was a small silence on his end. "I won't argue with a lady, but stay out of sight."

Chantal did not bother to say goodbye. Racing back to the car, she realized that Justin was possibly also about to be removed from

Banneret's residence.

She yanked open her door and told Gloria, "Back to Banneret's building. We might lose him." She meant more than losing the chance to follow him.

Back in town, at the street now all too familiar to both women, Gloria parked the car a block away from their target and headed toward a row of benches not far from Banneret's apartment building.

Gloria started to rewrap her scarf around her neck. She opened her mouth to speak just as rapid footsteps sounded behind them. Chantal turned first, her skin tingling with what she guessed must be fear. She did not want to, but she looked over her shoulder.

Zog. And two men with him.

"Run!" She grabbed at Gloria's arm, but Gloria was winding her scarf and she did not respond fast enough.

One of the men caught Gloria as Zog leapt for Chantal. But Chantal had already bolted forward and she sprinted right into the street.

A car screeched to a halt and her coat brushed its fender. She paused a fraction of a second between the vehicle's headlights, found herself uninjured and then darted through parked cars to the other sidewalk.

Still running, she smelled the burnt rubber of car tires as she glanced back to see the three men dragging Gloria through the garage doors.

CHAPTER 52

"Man, am I glad to hear your voice," Doby said on the other end of Laszlo's phone. "Do I ever need your help."

"What's wrong?" Laszlo said.

"You're in Geneva?"

Laszlo said "Yes," making a face of puzzlement when Jordi raised an eyebrow.

Doby rushed to explain, "Chantal Collins called me a few minutes ago. She and Gloria saw where Anne Kent was taken. I'm driving into Geneva now. I was on my way to get the police and go over there."

Laszlo was confused. "Chantal Collins. What is she doing here? And what does she have to do with Anne Kent?"

"Long story. I'll tell you when I see you. Can you help?"

"Yes. I'm here with Jordi Pujols."

"Thank God," Doby said, sounding as if he really did.

Laszlo was already standing up from the table and Jordi tossed the appropriate amount of Francs down for their beverages.

Doby was asking, "Where can I pick you up?"

"In front of the Palais Wilson."

"I'll be there in five minutes."

Laszlo slapped his phone shut and Jordi followed him out the doors.

Exactly five minutes later, Doby pulled his car into the curved drive in front of the Palais Wilson. The old but magnificently restored building faced the lake. An historical building, it had been used by the League of Nations, the predecessor of the United Nations, before the League fell apart with the start of the Second World War.

As soon as Laszlo and Jordi got in his car, Doby put his foot to the floor and sped down the road. He raced across Geneva while attempting to explain as much as possible, before arriving at Eaux Vives, the gated, hilltop neighborhood overlooking the Lake.

"And Anne Kent's in there," Doby pointed out a brick mansion with a fountain in the middle of a circular driveway. He continued driving and pulled over out of sight of the house.

Laszlo had taken note of the heavy iron gate and guardhouse in front. He turned to Jordi who was sitting in the back seat, "What do you think?"

"*Hombre,* I'm getting tired of subtleties. I think we should just go in and ask."

"Agreed." He turned back to face forward as if he could still see the layout. "There's one guard at the front gate, and perhaps one or two inside. Few people are expecting "visitors" in Switzerland. Surprise is our best weapon."

Several minutes later Doby drove his car up to the front gate and honked his horn. The guard came out and walked over to the driver's side. He leaned in enough to scan the empty passenger and back seats. "Can I help you?"

Doby acted impatient, "Yeah, I've got stuff to deliver here."

"Stuff. What stuff?" The guard looked dubious.

"In the trunk. The equipment."

"What kind of equipment?" the guard asked.

"Computer equipment." Doby said, as if there were no other kind. Rolling his eyes, he opened his door and led the guard to the back of the car. "Here, it's in the trunk."

"No one mentioned a deliver to me. Maybe you got the wrong place," the guard said.

"It's for some rich guy," Doby said. "He lives here, right?"

The guard did seemed to associate his boss with the vague 'rich guy'. He hesitated and then moved around to the rear of the car.

Doby reached to open his trunk, saying, "Their computer wasn't working, can't get on the Internet to read their email, so they asked me to come and fix it. Here are the parts." He thumped on the trunk and flung it open.

The guard found himself staring straight at Jordi who was had a gun pointed at him. He stood there as Laszlo walked quickly across the street, his Glock trained on the guard. Jordi got out of the trunk, reached under the guard's coat and pulled out a gun.

"Get in," Laszlo said.

"What?" the guard asked of his gun.

"Get in the trunk."

CHAPTER 53

Crouched in a narrow alley behind a dumpster, Chantal kept watch on the building across the street. Behind the sixth-floor windows a light glowed through a white curtain.

Her knees aching from the cramped position, Chantal felt her way backwards in the dark and sat down on the ground, resting her back against a brick wall. The icy cold of the cobblestone quickly permeated her red wool pants, and she hugged her knees close to her chest.

She had tried to call Doby after losing the men. No answer. She couldn't go back to the hotel. More than likely the men had either found the address in Gloria's belongings or extracted the information from her.

Chantal made fists both for warmth and anger. She had no way to get help, and Gloria was in the hands of those awful men. Only one option remained. She would have to try to get into the building, stupid as that seemed.

Great. That meant more waiting.

But not for long. After a quarter of an hour and cramp in her calf, Chantal saw the doors of the garage open. A black car with diplomatic license plates pulled out and down the street.

She slid to the mouth of the alley and as the garage doors began to close, she sprinted across the dark street.

★ ★ ★

Jordi moved to the back of the house. They did not want anyone escaping. In the distance, the lights along the lake shimmered in thin fingers of reflection across the black water.

Here at the house, the back yard swimming pool glowed a yellowy turquoise from its underwater lights. The skin of his hand holding the Glock glowed glassy green as he passed the pool. He crossed the patio to the back door, opened it and slipped inside.

Doby rang the front doorbell as Laszlo had instructed. A broad-shouldered man wearing a dark blue blazer and gray slacks opened the door. "What are you doing here?" he asked. "The gatehouse didn't…"

"Turn around slowly, hands up," Commanded Laszlo's voice and Glock.

As the man turned around, Laszlo raised his gun and brought it down hard on a well-alculated spot between the man's neck and shoulder. The man crumpled to the floor.

They had nothing to tie him with, so they moved quickly into the house. Laszlo looked around the opulent, marbled entrance. An enormous crystal chandelier hung above them and gold was the accent of choice. On one wall was centered an enormous painting of a man in Arab headdress with a large curved gold sword in his hand. He looked fiercely out from his black moustache at all who entered the hall.

Laszlo led the way into the next room, where eight men were seated around a long oval table. Two of the men wore traditional Arab robes and headwear. The other six were in Western clothing. The meal laid out in front of them was made with enough food to feed four times as many men.

Only those facing the door looked up when Laszlo and Jordi entered.

"Stay seated," Laszlo commanded. Those with their backs to the door whipped their heads around in the direction of the intruders.

A small man made as if to bolt, and Laszlo jerked the gun in his direction. The man eased himself slowly back into his seat and raised his hands to chest height.

"Where's the American girl?" Laszlo asked of the table in general.

"How dare you come into my home like this?" demanded a turbaned man at the head of the table. He spoke low and with a restrained rage. "I will have you arrested. In my country we would cut off your head."

"Saudi Arabia?" Laszlo asked.

"Yes. Get out of this house."

"Where's the girl?"

"Get out. Get out of my home!" the man rose, from his chair, restraint abandoned. He thumped his fist to his torso and yelled, "You do not treat Saudis like this."

"Everyone on the floor. You stay to the side," Laszlo said, pointing to the owner of the house.

Some of the men moved quickly, others took their time and attempted to preserve their dignity. Eventually, seven men lay face down on the floor.

"Come with me," Laszlo said to the Saudi.

"What do you want?" the Saudi asked, his voice once again dangerously low.

"A tour through your little house." Laszlo said.

"Thieves!"

"We will see who has stolen whom," Laszlo said through his teeth.

Laszlo grabbed the man by the arm and practically lifted him off the floor, shoving him in the direction of the entrance room. Jordi stayed in the room, gun trained on the prostrated diners.

"I'll take you upstairs," the Saudi said.

"No." Laszlo shook his head. "Downstairs."

★ ★ ★

Chantal squeezed through just as the gate doors shut. She had to pull the corner of Gloria's green coat from the clenched mental.

Moving along the wall, she glanced around the semi-lit garage. At the first parked car, she ducked down and tried to catch her breath. Slowly rising, she looked over the smooth and shiny trunk of her cover.

Several small lights shed an eerie visibility to the space. Counting the one she was behind, there were three black cars. All Mercedes, all with CD license plates. The white truck was parked at the end of the row which had several empty spaces.

Slowly Chantal made her way across the concrete floor, glad of her rubber-soled shoes. A workbench along one wall was neatly hung with tools, including three ball-pein hammers all in a row. She took the largest one off the rack, but the head swung downward with a weighted speed, almost clanking to the ground. Too heavy. She could maneuver the middle one. She also grabbed a roll of duct tape and stuffed it in her coat pockets.

As armed as she could be, she turned from the workbench and looked at the elevator. No. Stairs. She went to the door, easing it open, and slipped through an emergency stairway. Several small lights embedded in the lips of the stairs illuminated her way up.

Chantal shook off the impossibility of what she was doing and just tried to do it. After one flight of stairs, she pushed the door open enough to look through it.

A long hall with rooms off to each side. She pushed through and opened the door of the first room on the left. It was full of cleaning supplies. She made a sound of derision in the direction of the mop and bucket and started to close the door. She couldn't go from room to room, opening doors and looking inside.

A noise. Another door down the hall was opening. She ducked inside the cleaning closet, trying not to trip on a fallen roll of toilet paper. Leaving the door slightly ajar, she peeked through into the hall.

Directly across from her was the elevator. A man now faced it, back to her. He pushed a button and waited. He wore a gun holster on the back of his belt with a gun in it.

Chantal stepped from the closet. "Don't move and don't turn around," she said. "I've got a gun on you."

He began to turn around. "I know that trick," he said, laughing.

A moment later the ball-pein hammer came crashing down on his head and he fell to the floor with a thud.

CHAPTER 54

The sheik went in front of Laszlo down a flight of stairs into a small passageway with four doors.

"Open them," Laszlo said.

The man opened two. One was a storage room full of boxes and scattered tools and supplies. The other was a cellar full of hundreds of bottles of wine.

"Nice collection," Laszlo said. "Now open the other two."

The Saudi tried to open the first door, but it didn't budge. "It's locked," he said in mock apology. "I don't have the key."

"I have a key," Laszlo said. Keeping his gun pointed at the Saudi, Laszlo lifted his leg and crashed the sole of his booted foot into door near the knob. Inside sat two women at a table reading books. They looked Philippine. And scared.

"My domestic help," the man explained, attempting a smile.

"Why are they locked in here?" Laszlo asked the man and before he got a reply he asked the women, "Are you domestic help? "Laszlo asked."

"Yes we are."

"Are you being paid?"

The two women looked at the sheik.

"Don't worry," Laszlo said. "He can't hurt you, and I will let you go. You won't be in trouble with the Swiss authorities. Does he pay you?"

One of the woman tossed down her book. "No. He took away our passports eight months ago. We were never paid."

"They lie," the Saudi said.

Laszlo slapped him hard across the face and the Saudi staggered back in shock. "Open the next door," Laszlo said.

The man stayed still and held his hands to his face, expecting another blow.

Laszlo went to the door and kicked it in. Two women were each seated on a metal frame bed. Their left hands were handcuffed to the headboards.

One of them was Anne Kent.

★ ★ ★

Chantal stood there a second over the fallen man, wondering if she had just imagined knocking him on the head.

The hammer was still in both her hands. She set it down, then grabbed the man's feet, struggling to pull him into the cleaning closet. She managed to heave his torso against the shelves, knocking down several bottles of cleaner that thankfully remained sealed. So much for keeping quiet.

She took the gun from the holster and began binding his hands together with her golden scarf. She had a fleeting thought that Gloria would not find the thing so frivolous if she knew it was involved in her rescue. After reinforcing the binding with duck tape, Chantal wound more tape around the man's ankles. Then she took a broom handle and ran it from his hands to his ankles fixing it securely in place with the duck tape.

She patted her hands over his body and found a switchblade knife in his front pocket along with a key. His wallet was in his back pocket. She dropped the wallet and key to the floor and slipped the knife into her own back pocket.

Surveying her work, she noticed blood running down the side of his head. Her heart thudded with the awful thought that she might have killed him. She slapped him a couple of times on the side of the face and was relieved when the man opened his eyes and groaned.

"Talk to me," she said in French.

"Bitch," he said. "My head feels like shit." He shook it then thought better of the action, squeezing his eyes closed in pain.

"Where is Gloria? Is Banneret here? Where do I find them?"

"Go to hell," he said.

She took the hammer and tapped him on the side of the head where the blood was appearing.

"Ahhhh," he groaned.

"Tell me. One smack more, and you'll never wake up." She raised the hammer above his head.

He tried to raise his hands to fend off the blow and found them securely fastened together and to the broom. "No, wait." His voice was groggy.

"Where is she?"

"He'll kill me." His head swung faintly from side to side.

"Who?"

"Banneret." He managed to open his eyes and look into hers. "If I give you this information he will kill me."

"I'll kill you first. Where is Gloria?"

He hesitated, struggling for his thoughts. "Upstairs." His head fell back against a bottle of disinfectant and he passed out.

She waited a minute and then began to pat him on the face. She was faintly surprised when he regained consciousness.

"Where is she?" She asked.

His eyes were blurry. "She who?"

"Gloria. The woman who was taken in the park across the street, this evening, with the red hair."

"Her? She's in his apartment. Top two floors. He tests out many of the women." He had enough presence of mind to smile at this.

A memory of Yass and his violation surged through Chantal's spine and she almost lost her balance, crouching there next to this creep. "Which floor? Where do I find her?"

"I don't know. We rarely go up there. Everyone meets with him in his office on the third floor. His apartment is off limits. It's huge. Lots of rooms. The elevator doors only open on those floors if you know the code. Only two of us have the key, and we can only enter when called."

"You know the code?" she asked.

He shook his head, trying to resist.

"Tell me." Chantal hefted the hammer in her hand, but before she had moved it a centimeter, he gave in.

"Shit… 606. Then you need the key."

She picked up the key that she had dropped next to his wallet and asked, "This one?"

He nodded. It looked like it hurt to do so.

"What's on this floor here?" she asked.

"Rooms." His eyes rolled back in this head as more blood dripped off his hair onto the floor.

"And what's in the rooms?"

"Transients… people… seeking… work." He passed out.

Chantal ripped a strip of duck tape and pressed it over his mouth, disliking the feeling of his lips even through the silvery tape. She closed the door on him without glancing back at the disturbing sight of his blood pooling near the mop bucket.

She checked the hall to make sure it was clear, then crossed to the elevator and pushed the button for the top floor. As she waited, she remembered being in Rome at the outset of this search and thinking that she would ditch Gloria at the first opportunity. Now she found herself almost as worried for her rival as she was for Justin.

The elevator arrived, the doors opened and she stepped inside. On the wall was a small numeric keypad. She punched in 606. The doors closed and the elevator began to rise.

CHAPTER 55

"Who are you?" Anne asked, sitting up and ready despite the handcuffs. A calculation sparkled in her eyes where fear had shown in the other girls Laszlo had rescued.

"Miss Kent, you have been difficult to find." Laszlo said, not answering her question and finding he had little else to say. He was distracted by this woman's strength of spirit. And the fact that she was beautiful. He swallowed and asked, "Who is she?" pointing to the other woman, who was also attractive.

Anne looked pained, "She is drugged and I haven't been able to talk much with her. She has been here about a month." She clenched her jaw and fixed accusing eyes on the sheik. "It is horrible what that man there has been doing to her."

Laszlo turned to the sheik and said, "Get the key. Release them."

"I don't have it," the sheik said dully.

Laszlo walked over, searched the man's pockets and pulled out a key. He uncuffed the two women, Anne first. He lifted the drugged woman and carried her from the room, stopping by the supplies in the first room for a sizable roll of electrical tape. The Philippine women, who had stood well away from the sheik, followed.

Back upstairs, the other men—plus the kitchen staff Doby had rounded up—were still on the floor. The security guard from the back of the trunk and the one who Laszlo had knocked out were also on their faces on the floor.

The sight of his guests and employees lying on their stomachs enraged the sheik. His face flushed red under his white turban. "I will have you executed."

Laszlo, gun still in hand, ripped a stretch of tape from the spool and slapped it across the sheik's mouth.

* * *

Chantal's heart was thudding so fast, she felt like it was going to leap out of the elevator doors before she did.

But it was her gun that made it first into a small room with pale pink wallpaper. The only thing in the room was an oak door on the opposite wall.

Pulling out the key she'd taken from the now-bleeding man in the cleaning closet, she approached the door on thick carpet and stuck it into the shiny lock.

It opened with a muffled click. Grasping the doorknob, she leaned gently against the door and pushed it open. She found herself in an entrance hall that put museums and interior design show rooms to shame.

Reaching as tall as herself was an oversized bouquet of white lilies in a crystal vase on an inlaid table. Under her feet, a dark hardwood floor was polished to a shine that reflected her face when she looked down. Thick purple Persian rugs tessellated with objectless designs just beyond her toes. But she was most taken with original paintings by Picasso, Miro and Monet that hung on the three walls she looked at in turn.

Chantal was admiring the Picasso nude on her left when she decided she had better pay more attention to practical things like the spiral staircase next to it.

Walking across the plush rugs, she entered another large room with couches upholstered in green brocade. More paintings. She did not let herself look. Off to one side she saw a dining room and beyond that a kitchen. She moved cautiously from room to room, grasping the gun in her hand.

This floor appeared to be empty, so she ascended the spiral staircase, glad of all the thick carpeting.

From the landing, a long hallway stretched right and left. In the dim light she could see open doorways on both sides. The first led to an office with high ceilings. Bookshelves filled with the leather spines of antique and first edition books lined each wall. The next two rooms were bedrooms.

Chantal heard a noise and stopped. It sounded like a woman whimpering. She moved cautiously down the hall, following the sound to the last room. Peeking around the doorframe, she saw a king-sized bed across from the door.

Gloria lay splayed out on the bed, gagged and naked except for her bra and panties. Cords stretched from her arms and legs to each of the bedposts.

Without thinking, Chantal rushed to the bed, tossed the gun on it, and began untying one of Gloria's hands. She got one hand free before noticing that Gloria had been motioning with her head behind Chantal and trying to say something. With her hand now free, Gloria ripped offer her gag and said, "Behind you, he's…"

Chantal whipped around to see Banneret leaning against the frame of a side door. He wore a crimson silk robe and held a gun in his hand.

He was smiling.

★ ★ ★

Doby and Jordi went from person to person, taping their hands and feet. Laszlo kept his and Jordi's guns aimed at the group.

When all were securely bound, the three rescuers and four rescued women stood surveying the sprawl of well-dressed men slightly writhing in annoyance and discomfort on the marble floor.

Anne smiled without humor and said, "I don't think they were counting on a dessert of duct tape." She went over to the laden table and selected a leg of lamb and bit off a piece. "I'm starving." She poked into pots and platters, arranged herself a meal and pushed aside a place setting to sit on the table top and eat.

Laszlo approached her. "Are you alright?"

She smiled and swallowed a mouthful of flat bread. "Now that I'm no longer handcuffed to a bed awaiting violation, sure."

Laszlo nodded. "You don't seem too distraught by any of this, so I'll ask now. Are you willing to tell the press what happened to you?"

She did not hesitate, "Yes."

"Doby, my skinny computer friend there," Laszlo motioned with his shoulder toward Doby who was trying to explain domains to a confused-looking Jordi, "made a telephone call a few minutes ago. To Dr. Chevrolet, a lawyer in Geneva. He will be here in a minute. The Swiss television reporters have also been called. They might just arrive before him. After some interviews, we will call the police. Are you sure you are willing to participate?"

Anne set down her plate. She looked at the sheik and at the men on the floor. She then looked at the girl she had shared brief captivity with. The girl lay back in a chair, her eyes at half-mast. "For her," Anne said, "I want to do it for her and the others like her."

Laszlo turned to the two Philippine women who stood not far off. "Are you willing to tell your story?"

"Yes," they both said as Anne gestured for them to come and eat something. They went to the other end of the table and followed Anne's example.

Laszlo turned to Anne and said, "Doby will stay here with you. We have to go help someone else. Will you be okay?"

She met Laszlo's eyes and said, "I'll be okay."

They heard sounds from the entrance hall, and seconds later, in walked Dr. Chevrolet. Despite the hour, he was dressed as though ready to enter a courtroom. He stood in the doorway, taking in the sight before him. Ignoring all who were horizontal and incapable of speech—the major of his audience—he nodded to the standing men and said. "I can take it from here."

Jordi said to Laszlo, "We've got to go."

"You've got the address?" Doby asked.

"We know the address," Jordi said, already halfway to the door.

Laszlo started to join him, but looked back at Anne. She reached for a full wine glass and lifted it high. "Here's to the heroes," she said, looking at Laszlo.

"Laszlo," Jordi stuck his head back in the room.

Laszlo raised his hand and followed him out of the house. A car and a van with Swiss television logos pulled up as they were running down the drive.

Before jumping in Doby's car, Jordi said to Laszlo over the roof, "*Hombre,* you have eyes for the lady."

CHAPTER 56

"What a pleasure to see you, Ms. Travers," said Banneret. He tilted his head and the lamplight illuminated the white hair at his temples. "Or should I say Mrs. Collins? You are a resourceful woman."

Chantal made a move for the gun she had placed on the bed. A shot rang out and foam spurted from the mattress by Gloria's feet. Gloria kept an eye on Banneret, surreptitiously using her free hand to loosen the bound one.

"I wouldn't," Banneret said to Chantal. He walked over and picked the gun up from the bed, twirling it in his hand.

"Let her go," Chantal commanded.

"Why should I? She is my dessert for the evening, and now fate is good to me. You shall be my aperitif."

"You are sick," Chantal spat out.

He laughed. "No. Just someone who knows what he likes, what he wants." He looked at her as no respectful man would.

Chantal was shaking with fury. "To dominant women? Is that what you want?"

"Ah, you are egocentric. No, men too. People. Isn't that what it is all about? Power over people. But I don't care to explain myself. Get undressed and get on the bed."

"I am egocentric? Look who wants the power." Chantal laughed then straightened her face. "Where's Justin?"

"Oh, you are looking for your precious Justin." He widened his eyes in mock forgetfulness, "Why how could I have forgotten to reunite this happy little family. Ladies, your husband."

Both Gloria and Chantal looked at him as if he was crazier than they had thought.

A curtain hung across one corner of the room. Banneret moved to the curtain, a gun in each hand. Keeping one of the weapons trained on Chantal, he used the other to draw the curtain aside.

Justin sat tied to a chair, his mouth taped shut. The rest of his visible face was battered and bruised. His eyes were alert.

Banneret stood over Justin, his fine robe contrasting with the filthy garments of his prisoner. Banneret watched Chantal and Gloria to see their reactions. He seemed pleased. "Your husband is a stubborn man. But I do believe he will cooperate now."

"Let him go. We will give you Tapic's money."

Banneret smiled. "You think it has to do with money? The money is nothing."

"What do you mean?" Chantal asked. Though ungagged, Gloria said nothing, trying to remain as inconspicuous as possible to untie her bound hand.

"Enough of this," the owner of the bed said to Chantal. "Time for you to get undressed and on the bed next to wife number two."

Justin tried to speak but only a muffled moan escaped the tape.

Banneret looked at him, "Now fancy that. He is trying to say something. Once he sees what will happen to his two women right before his eyes, then he will articulate more clearly. You see, he has something I want."

"What can you possibly want from him?"

Banneret laughed, "We already mentioned it. Power. On the computers in Tapic's office we had information on every major politician in Europe. Even on those in the United Nations and of course leaders in the U.S., including the President himself. From secret bank accounts to their sexual preferences and partners. With that information, the possibilities are enormous. Now it is time for Mr. Collins to tell us where to find that information."

"He doesn't know," Chantal said, taking a step forward.

Banneret jerked the gun straight at her, his theatrical humor fading. "He knows. And he will tell me what he knows. For the last time, get on the bed, and I will replay the scene with our famous Yass. I trust you had an enjoyable holiday in Tunisia? You see, Jacques Tapic arranged it. He was my business partner."

Chantal's entire body lit with a surging hatred that burned through to the surface of her skin. She started to sweat with the heat of it and would have gladly stripped off her clothing in other circumstances to cool herself, but she said to Banneret, shaking, "I am not getting undressed."

Lightly, Banneret retorted, "Then I will be forced to do it. A little struggle excites me." He put the guns at the foot of the bed, reached over, grabbed Chantal's blouse and tore it open, her coat still over it. She stepped backward out of instinct, and he closed in on her, grabbing her neck with both hands. He began to squeeze.

Chantal fell back against the wall, but Banneret stayed with her, choking and overpowering her. He left one hand on her neck forcing her chin up, and with the other he finished ripping her blouse open in the front.

She clawed at the hand at her jugular and tried to look down and see where to strike him. The wound near her ribs throbbed and she started to see patches of black as less air made it to her lungs.

What to do? Then she remembered—the cleaning closet souvenir. He had her pressed against the wall. She gave up trying to remove his hand and struggled instead to reach behind her back. Her hands closed around the knife.

She pressed the release button. As the blade snapped forward, she plunged it into Banneret's stomach, just under his heart.

It took a moment for Banneret to release his grip. When he did, he stood back in shock, looking down at his bare stomach. His robe had fallen open in the struggle, and his naked body was now exposed, a knife handle protruding from his belly.

Banneret crumpled to his knees, mouth working open and closed but no words coming out. He fell to his side on the floor, and a red stain began to grow on the thick white carpet.

"So much for your power," Chantal said, yanking the knife from his body and using it to cut Gloria's bound hand and feet. "Get dressed, I'll get Justin."

Gloria nodded, still partially in shock. Chantal ran to the corner where Justin was heaving at the cording that anchored his wrists to the back of his chair. She ripped off the tape while saying, "Sorry," and then used the bloodied knife to saw off his bindings.

Gloria was pulling on her pants when they heard yelling and two shots fired in another part of the building. Had someone found the man in the cleaning closet, Chantal wondered?

Finally free, Justin struggled to stand up and managed a weak smile but said nothing, only holding Chantal's eyes with his own for two full seconds before turning toward the bed, taking the two guns, and handing one back to Chantal.

Gloria tied her shoes and followed Justin out the door. Chantal took one last look at the red heap in the middle of the room.

"You evil man," she said, closing the door.

★ ★ ★

They took the elevator down to the ground floor and saw several women coming out a door, tears of relief on the faces of the women. They heard several more shots and Lazlo and Jordi quickly emerged through the door, guns in hands.

With disbelief in seeing his old friends, Justin exclaimed, "What are you doing here?"

"Taking care of an ugly mess," Lazlo said.

Justin nodded his head and said, "It's crazy. I understand."

EPILOGUE

ora, crossed the monastery sitting room and reached for Sophie, asleep in Chantal's arms. Chantal whispered, "Thank you," and let her fingers cup the crown of her daughter's head as Dora smiled and carried the tired toddler off to bed.

Justin, Chantal and Gloria were left in the dark and quiet. A low-burning fire cast thin light on their tight faces. Justin realized it had only been a few days ago that they had sat around the fireplace in his Llanca home.

Justin's face was still swollen, one eye still black and blue. But after some basic first aid and a shower, he looked a world better than he had in Geneva. As for how he felt, well, that would take a bit more time.

He glanced at the two women sitting across from him on a leather couch and leaned forward in his chair. "We should leave here," he said. "I thought this would be a place to heal from physical—and other—wounds. But it looks like I was the one who picked up additional scratches." He smiled and touched his face.

"We are just happy you are alive," Gloria said. "I, er, we," she looked at Chantal, "were so worried about you."

Justin smiled, "And I was worried about both of you too."

Chantal softly asked, "You are sure you are alright?"

Justin's smile was weak this time, and he waited to speak until a particularly painful memory passed. Eventually he said, "I thought they wanted to know where the money was. I didn't want to tell them because I didn't want to endanger either of you. It took me a long time to figure that they wanted something other than the money."

"Banneret wanted power," Chantal said without hesitation. "By having that information on all the politicians he would have had tremendous control in the European Union and the United Nations. He even mentioned the President of the United States of America."

They were quiet for a moment and Chantal continued, "Dr. Chevrolet did a great job."

"Yes he did," Justin agreed. "Somehow he made everything make sense to the police. I suspect the Arab sheik will spend many years in prison for kidnapping Anne Kent." He settled back in his chair at this thought.

Gloria twirled a strand of red hair in her fingers. "And Banneret. It must be quite a shock for the United Nations. The world learns that

one of their directors was implicated in drug and human trafficking."
She looked at Chantal.

Chantal looked at her hands. "I took a life." She folded her hands
and looked at Justin and Gloria in turn. "But I am not sorry."

Gloria laid her hand on Chantal's knee. "Neither am I."

Justin closed his eyes, trying not to picture Gloria bound to Banneret's
bed. He also tried not to imagine what would have happened had
Chantal not been there.

A log snapped and split, falling into the ash.

Chantal asked, "Why didn't you tell us about the money?"

Justin went to the fireplace and set another log on the struggling
flames. "I wanted to, but only when the time was right." He poked at
the pyramid of warmth with the stoker and turned toward them. "We
had so many things to think about. I thought it would just add to the
pressure. I have barely even absorbed it yet."

"And Dora knew." Chantal said. "Why didn't she tell us?"

"She wanted me to tell you when the time was right."

"Even though I work with accounts all day, those numbers are so
big, I can't grasp them as being ours," Gloria said.

"Yeah," Justin tossed up his hands. "What to do?" He was not just
referring to the money.

"What do you want to do?" Chantal asked.

Justin ran an bandaged hand through his hair. "I love you both," he
said, not making eye contact with either of them. "But it just seems
not right to have you both as wives. I cannot internally work it out
but maybe I am restricted by cultural conventions? And how could it
ever work out? This is something that none of us chose but we find
ourselves in this irreconcilable situation."

"Then chose and make it easy for us," a low voice said.

Justin looked up, not knowing whether Chantal or Gloria had said
this.

★ ★ ★

After lying in bed for a sleepless hour, Justin gave up trying to
figure out whether they had solved anything in their conversation that
evening. He thought not as he fell into a fitful sleep.

Justin woke to a noise in his room. For a second, he thought his
captors were coming to drag him from drugged sleep and he started
to sit up.

The clock said two a.m. in digital red numbers. The bed moved, then someone lifted the covers and a woman slid her arms around him.

"Hello Justin."

This time he knew who was speaking.

⋆ ⋆ ⋆

Chantal could not get to sleep. She was thinking not only of the fireside discussion this evening, but also the one she had had with Gloria in the farmer's cabin in France.

Gloria was right. The two of them would have to make the decision. And that decision could not be based on fear or jealousy.

Staring at tree shadows on her moonlit ceiling, Chantal finally understood that it was love—not physical or romantic love but a more general human love—that Gloria understood. Gloria had acted out of this kind of love.

Chantal knew she had not. She had been competing with Gloria body and soul.

Her reason? Simple. She wanted Justin. And wanted him for herself alone. In fact—and her body bristled to a sleepless awareness—she wanted him now.

She rose from bed, pulled on her robe, and walked out into the hall toward Justin's room. The door was slightly open, and before she saw them, she heard Justin and Gloria.

She realized that a heavy jealousy lay in her heart where she thought love was. Weighted down by this gravity, she stood watching as Gloria pulled Justin's head toward hers and kissed him. Tangled together in the dark, they looked like a single being.

Chantal remembered Rodin's statue, *The Kiss*. Masculine united with feminine. Rodin had believed that man and woman were created as one, and the relationship between them is a constant search to rediscover that oneness.

If Justin and Gloria were one, where did Chantal belong? She turned and went to her room.

⋆ ⋆ ⋆

Justin woke to the sound of the shower in his bathroom. A faint worry creased his forehead, but he knew he was no longer in captivity, so what...?

Gloria. They had spent the night exhausting each other. He smiled a tired but pleased smile. Then he thought of Chantal, and the worry lines and guilt returned.

Gloria was singing a Spanish melody in the shower.

A telephone began ringing. His. He remembered that Doby had given him a mobile telephone so they could stay in contact and discuss any of the events that had taken place in Geneva, if necessary.

Justin grabbed for his boxer shorts and the telephone. "Hello?" he answered, cradling the small phone between shoulder and ear and pulling on the boxers with his free hands.

"Justin?"

"Yes."

"This is Stefan."

Justin looked at his watch. It was eight o'clock in the morning. "Stefan, I've never heard of you rising before eleven o'clock." He laughed then asked, "What's going on?"

"I have several pieces of urgent information for you."

"Urgent?"

"Yes. First, all the computers from the Nice offices were taken out of Doby's workshop while he was gone." He paused to let that sink in. "Somebody now has all that sensitive information."

"Do you know who?"

"I have no idea, and every idea. With information on every important politician in Europe, the U.N., and the United States, the list of interested parties is daunting."

"Why is this urgent?" Justin asked.

"It isn't to us, exactly. We'll have to sit back and wait. And Doby did make a backup of all the data. He is going to start analyzing it today. But there's something else." Stefan paused. "Laszlo got a telephone call from Abdouelle in Paris. Do you remember him?"

"Yes, I visited him in August. He's a creep."

"How very American of you. He sells information. Anyway, I have bad news."

"Which is?"

"Abdouelle said that Yass visited him."

"But Yass is dead. I shot him myself." Justin could still feel the bullet exiting the gun and the sense of satisfaction that the man who had raped Chantal would never harm any one again. Alive?

Stefan kept on, "Abdouelle said that Yass looks terrible. But he is alive and crazier than ever. He was asking Abdouelle about how to find his concubine and his child. He's cracking up. And he's after Chantal and Sophie."

Justin had promised Sophie that man would never harm them again.

The taste of those words went sour in his mouth.

They were in a remote section of Spain. Yass could not find them here, could he? Justin tried to keep his head in the conversation and asked, "Do you know what Yass is planning?"

"He already checked out your house in Llanca, and found no one home. Someone there told him you had moved back to Paris. That seems to be what most of the locals think."

Justin sank more, then sat down on the edge of the bed. All his powers of reasoning and decisiveness left him. "What should I do?"

"Stay where you are. I would like to get Laszlo down there to help you, but Sam Oliver has asked him to act as a bodyguard for Anne Kent. Laszlo was more than willing. I suggest you contact Jordi to see if he can arrange some security for you. And if you need any additional help, please let me know."

"I'll call Jordi right away. And Stefan," Justin looked at the closed bathroom door where Gloria's singing had ceased. "thanks for your help."

Justin hung up, grabbed his robe and headed for Chantal's room. He knocked on the door and waited for a response. None. He knocked again and then opened the door.

Chantal's bed was unmade, her bags gone. He scanned the empty room as if she would materialize. But on closer inspection, all he noticed was an envelope with his name written on it. He went to the table where it lay, white and ominous. He held it in his hands a full minute before steeling himself to open it.

Dear Justin,

I have been thinking about our situation—how could I not? I know that you love Gloria, and I have decided that I want you to be happy with her.

Thinking of you is what kept me alive over the past year, but now that I am free, I will try to find my life in other things. I have always loved you and always will. I am returning to Paris with Sophie. Dora will join me there. I will find my sister as I know she has recently gone through some difficulty. I am not yet sure where we will stay.

If you need to contact me, please send me an email. Please tell me—what should I do?

With all my love,
Chantal

AUTHOR'S NOTE

One theme in this novel is about human trafficking. While the story is fiction, it reflects what is happening in reality. The UN Office on Drugs and Crime recently announced that 2.4 million people across the globe are victims of human trafficking at any one time, and 80 percent of them are being exploited as sexual slaves. Their report says that $32 billion is being earned every year by unscrupulous criminals running human trafficking networks. Another UN study says that the number of people being trafficked into Europe is on the rise, yet the number of arrests is on the decline.

While the UN, the European Union, and the United States Government are calling for tighter controls on this practice, sometimes it feels like empty words, and their failure to do something makes it seem they are indirectly culpable. In fact, there have been a number of cases where UN workers at refugee camps have traded food for sex, exploiting under-aged girls. There are few penalties being charged and the UN investigations into these cases seem to be lost in a bureaucratic sea of oblivion. The world must be made aware of the immeasurable human suffering caused by this, and something must be done about it.

Another underlying theme in this book has to do with social conventions. In *Pursuit* we find two women who both love the same man. In fact, they find themselves in a bizarre situation that is not of their own choosing. Within their worldview is a belief system of marriage relationships as being between one man and one woman. So, how can they find reconcilation?

Has society imposed a set of standards that doesn't fit their unusual situation? If anything, the two woman are not relativists who believe that anything goes, where you just make up your own rules as you go along. If they go against social standards, upon what presuppositions should this be based? In the end, they need to ground their decisions on something concrete.

It looks like Chantal has indeed made the decision for them as she heads back to Paris to find a new life and join up with her sister who has problems of her own. She doesn't know that Yass, an evil man who has caused her great pain, is on her trail.

That leads us to Blue Fate 6, which I expect will be the concluding novel in this series. The Blue Fate series began with the story of Hank Morgan, so it is fitting that Hank Morgan comes back on the scene in Blue Fate 6.

Please let me know your thoughts about *Pursuit* as well as any of my other novels. Authors love to hear from their readers.

Thanks for taking an interest in my books,

Cass Tell
Costa Brava, Spain

Your opinion is important to me!

I hope you enjoyed my book and I'd love to receive your feedback.
As the book is still fresh in your mind, please leave some comments
or a review on any of the following websites:

Amazon — www.amazon.com
Barnes & Noble — www.barnesandnoble.com
Goodreads — www.goodreads.com

And I invite you to visit my website www.casstell.com to find out
more details about all books in the Blue Fate series and my other
books.

Thank you!

www.ingramcontent.com/pod-product-compliance
Lightning Source LLC
Chambersburg PA
CBHW061442210726

48287CB00007B/2320